She stared at the sprawling body of a woman in the water.

'*She is down there*,' the voice whispered, stiffening the hairs on the back of Kate's neck. No! She slams down the lid of her laptop computer. That was where the picture and sound had come from. But it doesn't help. On her first vacation ever, Kate is plagued by visions she doesn't want. Now she has no choice but to place her trust in a Colorado sheriff, who wants to be more than a friend, even though Kate has serious doubts about his motives.

In the sequel to *One...Two...Buckle My Shoe*, *Death Has No Dominion* takes the reader on a journey into the mind of a psychopathic killer. And the reluctant psychic detective, Kate Macklin, is the only one with any chance to stop him from unleashing his insatiable thirst for vengeance.

Kate was the only thing that could tie him to the crimes, so all the killer had to do to escape was to eliminate her...

"I know. I hope to learn how to block out some of the images when I want to." Kate had the feeling the Catman was better at blocking than she was. She motioned toward the black plastic-wrapped body. "The woman in the river called to me so clearly. She wanted to be buried. She needed to be found."

"Now that's over, will you leave?"

"It's not over. He has to go on killing." A flash of an older man lying dead on a hard-packed earthen floor intruded. A figure above him tilted his head back to laugh. She shivered.

"Here, take my jacket," Dillon began, pulling his arm out of the sleeve.

She stopped him. "No, I'm not cold. It was a feeling that he has to come back here. It's as if he left something valuable behind." That idea was new, and the first time it had entered her thoughts. He needed to return to Plenitude for some reason. "It may be the only mistake he's made by killing two women in the same town. He feels angry and humiliated knowing this. I brought it to his attention and he has to do something to change it."

"There's one way he could change the past and that's by eliminating you, the evidence of his mistake."

That was smart of Dillon. She didn't pursue that line of reasoning, fearing he would make more of it than he should. "He may be stalking someone right now. He isn't ready to stop killing. He gets off on the fear and terror of his victim before he kills. It feeds his sickness, his emptiness."

Kate knew he would return. Like an unsatisfied lover who can never leave, he would come back for her. All she had to do was wait.

KUDOS for *Death Has No Dominion*

In Death Has No Dominion (love the title!) by P. K. Paranya, which is a sequel to One...Two...Buckle My Shoe, this time reluctant psychic Kate Macklin is taking a long-deserved vacation, or so she thinks. Traveling on a train through the Colorado Rockies, Kate gets another cryptic message from her computer: "She's down there." It's the last thing that Kate wants or needs to hear. But despite her desperate desire to do so, she cannot let the message that a woman has been murdered go unanswered. So Kate hops off the train and into the frying pan, so to speak. She takes up residence in a small hotel in a small Colorado town and runs into the small town sheriff, who takes an unseemly interest in her. Is he trying to help her solve the murder, or is he trying to shut her up? She doesn't know, and neither do we. That is part of Paranya's brilliance. I love the way she develops her characters. They seem so human and real. *– Taylor Jones, reviewer*

I love the way P. K. Paranya writes, from her characterization to her vivid descriptions. I always feel like I am right there in the book with the characters. It is a gift that some authors have and Paranya has it in spades. I shivered in the cold Colorado winds right along with Kate, and I shook my head in confusion, right along with Dillon, even while I suspected him of murder—just like Kate. Too bad I didn't get to sleep with him, too! Sigh. Death Has No Dominion is a chilling story about a psychic killer who is always one step ahead of the cops, and when Kate comes along to mess up his carefully laid plans, he is one step ahead of her, too. Plus, he knows who she is and where to find her. And he is coming for her. She doesn't know who he is, or how she will recognize him. But she does know he is coming. It makes for a real edge-of-your-seat suspense/thriller. I loved it. Well done, Paranya! – Regan Murphy, reviewer

DEATH HAS NO

DOMINION

P. K. PARANYA

A BLACK OPAL BOOKS PUBLICATION

GENRE: PARANORMAL THRILLER/ROMANTIC ELEMENTS

DEATH HAS NO DOMINION
Copyright © 2013 by P. K. Paranya
Cover Design by Jackson Cover Designs
All cover art copyright © 2013
All Rights Reserved
Print ISBN: 978-1-626940-48-2

First Publication: AUGUST 2013

Published by Black Opal Books **http://www.blackopalbooks.com**

Though they go mad they shall be sane,
Though they sink through the sea they shall rise again;
Though lovers be lost love shall not;
And death shall have no dominion."
– *Dylan Thomas 1914-1953*

CHAPTER 1

Kate Macklin stared at the grotesque body of a woman in the water. '*She is down there.*' The voice whispered into her ear, stiffening the hairs on the back of her neck. No! She put her hands over her ears, as if she heard the words out loud. She slammed the lid on the laptop computer, knowing it wouldn't help. But that was where the picture and voice had come from.

Out of the window of the Amtrak car, Kate glanced down into a deep gorge alongside the train tracks. The river crashed over the rocks, exploding in spumes of white, high into the air. The Colorado countryside in the fall appeared brilliantly clear and sharp. A sudden stab of unreality pierced Kate, and she closed her eyes.

In the past, she had seldom ventured out of her house. Now here she was, Katharine Macklin, speeding through another state, toward a destination she hadn't yet determined and enjoying every moment. Until now.

Without warning, Kate's fingers grew cold on the edge of the laptop and a sinking feeling settled in the pit of her stomach. Her skin was as clammy and damp as if the spume sprayed over her from the water below. Slowly, cautiously, she opened the computer, expecting--hoping to see the familiar spreadsheet with figures from one of her bookkeeping jobs.

Slowly, in horrifying detail, pixel by pixel, the contorted body of a woman sprawled in death appeared in the center of the screen. Kate opened her lips. A low moan escaped her clenched teeth. She wanted to slam the computer lid down again but shock from what she had just seen paralyzed her.

The woman lay on her back underwater, her eyes wide, with long dark hair floating like seaweed about her head. It was her mouth, open in a silent scream that Kate focused on, feeling the woman's terror as she died.

The picture zoomed in closer, forcing Kate to view the wound on the woman's neck. She saw a wire noose, embedded deep in flesh, and twisted behind the head by small wooden pegs.

With shaking hands, she folded up the laptop. She'd get no work done now.

It has started again.

"Are you all right, Miss?"

A quavering voice came from the other side of the aisle.

Kate looked at the tiny, bird-like old woman sitting across from her. She appeared to be in her nineties, at least.

"Thank you. I'm fine."

The elderly woman gripped her worn brocade bag and stood up. Kate felt her tenseness slowly evaporate, and the chills leave her body. It was good to have a distraction.

"My name is Sarah. Sarah Jenkins." The woman stood waiting in the aisle for Kate to remove the laptop from the vacant seat.

Despite her reluctance to touch the machine again, Kate picked it up and leaned it against the wall, on the floor by her leg.

As soon as Sarah Jenkins nestled in the seat, she turned her bright, black-eyed gaze on Kate, waiting.

"Oh, sorry. I'm Katharine Macklin. Friends call me Kate." She didn't have that many friends, but it made her feel agreeably ordinary to say the words.

Sarah reached into her bag and drew out two granola bars, handing one to Kate.

Good. Maybe the woman wouldn't be able to talk around a mouth full of nuts and caramel. No such luck.

"This is my thirty-second train ride. I dearly love the rhythm of the moving train. It's addictive. Don't you think?"

Kate's noncommittal nods seemed to spur Sarah on. "Where are you going? I don't mean to be nosy, but when I reached ninety, I figured I was allowed certain liberties," she said as she smiled and touched the frail hand holding tight to her purse.

"I don't blame you. When I reach the age of ninety, I'll surely remember your words."

Sarah's laughter reminded Kate of glass wind chimes in a gentle breeze.

"To tell the truth, I'm not sure where I'm going. This is my first vacation ever and I was just going to stay on the train until I saw something I liked, but…"

"Are you a writer?" Sarah pointed to the laptop on the floor.

Thinking back to her daughter Annie, Kate recalled the last, tragic connection through the computer. She'd never wanted the gift, as her mother had called it. But her psychic ability came from a dark Scottish heritage. Using a computer worked like a crystal ball might have, but why did her psychic abilities always bring pictures of death?

Kate glared at the offending machine. "No. I'm not a writer. I do bookkeeping at home."

"And you brought work with you on vacation?" The beady little eyes crinkled at the corners. "Shame on you."

"You're right. It was a dumb thing to do."

She would never have brought it with her if it hadn't been a shiny new toy, a gift from Captain Murphy's precinct for her help on the Shoe Man case.

Kate turned to stare outside in a desperate attempt at calmness. The window reflected a thin-faced woman with frightened eyes. Sgt. Slater had told her she was beautiful. How absurd that had been, but for a while, she'd believed him.

"I like your outfit."

Sarah's chatter interrupted Kate's gloomy thoughts.

Kate smoothed out the long skirt of her embroidered denim dress. First new dress she'd bought in years. It seemed especially appropriate to wear through Colorado. "Thanks. I picked this up a couple of stops ago, when the train had a long layover."

The effect of Sarah's talking forced Kate to return to a sense of reality. Something she deeply needed.

"When does the next stop come up?" Kate asked, interrupting the monologue.

"Soon. Very soon. That will be Plenitude, my home. Lived here all my life. Used to be just a ranching community, but it's a nice little town now."

"You must be happy and satisfied, living here that long."

Sarah smiled. "How would I know? Never been anywhere but on those little train excursions I take now and again. Like I said, the town is nice. People complain about not getting cell phones to work here with all the mountains and trees, but I wouldn't have one of those things, anyway."

Kate didn't own a cell phone either. Who would be calling her? Before she could say anything in answer, the frail-looking woman scrabbled up with surprising agility from the enveloping seat to gather her purse and luggage.

"I think I shall go to the little girl's room before getting off. Sometimes Jasper stops only long enough to throw down a bag of mail, but he knows I'm riding today. It was a pleasure visiting with you, my dear. Excuse me?"

Kate watched as she made her way down the aisle toward the back of the train.

A voice came from somewhere inside her head. '*There she is. She is down there.*'

Not wanting to look through the window again, but unable to turn away, Kate peered over the trees into the swiftly running river. As they passed one point, the river widened and grew calm.

The water was deepest there and Kate remembered seeing in the computer, where the woman lay at the bottom of the deep water. Could be the woman wasn't in the river at this moment. Was she dead already, or was Kate seeing the future, an event she might be able to stop from happening?

She turned away from the window, willing serenity to return. The voice continued to whisper.

'*She is down there.*'

Her throat felt dry, making it hard to swallow, but she couldn't help picking up the laptop again. Maybe it had been a momentary aberration, stress from being in an unfamiliar situation.

When she touched her fingers to the switch of the computer, the keys hummed beneath her hand. It was supposed to turn itself off when the hinged top closed. A sense of urgency made her hands tremble and her heart palpitate beneath her sweater. She had two choices. One choice would be to go up on the observation platform and fling the laptop as far as she could over the side of the gorge or...

No good. She could never escape from her visions.

"The next stop is Plenitude." The conductor moved down the aisle with his announcement.

Kate gathered her belongings in frantic haste, fearful that if she missed the stop, the woman in the water might be lost forever. Twice she dropped her purse, her fingers cold and numb. She pushed past a slow-moving passenger in the aisle, her concentration so strong she barely mumbled an apology when the train began to brake for a stop. Sarah Jenkins had mentioned the conductor was quick with his stops. Kate ran toward an exit.

Something—someone cried out to her for help. She hoped this time it wasn't the killer summoning her.

CHAPTER 2

The train slowed and stopped. Kate stepped down onto the platform, hating to leave the security of the train. The image of the dead woman flashed across her mind, and she almost turned to go back. Too late. The engine revved up speed, the cars lurching down the track.

Rails spanned a suspension bridge alongside the station. Beyond the bridge, the train disappeared over a hill. At the beginning of the walkway, Sarah waited for her and they fell into step together. Kate shifted her longer stride for the arthritic hesitancy of the old woman. "How did you manage to get your luggage?"

"Oh, the conductor brought it to the back for me. You didn't mention getting off here," Sarah said.

"No, it was a last minute decision," Kate admitted, thinking Sarah didn't know the half of it.

A wooden sign at the front of the station announced the town of Plenitude, Colorado. They passed through the narrow railroad building and stopped to look down upon a prosperous little community nestled between a mountain and a river gorge.

The village just before this stop was Gold Hill. Was she supposed to be in Gold Hill or Plenitude? There was no assurance of her choice. She was here now, and if she should be somewhere else, something would tell her.

"This must always feel like coming home," Kate said.

"My yes, it does, child. I never get tired of leaving for a bit and never tire of coming home."

Sarah walked ahead on the narrow sidewalk, and Kate followed with a suitcase in one hand and her purse and laptop in the other. A familiar panic rose in her throat and choked off her breath in the high, cold air. She should be back home, in her cozy suburban New York house with Rasputin, her cat. She hoped he would be all right in the kennel. He, too, hadn't been one to venture outdoors in years, taking his cue from her.

"Do you have a family? Are they coming to join you?" Sarah couldn't stop asking questions although she seemed breathless from the high, thin air. "Soon the ski season will begin. I love snow even if these old bones don't care for it anymore." Sarah spoke in a high-pitched voice in sentences that lacked periods.

Kate was not comfortable talking to strangers and had not spoken to anyone about her personal life since—she couldn't remember when. What could it hurt? She wouldn't be here that long.

"I don't have a family. My husband, Mac, was killed in an accident on the job. My daughter Annie died two and a half years ago, killed by a hit and run driver. She'd be fourteen now. I do have a cat named Rasputin." Kate carefully let her voice go into neutral, trying out the new idea of confiding in someone.

Sarah stopped walking and, with a "Tsk, tsk," laid her hand on Kate's arm. "Dear, that is so sad. Of course, I should talk. My husband and three children are gone, and without leaving one grandchild behind for me." Her voice turned peevish. "I've outlived them all."

Kate thought of the empty years. "It's never easy."

"Time will heal all, eventually," Sarah pointed out, taking her hand away and beginning to walk again.

"You're right. I never thought it would, but now I can remember Annie sometimes without feeling guilty." It was like a scar that had healed over, leaving rough edges to chafe from time to time. She used to pick at it often but eventually she left it alone to mend.

Sarah shifted her belongings to the other hand. "Guilt? Guilty for being left behind? I had that. Quite a bit, at first. Then I got used to it."

"Can I carry that for you?" Kate touched her shoulder, feeling the sharp bones beneath the woman's navy blue cardigan. Sarah shook her head and looked as if she was waiting for an answer. "Well, yes. I felt guilty because I knew Annie was mad when she left home for school that day," Kate continued. "We were arguing a lot. I couldn't have been much fun for her. I drank a little then, too, which didn't help."

At Sarah's inquisitive look, Kate hurried on. "Oh, not that much, just a couple of glasses of wine at night to help me sleep. Still, it made Annie uncomfortable. The day she died we'd argued and she forbade me to meet her after school." It had only been five blocks. Five short blocks that had robbed Kate of her daughter's presence for a long time.

They walked in companionable silence until Kate spoke. "This seems like a pretty little village." At the same time she wondered long would she need to stay in this strange town, waiting for another vision.

Waiting. The word flowed around her mind with silky apprehension, sliding into her thoughts like the ominous whisper, '*She is down there.*' Someone, something was waiting here for her. She felt it now, slipping through her thoughts.

She zipped up her ski jacket, grateful for the thick pullover sweater under it. She had hoped by fall that the tourist season would flicker out, to let her enjoy a quiet vacation. "Aren't you cold in that light sweater?" she asked Sarah.

"Me? Goodness no, my dear. I was born and raised here in Colorado and I'd have to be knee-deep in snow now to feel any discomfort from the cold."

The small town nestled against the side of a pine-forested mountain, which could have been a mammoth glacier millions of years ago. The air filled with tiny brilliant prisms in front of her face from the crisp, clear cold. Kate inhaled the sharp woodsy smell.

The buildings had cutesy-pseudo gold mining era fronts while the sides and backs were of prosaic board and brick. Curious, Kate paused in her walking to peer into the alley behind a row of buildings. Beat-up ancient garbage cans, spilling over with boxes and trash, crouched at the back of each store as if hiding in shame. Seeing the rear of the buildings took some of the naiveté of the small town away, leaving a sense of sly furtiveness.

A good town for secrets.

"You live near here?" Kate asked. Hey, she was getting good at casual conversation. It felt liberating.

"Not far. Nothing's very far away here," Sarah said without explaining. She paused to lift her head and sniff the air. "Hmm. I never get tired of that clean pine smell. We lived on a ranch out of town most of the while the children were growing up, but now I live in town, not far from here. Any idea of where you're going to stay?"

"Nope. Haven't given it much thought."

"How wonderful! I adore people with spontaneity. So many adults have lost it over the years, you know." Sarah's dark eyes twinkled and her smile showed white store-bought teeth that seemed just a little too large for her. Probably bought them through mail-order years ago.

"I'll need a room," Kate said. "Not too expensive." Then she had to find the town library. It would have been faster and easier to go straight to the sheriff's office and inquire if they had found anyone dead in the water lately, but she quickly dismissed that idea. She didn't even know if the woman was dead. From past experience Kate had learned it didn't pay to give away too much information in the beginning.

"You wouldn't like where I stay," Sarah said. "All of us are old. Really old. But just up the street is The Antlers Hotel, a nice place, not expensive. It's ancient too, but not colorful enough and visitors hardly bother staying there. Ralph's a hoot. He's the owner. Like me, he's lived here all his life. We call him the weatherman behind his back. That's his idea of small talk, always about the weather. We have two kinds of weather, cold and colder." She giggled.

"What a strange name for a hotel," Kate said, but when they drew close, she understood. Hundreds of moose, deer, and other varieties of animal antlers were attached all over an ancient wooden building, including up on the roof and gables. It seemed as if that kept the building from collapsing.

"Come in," Sarah urged. "I'll introduce you to Ralph. He's an old fogy, but he's got a good heart. Nosy as all get-out though. He'll know all your secrets in a few minutes."

Like someone else I just met, Kate wanted to say, but she turned away to hide her smile.

No one was at the desk, although the door squeaked when they opened it. Sarah hit the bell hanging over the counter with brittle impatience.

The small lobby was designed to look antiquated, but elegant. The stairwells gleamed darkly, and the front desk hid behind a facade of polished cherry wood with the top surface tiled in small squares, sprinkled with flowers and greenery. On the whole, it seemed cozy, but in another sense, reclusive. Why did she keep thinking of this town as having its own identity, one of furtive silence? Was there something hidden here that would have to be dug out? She hoped not. Her energy level, never high, had just plummeted.

A thin, wiry old man shuffled out from behind a nest of fake greenery. By his tousled hair, or what remained of it, she knew he had been dozing. He smelled vaguely musty, like the lobby.

"Ralph! On duty as usual," Sarah said tartly.

The man frowned, picking up the bickering as if they'd been doing it for years. "Don't torment me, old woman. I was just resting." He pulled his half-glasses down from his forehead and peered at Kate.

"This is my friend, Kate Macklin. I want you to be nice to her. She's not one of them touristy people. She's on her first vacation. And she doesn't even own a cell phone," Sarah added with a triumphant air.

More than Ralph cared to know obviously, by the impatient wave of his hand when he shoved the register forward for Kate to sign.

"I'll be going on now, dearie. But I'll check on you once in a while until you leave. Make sure this scoundrel here don't take advantage of you."

"Git along with you, Sarah. You're the town troublemaker."

Sarah laughed as if he had paid her a huge compliment. She motioned Kate forward, stood on her tiptoes, and bestowed a dry, whispery kiss on her cheek.

"Bye for now, Sarah. I enjoyed talking to you." No need to ask where she lived in case she needed to ask some questions later. Ralph was sure to know.

Once checked into the downtown hotel, Kate looked out onto the street, thinking of the changes in her appearance and personality over the past months. She had gradually emerged from her morass of guilt and fear. Guilt for being alive when both her husband and daughter were dead, the fear of leaving her home, and wondering what terrible catastrophe would happen to her next.

Everyone important was gone from her life and here she was, supposedly on a long vacation to shed the past. Would she ever escape? Or was that a part of her, always trailing behind like a jet trail in the sky?

The temptation had been so strong to pass this town by, to continue on her travels. Still, she had little choice. Her psychic ability told her enough to realize that something strange had happened or was happening here. Someone had called out for help and she was the only one to hear the cry.

Kate climbed the stairs to the second story, to avoid the ancient elevator. She looked to the end of the hallway to see another set of stairs climbing upward but noticed cobwebs attached to the railings. They didn't appear to have many guests at this hotel.

As soon as she unpacked, she changed into a soft gray, woolen pantsuit and decided to take the elevator down to the lobby. It squeaked and groaned mightily, but when the doors flew open, she felt she had accomplished something important, sloughing off a corner of another phobia.

The euphoria didn't last. Familiar feelings of doubt assailed her, causing her to want to rush back up into the safety of her room. But her room wasn't the secure shell she needed, not as long as her computer screen displayed the dead woman.

Kate closed her eyes, again seeing the woman with long hair flowing about her head, the noose of wire biting into her white neck, eyes open in terror with the sure knowledge that she was going to die.

"Are you all right, Miss?"

Ralph's voice came from a distance and she opened her eyes, still expecting to see the woman in the water. The elderly man walked from behind the desk, his face folded into wrinkles of concern.

"Thanks. I'm okay. Just a little tired from the trip. Do you have a library here? Maybe I'll just go sit a while and look at magazines."

He patted her shoulder gently, his hand like dry branches against the material of her sweater. "Oh, my yes, we have a fine library. Best in these parts, for the size of the town. Donated by some of the country club crowd, the winter people."

Kate felt grateful for the detour in her thoughts. "The winter people? I'd have thought your summer trade was more important."

"No siree. The summer people are cheapos. Families with noisy, ill-behaved kids. It's the winter folks that support this town." He paused, cocking his head to look at her, as if deciding which she was.

"I'm neither one, if you're trying to fit me somewhere." His expression of monkey-like curiosity amused her. "A friend told me about this town and I just stopped off on my way somewhere else to check it out." A little white lie never hurt. How else to explain her being here?

"That's good. To tell the truth, I like the in-betweenies best of all. They come to see what's here, bide a bit, and leave quietly."

Kate wanted to hug the old man. He was so satisfied, so settled in his opinions, which he drew around him like a wool blanket on a windy night.

When she left the hotel, the dispossessed feeling hit her again, as if she stood out in the nippy wind, naked in the center of the town. She pulled her jacket tighter around her neck and raised her shoulders. She was okay, she could deal with the past now.

Her pulse sang in her veins, her temperature rose, she felt the flush in her cheeks. It was a matter of unraveling the ball of yarn to get to the center of the cry for help. It couldn't be that tough, could it?

A woman lay dead, or would die. Murdered and thrown away in the water. That was Kate's immediate problem. Was she to stop it from happening or was the body missing? Eventually the computer would tell her what her mission was.

Caution took over her rush of adrenalin. Something warned that her that prying would not be welcome in Plenitude.

In spite of the inner warning, Kate hurried, her responsibility now clear in her mind. She had to find out about the woman, to save her, if she was still alive, before a terrible fate overtook her.

CHAPTER 3

Where to start? Probably with either the library or the local newspaper, if the town had one.

As if in answer to her musings, Kate looked up in time to see the clapboard sign of *The Sentinel*. Pushing through the door was like going a century back in time. The counter looked realistically ancient, as did the person behind it. Was everyone old in Plentitude?

"Yes?"

The woman stared rudely at Kate. Half-glasses perched on the end of her nose. Did the glasses cause her nasality?

"I need some information." Kate took a flying leap at the truth but didn't come close. "I'm looking up an old friend who's supposed to live here, but I can't find her."

The woman raised plucked eyebrows. "What's her name?"

"Uh, oh, that's the problem. I haven't seen her since high school. We were going to have kind of a reunion and I lost her address and her married name. All I remembered was the town." She hoped the woman wouldn't insist on a first name, although she could make one up, but then that might change the outcome of her quest.

The woman's lips pursed, she gathered her patience with a huge sigh. "I've been here ages. What does she look like?"

Kate managed a small smile in gratitude. "She's about my age, thirty-four, has long, dark hair, she's shorter and rounder than me..." Kate faltered, reluctant to dredge up the details from her vision of the dead woman.

A short laugh issued from the pursed lips. "Not much there. Sure she wasn't just passing through? We get a lot of women your age taking the rafting trips."

Kate didn't like her comment about women her age. "What do you mean by that?"

"What I meant was, women from the city, they come here to go rafting in the summer. Meet lots of men. Younger men." The clerk looked inside her coffee cup on the counter, as if her cream had curdled.

Kate hoped it had. "I really don't know about that. I thought she lived here. You don't know anyone living here fitting that description?"

A closed expression on the woman's face told Kate the conversation was finished.

"Was someone like that here a while ago, with the long black hair." It seemed as if the woman needed to impart *some* gossip. "She caused a little stir when she turned up missing, paid a week's rent on a car and never came to claim it. But they figured she just took off with someone."

They? They who? The sheriff's department? Kate opened her mouth to ask another question, but the woman turned a formidable back upon her to show that the interview was over. So much for small town hospitality.

"Thank you for your help," Kate muttered with as much grace as she could manage. Just as her hand touched the doorknob, the woman spoke again.

"Check the library. They might have old newspapers from Gold Hill, that's the next town up the river."

Kate nodded and pushed through the door.

Odd. Why would Gold Hill have information on someone here? It could be a wrong guess on her part and the woman in the river might be from Gold Hill.

Something told her no.

When she passed by a small diner, she remembered not eating breakfast. The smell of fresh baked bread drew her inside.

She pushed open the door and paused on the threshold. One of her more unshakable fears was of eating alone with strangers staring at her. Resolutely, she moved forward and the warmth of the room encircled her in a comforting way. The noise level lowered immediately, but before she made up her mind whether to leave or not, the buzz of conversation started up again. Everyone was talking to everyone else. This must be one of those local cafes the guidebook mentioned, with excellent food and only the natives frequented the place.

Not wanting to take up a table, Kate sat on a stool at the counter. The mirror behind the counter reflected the patrons, who weren't paying any attention to her. But she did feel someone observing from the next stool.

The man regarding her so seriously didn't look away when she turned toward him. His dark mustache, the thick, slightly gray hair, and narrow body with wide shoulders made her think of the movie star, Sam Elliot. His nose was too prominent for him to be exceedingly handsome, but he certainly was masculine. She judged him probably five or so years older than herself.

Kate looked away quickly, conscious that she had been staring back. An uneasy thought threaded through her mind, that more than his rugged good looks bothered her. She knew this man—or would know him.

"You look as skittish as a Blue Tick just let off the leash," he commented in a low voice, as if not wanting anyone else to hear. "Relax. Have a cup of coffee. We don't bite."

"Blue tick?" Kate asked inanely, not knowing how else to reply and not wanting to discourage him altogether.

He laughed. "Hound. Blue Tick hound. Let me guess. You're from the city. A big, northern city."

"Maybe," Kate answered, cautious in the way of big city residents. She had already started a network of lies about why she was here.

"Try the special. It'll warm you right up." He reached for his hat on the next stool and stood. "*Adios.*" He touched a finger to his wide brim. When he turned, she caught a flash of gold on his chest. Before she had time to wonder if he was some kind of town official, maybe someone who could help her, the door jingled and he was gone.

"What'll you have?" A bored waitress scooped up the money he had left behind and began clanking the dishes away beneath the counter top.

"Coffee. Black. And what is that smell of baking bread?" she asked.

"That's our fresh cinnamon buns. Want one?"

"Yes, please." In spite of the stranger's idea for the special, she did not intend to face an enormous platter of bacon, eggs, and potatoes, which was probably what he had had.

Kate wanted to ask who he was, but too many people would hear. She swallowed the strong, black coffee, remembering how much Detective Slater had enjoyed his coffee, with at least four teaspoons of sugar. She missed him a lot, but Slater was part of the baggage of her past she had to let go. The next stop was the library. She hoped the librarian would be a bit friendlier than the woman at the newspaper was.

ℰℐℰℐ

When Kate walked inside the library lobby, the sudden warmth and silence settled over her shoulders. Why was she pursuing this? She was playing detective with no idea of which way to go next. Her distress was because of the sense of urgency hanging over her head, as if she could prevent something terrible from happening.

"May I help you?"

The young woman behind the library information desk seemed amiable. Not like the person at the newspaper.

"I'd like to look at some back issues of the Sentinel."

"How far back? We have them on microfilm for several years, and then we store the film away. I can get you back issues from twenty years ago or more, if you'd like."

"Oh, I don't think so, not that far." Kate tried to recall the scene on the computer screen. The trees were full-leaved, not like now with the aspen and others turning colors or limbs already bare. "How about the summer editions of this year?"

The librarian explained how to operate the reader. Kate jotted down her starting date. If she was not careful, she could miss valuable information by missing one edition.

What was she looking for?

A missing person, probably.

The library was quiet, with the crisp turning of pages occasionally to interrupt her concentration. Apparently, not too
many people frequented the library this time of the year. Hours
passed and still Kate sat glued to the chair, with a fragmented
idea of what she might find.

Finally, just when she began to think about giving up, an
eerie premonition made the hairs on her arms feel as if they all
marched up and down her skin, telling her that she was getting
close.

Whatever she searched for would soon turn up. She
blinked to give her tired eyes a break and rubbed futilely at the
headache forming just above the bridge of her nose. One by
one, she continued to turn the pages, the creepy feeling still
there but getting stronger.

Down at the very bottom on the second page of a July issue, a short article caught her attention. 'Do You Know This
Woman?' The article described the approximate age, weight,
height, coloring, and long dark hair of the missing person. She
had vanished from town, leaving her rented tent and a few belongings behind.

The description matched that of the woman Kate had seen
in the river.

She rubbed her eyes again and zoomed in on the article. A
sense of regret and futility swept over her. She was too late to
save this woman from a killer. Why then had she been sum-
moned and by whom or what?

The article continued, stating that authorities had presumed the young woman had been a summer visitor, since they
didn't find a purse or identification in her tent. It went on to
say the authorities had dismissed the idea of foul play or rob-
bery, because there was nothing disturbed at the campsite to

denote a struggle. Trackers found her footprints in the woods, but she might have met another camper and walked away.

Had they ever learned her identity? Kate had a strong conviction that the body was still there in the water. Otherwise, she would not have seen it so plainly at that exact spot in the river.

She continued to go through the next few issues to see if they had discovered anything more about the missing woman. Someone murdered the woman, of that Kate was certain. Why would the local authorities assume the woman had walked away? Was anyone still looking for her? There was a possibility the newspaper, the pulse of small towns such as Plenitude, might have deliberately played down the incident, fearful of frightening the summer people.

Kate's eyes drooped with weariness, and she decided to quit reading. She jotted her stopping place on a note pad and tucked it in her purse. The woman was dead in the water, beyond help. Why did she continue to have this sense of urgency, as if something terrible was going to happen?

When the library doors closed behind her, Kate inhaled the clean, cold air and stood for a moment on the steps, clearing her mind. In the next block, she spied a grocery store. The hotel room contained a compact refrigerator, and she remembered it had been a while since she ate. She bought sandwich spread, bread, and ginger ale. Since she lost Annie, the thought of eating meat made her sick. What one circumstance had to do with the other, she didn't know. Maybe it was the blood— blood she had seen spilled on the highway when the car ran over her only child.

In spite of the sense of hiding away in the comfortable, high-ceilinged hotel room, Kate felt edgy. She walked quickly, envisioning opening the first of several paperbacks she had bought, preparing for a night of relaxation. By tomorrow, things might appear normal and she could leave this place to get on with her vacation.

She thought about Rasputin, her cat. Was he okay in the boarding kennel? Since she found him as a kitten in the alley years ago, they had never spent a night apart.

In the beginning when she started seeing the visions on her computer screen, the cat seeing them, too, let her know she had not gone around the bend. When he saw the pictures, his back arched, his hair stood on end and he ran for his hiding place behind the refrigerator.

Kate waved at Ralph, who sat behind the desk, and took the stairs up to her room. She fluffed her pillows and tried to read. The mystery didn't hold her attention for long. When she dozed off, her hand relaxed and she dropped the book. When it fell to the floor, she bent to retrieve it, noticing the clock read 2 a.m.

On the nearby dresser, Kate saw a thin streak of light coming from the computer she knew she had turned off. A cold prickly feeling crept over the back of her neck and her heart seemed to skip a few beats. She rolled over and put a pillow over her head, but that didn't work. Slowly, reluctantly, Kate arose, walked to the computer, and opened the lid.

She stared at the picture waiting for her.

Wide-awake now, she tried to swallow past a dry throat, as she watched a scene form and re-form across the screen. It wasn't of the woman in the river with the wire around her neck. For that she was grateful. Her gratitude did not last long, when she felt herself being drawn into the computer picture.

e/oe/o

She walked up a dark road, past a mailbox with a name on it, up the steps of an old, two-story house. The nails holding the wooden steps together shrieked beneath her feet. The damp, pre-dawn chill penetrated her clothing.

On one side of the wooden porch was an old fashioned swing attached with chains to iron rings. Old furniture lay scattered about the lawn. The whole place resembled a museum. A very spooky museum.

The ethereal figure of a man emerged from the bushes and glided toward the house. He peered into the window before turning and walking to a large tree with branches hanging over the roof.

Cat-like, he leaped upward, grasping branches, never miscalculating, and arriving at a large, perpendicular branch. The shadowy form paused a moment, leaning forward to look through a window and then swung up to the top branch, a position that seemed impossible for a human being to reach. He concentrated his gaze on the roof for several minutes, and then, leaped onto the roof, flattening himself against the steep incline. Both hands stretched out, his fingers splayed, holding onto the shingles.

It seemed as if he must have practiced this exploit many times before. He slid down to the eaves, clung to the cornice for a heartbeat, dropped lightly down to the tiny balcony, and stepped through the open window.

Unable to pull herself out of the dream-like trance, Kate opened the screen door. A loud squeak broke the silence. In the front foyer, she looked up the narrow, dark staircase. That was where she had to go. Her back felt vulnerable. Eyes pierced her skin. The urge to turn—to see if anyone watched her—came and went. She could not move any direction but forward. She seemed programmed to do certain things, with little leeway or latitude to alter her steps.

She knew she was supposed to go up those stairs and struggled to pull free, bound in a dream world with no way out. She slid her hands along the worn banister rail and slowly climbed the steps. At the top of the landing, she didn't pause, knowing which way to go—toward the room with the door ajar.

No! I cannot go in! Did she say the words aloud? Unable to turn back, she slowly pushed open the door.

Gloomy darkness closed in around her with only the feeble glow of a hall nightlight penetrating into the room. She avoided looking at the bed, and moved, captive within her own body, toward the balcony to look out on the pale dawn.

Her heart leaped when she saw the figure below, staring up at her from the cover of the dark trees. Could he see her? What had that meant, seeing him climb the tree and come inside the house? Was he a part of this walking nightmare or was he in a different time plane? She felt a malevolent savageness in the shadow and pulled back into the comforting darkness of the room. Catman. He was like a stealthy cat, tail twitching, waiting to pounce.

She had no choice. He would never allow her to break away. Kate moved toward the bed, dreading each step.

A young woman lay in the center of the bed, nightgown primly down around her legs to her ankles. Her dark brunette hair sprawled over her pillow as if arranged. Was she sleeping?

When Kate drew closer, she saw the woman's face gleaming whitely in the semi-gloom, eyes wide with fear, mouth open in an unheard scream. Around her neck, a wire noose bit into her flesh, a thin necklace of blood surrounding it.

Kate's gaze traveled down to her arm, flung outward. The upper part, a soft white, showed a small strip of darker skin, neatly incised. The cut was made so precisely it barely showed, obviously done after death, since there was barely a tiny sliver of blood left behind. Kate sensed it was not a mutilation. Was it a ritual killing? Something the killer had to do?

The back of Kate's neck prickled with the sensation of someone staring at her—the watching, waiting man outside. He knew she was here. Fear lined her mouth with dry cotton, and she gasped for breath.

ᏽᎧᏽᎧ

Enough! An oozing blanket of spongy warmth began to envelop her, as if she were drowning in blood. She had to get out of this! With a supreme effort, she closed her eyes and pulled herself out of the dream, reaching instinctively toward the computer to slam the lid shut. Her fingers felt icy cold on the little machine but the touch had broken her journey. She staggered back to bed.

When Kate awoke, her body bathed in sweat, she imagined a spigot turned on inside her, letting all her blood leak out, leaving behind soft, jelly-like bones held in by her outer skin. The incongruity of the sun shining in through the window added to her confusion.

This woman was not the same one Kate had seen in the river.

CHAPTER 4

Kate rested a while, letting the rays of sunshine warm her body. The previous night had turned cold but she lay in her pajamas on top of the bedspread. Until now, she hadn't felt the chill and did not remember getting out of her clothing and into her pajamas.

She sat up, running fingers through her hair. When her hand brushed her bare neck, she knew she hadn't been dreaming, but had seen another body with the same wound around her neck as the woman in the river.

It had happened again—a journey psychics called astral projection—a traveling of the soul or spirit through time and space.

She rubbed the goose bumps from her arms, grateful she had not experienced distant viewing this time, locked within the killer's mind. Yet, he had stood outside at the edge of the woods, and she had felt the evil floating upward.

Was the woman living there alone, unprotected? Kate shivered, pulling on a fleecy robe. "This woman I saw last night is not the one in the river." Her voice broke the silence.

She was used to talking to her cat. The coffee was left over from the day before, but she didn't mind. She needed caffeine and plenty of it.

If the woman in the old house was not the one in the river, that meant there had been two murders committed. Two women had died by the same method. When? Where? How far apart? Was the same killer loose, a predatory monster or a sick person wreaking vengeance in this little town? In other towns? She tore off a partially blank sheet from an advertising brochure on the nightstand and began noting the similarities in both murders.

Both women had died a violent, agonizing death. Both women had seen the killer clearly before their last breath. Kate had the sickening feeling that if she had stared deeply into the open eyes of the woman in the old house, she would have seen the reflection of the face of the killer.

She remembered the mailbox before going into the yard. What name had been on it? No matter how hard she concentrated, it would not come to her. Too much had happened, making her mind thick and sodden. Her thoughts were bogged down in a swampy mire, so that she had to pull each idea out, one by one, using all her energy.

Two murders should have blown this little town apart, yet the notice she found in the paper mentioned only a missing person. The newspaperwoman hadn't said anything about a murder of a young woman with long dark hair. Wouldn't she have told her about the death in the old house? Surely, it wasn't some conspiracy to protect the town's precious tourist trade.

Kate decided to make another trip to the library before she talked to a sheriff. She was not ready for that yet.

She washed down the dry muffin brought home the day before with another cup of stale coffee, just to get something in her stomach. She dressed hurriedly in new jeans and a flannel shirt bought especially for the trip. Her first pair of jeans—hard to believe. She left the hotel without catching sight of Ralph.

At the library, a balding gray haired man sat behind the reference desk. Kate nodded to him and walked back to the microfilm. Fast-forwarding the film to the date where she stopped reading the day before, she continued her search. The monotony of reading through a small town newspaper was soothing after the nightmare of last night.

One headline caught her eye and curiosity made her pause. She did not recognize the town but it must have been close by to have *The Sentinel* include it in their issue. It told of a tragic accident at a visiting circus where an experienced trapeze artist fell to his death. An unexpected chill ran up her spine and she hastily turned the handle to get away from the article. She didn't need to read about any new tragedies, she had enough on her plate.

Moving ahead, the next headlines blazed onto the screen, and she stopped the rolling screen to read.

Elizabeth Bartlett, murdered in her home. The name on the mailbox from her mind-journey lay just out of reach of her memory, but Bartlett didn't ring true. It would come to her in time. According to the article, the young woman was the daughter of the town's previous mayor. She had lived alone since moving into her parents' old homestead. The authorities were checking out clues but their one lead so far was the possibility of a jealous suitor; since everyone else questioned had alibis.

There were several articles, each smaller than the previous one, about the authorities checking out the murder, but reading between the lines, it seemed as if the search had ended. Disappointment settled over Kate's shoulders and she put her head down on her arms for a moment. She realized that both women were dead, and she had not come here to protect them.

Kate made copies of the articles and took them to the front desk. The librarian looked happy that someone needed his help. Sliding the copy of the article about the murder toward him, Kate carefully managed a few delicate lies. "I'm looking for a friend of mine, an old high school chum. I hope it's not, but this looks as if it could be her. We were supposed to have a sort of reunion here last July, but I couldn't make it."

The man pulled the paper toward him. After glancing at the column, he took off his reading glasses and stared at her. "And?" His voice sounded impatient for the first time.

"I wondered, since this is such a small town, if you might have known this woman. There isn't much about her in the article."

"Everyone knew Betsy. She taught school a while, but went away, Chicago I think, to study art. Moved into her folk's old house at the edge of town so she could paint without interruption, I suppose. It had to be spooky out there in the woods alone. Maybe that was why her marriage broke up. Her husband didn't want any part of living out there, I heard."

As if realizing he rambled, the librarian backed up a little to put some distance between them. "I'm sure this isn't the same person you're looking for. Betsy was born and raised around here."

And I'm obviously an outsider. Kate knew his thoughts without needing to be psychic.

"Then what about this woman? She could be the one I'm looking for." Kate pushed forward a copy of the article about the missing woman the authorities presumed had walked away.

He put his glasses back on and read it.

"Don't know anything about her. Nope. She was a tourist passing through. Some folks remembered her enough to give the sheriff her description, looks like, but I didn't know her."

She sensed an underlying hostility behind his polite words.

"Said I didn't know her," he repeated when she didn't go away. "Why would you ask me?"

"Why not? You live here. Small town, everyone knows everyone," she countered, irritated at the doors always slamming on her questions. The trick of turning suddenly aloof was supposed to be a big city maneuver, to keep people at a distance. She didn't expect it here, in this quaint little village.

"I never keep up with the concerns of outsiders. Got enough to occupy myself."

"Outsiders?"

He shrugged impatiently, shoving the copy back to her side of the counter. "That's what I said. People passing through all look the same to me. They come here expecting excitement, whether rafting or hunting or skiing, then decide they can't take the quiet."

So he thought this town was for people born and raised here. How provincial. Suddenly Kate felt as if she were in the middle of that movie about the Stepford wives, where everyone was like a clone.

Kate waited while a customer checked out books. "Where might I find out about her?"

"Most likely ask Sheriff Albarade." He looked at the big clock on the wall. "You'll probably find him in his shop, The Outfitters, about now." He turned his back to work on a stack of books and ignored her.

A wave of excitement caused her to lean against the counter for support. Albarade. The name on the mailbox at the old house. The dead woman's name was Elizabeth Bartlett Albarade. Was she connected to the sheriff?

"Excuse me. Two more questions." Kate ignored the old man's frown and the pucker of his thin lips as he turned back to glare at her. "Is the sheriff the only one named Albarade in Plenitude? Was Elizabeth Bartlett any relation to him?"

"Yes to both questions, young lady. You ask a lot of questions for a passerby. Anyway, it's a matter of record. Betsy and Dillon Albarade were married—for a while." He turned away again.

"Thanks," Kate said, pushing through the heavy library doors, inhaling the sweet, cold air outside. Interesting piece of information. A divorced husband killing his ex-wife for one reason or another happened all the time. But a sheriff garroting his wife and possibly a woman who looked like her? Who would suspect an upright member in such a tight-knit community as Plenitude?

Kate walked down the street looking in each shop window. What was an outfitters shop? The librarian might have told her how to find it. These people could be so rude. Still, Sarah Jenkins and Ralph at the hotel had been nice. Maybe they were pleasant because she hadn't asked them any questions to cause discomfort. She would need to question Ralph later, since desk clerks in hotels probably knew everything going on in town.

Talking to the sheriff was the last thing Kate wanted to do. Even though she was out of her comfort zone and doing things she had never dreamed of doing in her life, she still held an abiding fear of authority figures. There was time to back out, leave Plenitude, and continue her vacation. How could she help either of the two women now?

If that was true, why did the woman in the river call out to her? Why did she see the body in the old house? When the truth hit her, it knocked her breath away. She half-stumbled to a nearby bench and sat, stunned at the simplicity of it.

The woman in the river wants to be buried. Like Annie, she wanted to be found and put to rest wherever it was she was supposed to spend eternity. In peaceful surroundings, not thrown away like so much garbage.

Relief flooded through Kate at the knowledge that the victim, rather than the killer, had called out to her. All her research into the Shoe Man case had given her insight into how the mind of a murderer worked. She sensed this killer had something to accomplish in his lifetime, some formalized ritual he had to perform. That made him a predator stalking and killing his prey.

Kate inhaled sharply, jolted hard by the horror of her theories. She let her breath out slowly as she realized that no one knew who the killer was, or where he was, or even what he was doing. Even worse, she seemed to be the only one who cared.

CHAPTER 5

Kate found The Outfitter's Shop on the one long main
street in town, just past the diner. When she entered, a
bell clanged over her head. The smell of leather permeated the pine walls and floor. For a moment she stopped in
the threshold, staring across the cluttered room at the tall
stranger she recognized from the lunch counter. On his shirt, he
wore a badge. A leather belt with two guns hung behind the
counter on the wall within easy reach.

He stood talking to a customer, bending his head to the
shorter man. He looked up, regarding her with a steady gaze
for a long moment, and nodding briefly to acknowledge he remembered her. He turned back to the customer who listened
intently.

Interested, she moved closer to observe. His hands were
large, but he worked deftly with a delicate object trapped in a
little vise on a table. He twisted a wire with skillful ease, wrapping it around the top. For a brief second she saw the flash of a
woman's neck intermixed with hands and a thin wire leaving a
narrow necklace of blood behind. It would take strong hands.

Her legs trembled with the wild thoughts racing through her mind.

He reminded her of an old time western hero—or villain. He wore scuffed boots and a denim shirt, his long legs encased in Levis. Thick, dark hair curled slightly around the bottom of the baseball cap he wore. The cap had a Cubs emblem, but looked old, before rooting for the Cubs was cool. When she had seen him earlier, he'd sported a Stetson.

Kate listened to the conversation about fishing for trout and rafting down the rapids while she pretended to examine sleeping bags hanging against the wall. What was she going to tell him? That she saw two bodies on her computer? She dared not trust anyone. What if he were involved? He might have gotten away with murder. Twice. Kate concentrated on what kind of story to offer, to trade for information. If he'd wanted to kill his ex-wife for some reason, maybe he would kill another woman just to throw everyone off track. She had read novels about that.

Before Kate had a chance to give it more thought, he was at her side, looming over her. How did he get there so quickly and quietly? She was not aware that the customer had left, since she hadn't heard the bell.

He looked down at her, his eyes squinting under the fluorescent glare of the overhead light and grinned.

"You're the lady from the Hole-in-the-Wall."

She returned his smile. "Is that the name of the restaurant? Good idea. It was the first thought that came to my mind. I'm Katharine Macklin, most people call me Kate."

"Dillon Albarade," he answered.

Browned to a rich mahogany by the sun, wrinkles of good humor around his eyes conflicted with the hard lines near his mouth, partially hidden by his mustache. His eyes intrigued her. They should have been chocolate brown to go with the rest of him. Instead, they were startling hazel-green, flecked with gold, surrounded by lashes that any woman would have envied.

"I see you're checking out camping equipment. You don't strike me as the outdoor type." His voice was a deep baritone, his teeth white and straight beneath the mustache. He was laughing at her!

Kate tilted her chin in that way her husband used to call her stubborn Scots look. "As a matter of fact, I wanted to try rafting." She had never ever given that a second thought in her life. Why would she say that?

For a split second decision, it seemed vastly preferable to catching some poor misguided, slimy fish on the end of a hook. She had seen the sign mounted on the wall, *Fishing spoken here.*

"What were you doing with that vise?" she asked, diffusing her annoyance at his look of amused skepticism.

"Come on over here, I'll show you."

He led the way to a beat-up table with a coffee maker taking up most of the space on a corner of it. He poured two cups and motioned her to sit.

"I tie flies for fly fishing. I also teach anyone who wants to learn how to do it. Some are all thumbs and some learn real quick."

She shook her head. The only time she had remembered hearing about fly-fishing, she thought anglers had used real flies. Now it made more sense, but she was not going to tell him that. The next thing he would ask is why she was here, in the off-season. It worried her that she had to leave a skein of lies trailing behind her everywhere she went in this little town. She did not like lying. It didn't feel good. Nevertheless, what choice did she have?

"I'm a reporter for New York Country time," she began to ad-lib. "It's a Sunday supplement kind of paper. They want me to write an article about rafting the river." Maybe telling him she was a reporter would make it more logical when she started asking questions about the women.

"And they sent you to do it?" A dark eyebrow winged upward and he laughed. The sound might have been pleasing had he not aimed it at her.

"Why not?"

"You're about as big as one of our mosquitoes," he said, still grinning. "I'd have to anchor you down in the raft so you wouldn't fly out at the first sign of white water."

"You're one of those macho red-necks I've read about, aren't you?" she accused, past caution now. "My size doesn't have a damn thing to do with my qualifications for anything." Besides, she was not small, she was actually tall. Maybe her slimness made her seem smaller. No one had ever mentioned her size before as a drawback.

He held up his hands in a gesture of surrender. "God preserve me from a woman who thinks she can do anything. I did come off like some overgrown macho jerk, didn't I? How about another cup? This is my slack time, not many customers around."

"My husband and I—we used to do some rafting," she began a new layer of lies, not knowing how to stop now. Mac was city-bred, as she was, and probably would not have known a raft from a canoe. She twisted the finger a wide gold band used to encircle. She had removed the wedding ring about ten months ago.

"Well, that's different. If you've got a husband to watch you and be responsible, we might take a trip on the river."

"Mac died years ago. Accident at work, a steel girder fell on him." Why did she tell him that? Talking with Sarah Jenkins had been the first she had spoken about Mac in a long time. Annie had never wanted to talk about her father.

"Sorry. That must have been rough."

"Things happen."

"I lost my ex-wife. It's never easy."

The name on the mailbox in front of the old house pushed at her memory again. She tried to hide her dismay at his confirmation of her suspicions. As he spoke, Kate saw the complete name on the mailbox. Elizabeth Bartlett Albarade. The article in the paper mentioned Elizabeth Bartlett, which had done nothing to trigger the remembered vision. She had probably taken back her maiden name after the divorce, but hadn't bothered to change it on the mailbox.

"Ah, she died, and so young? I'm sorry." Kate was not good at fishing for information, but she needed to know.

"She was killed. Just last summer."

Kate had no warning before she looked into his eyes and caught the image of the dead woman on the bed in the old house. She shivered.

"Did they...did you find the murderer?" She knew the answer to that before he spoke.

He stared at her, then took off the baseball cap and slapped it angrily against his pant leg. "Hell no. Not a trace of a clue left behind. We only know she was choked to death and left like a discarded piece of trash. But I didn't say anything about murder." His eyes narrowed into what she supposed was his sheriff's mode.

"I read something about it in an old edition of the paper. At least, he didn't violate her."

His eyes narrowed. "What's going on here? How'd you know that?"

"It was in the papers, wasn't it? I was checking some back issues in the library for some local color to use in my article and came across the headlines. Last July it was."

"Yeah. July. I don't remember those details being part of the news. We had to be careful what we let out, so when we caught the bastard we could tie it all together."

The woman was not choked with hands, like strangled. Law enforcement, even in this back woods town, would have termed it ligature strangulation. That must have been part of the details of death that the authorities were keeping a secret.

Albarade's lean strength was obvious as he kicked back the chair to stand in front of her. Something about him frightened her. Like that shadowy figure outside the old house. Could that have been him? This man projected the same sense of strength and restrained vitality. Surely, Betsy would let him inside without him going to such lengths as to climb that tree and get on the roof. Maybe they didn't part friendly.

"The newspaper article called her Elizabeth Bartlett."

He sighed and hooked the chair out toward him with his booted foot, sitting down again. He leaned backward gracefully, balanced on the chair's two legs.

"She wanted her own name back, went to court for it."

"I guess your name is a bit unusual," Kate said.

"My mother was Anglo, my father Basque."

His clipped words made Kate think he was speaking against his better judgment, talking to a stranger.

"That's where your unusual first and last names came from," she said.

"Yep. My father's name was d'Albarade when he came to Colorado. My mother wanted to call me Dylan after her favorite poet, but my grandfather insisted on spelling everything his way. So I wound up as a Dillon Albarade."

"Mmm, that's interesting."

"You sure ask a lot of questions."

"Don't all reporters?" she countered.

Dillon stood and took a few steps to look out the window. Kate couldn't see his expression, but his voice sounded cracked and filled with pain. She closed her eyes, trying to get an idea of his thoughts. Sometimes that happened, but not this time.

"I hated that old place, where Betsy died. It always gave me the creeps. She and I, we didn't agree on much, but we parted friends. For that, I'll always be grateful."

Kate hated to push too fast and make him suspicious. "How about the rafting? Can you take me? Some place mild, just so I can get the feel of it."

"I may have one more party to book, not sure. It's too early for the hunting season." He turned away from the window, the backlight making him look huge and threatening for a moment, before he moved forward. "But I don't see you out on the water. Too dangerous."

"I can take care of myself," she lied.

He did not look convinced. She needed to have time alone with him, to pick his brain, but he was cautious. It wouldn't be easy.

The phone rang and while he spoke to a customer about hunting deer, she wandered around. In the back of the room, a little glassed-in cabinet held some rock specimens, a couple of big, ugly knives, and a long, awkward-looking pistol that might have been an antique. She peered closer and saw the Colt signature. A small leather book lay next to the pistol. Her fingers itched to touch it, to open the thin, butter-soft pages. She loved the smell and feel of old books.

He walked up behind her. "Just odds and ends I've collected."

"That little book—is it a prayer book or a bible? It looks very old."

Dillon opened the door and took it out, blowing off a fine spray of dust.

Kate followed him back to the table. He opened the book carefully, as if it had been made of the finest parchment.

"This was my mother's proudest possession. Dylan Thomas was her hero, if she ever had one. Thomas was a fellow countryman, from Wales. My grandfather brought our family over when she was only a child."

Kate liked the feel of the buttery-soft old leather when he handed it to her. She barely skimmed a page with her fingers, not wanting to mar the delicate paper. The sorrow, the loneliness of a woman of gentle rearing, living on a ranch and trying her best to survive in the harsh reality of pioneer life emerged as a vivid picture in her mind through her fingers.

"She loved you very much."

Dillon looked surprised at her comment. "Yes. I guess she did. God knows I loved her. I think reading helped her hold on to her sanity over the years. When she was a young girl, she fell in love with my father, who owned a sheep ranch next to my grandfather. Of course, Grandfather would never have let her marry him, even when he found out she was pregnant with me. When Albarade disappeared she didn't know if he had been paid off or if her father had him killed."

"As a young boy, you knew all this?"

"I found her diary after she was gone."

"After she was gone?"

"The old man wouldn't let her take me away and I guess she couldn't stand it, living there, not knowing if her own father killed her lover. She left one day and we never saw her again."

That might make a man angry with women enough to hate them. Angry enough to kill?

"When I was fifteen, I left him, too. Never went back. Didn't go to his funeral."

"Do you really think your grandfather killed or had your father killed?"

"He never admitted it. The ranchers and the townspeople must have made my father's life miserable. Even though Albarade and my grandfather came to this country around the same time, that didn't seem to matter back in those days. Albarade was Basque—a brown-skinned outsider while my grandfather was Anglo. Even if he was a foreigner."

"That's sad." She didn't know what to say. He sounded as if his bitterness had not worn away any over the years.

"My mother had the last word. I don't know how she found the courage, but she stood up to the old bastard and told him my last name was Albarade and had it put on my birth certificate."

"Good for her."

"The old man left the land and ranch to me, but I never set foot on my grandfather's property after I left. He broke my mother's heart, forced her to abandon me, and I'm sure he killed my father."

Kate gave the book back. "Read your mother's favorite passage." Kate already knew what it was, coming to her in its entirety, and spread out in her thoughts, as if he had already read it.

"I memorized a lot of his poems when I was a kid. It always tickled my mother to have me recite this one especially.

"Though they go mad they shall be sane,
"Though they sink through the sea,
"They shall rise again;
"Though lovers be lost, love shall not.
"And Death shall have no dominion."

"That's beautiful," Kate finally said to break the silence. It also confirmed the possibility that Dillon Albarade could be the killer. A man who murdered two women might think that way.

He was bitter and angry over what happened so long ago. Death shall have no dominion. Did that excuse killing in his own mind? Maybe because his grandfather had done it? That didn't make sense. Why would he kill two women merely because they resembled one another? Was it some elaborate scheme to get rid of Betsy and then someday when the body in the river was discovered, if there had been any suspicions toward him, he would be vindicated? Make it appear to be a stranger passing through town killed them both?

"You're the sheriff." Kate changed the subject. "I assume you discovered the body. Didn't you call for help from the outside?"

"Of course, I did. Betsy was the first murder we had since gold rush days. About the only thing that happens here is when the town council's parking tickets mount up and I have to serve notice."

"Must be boring."

"We like it that way. That's why I kept my outfitter business. I'm on call twenty-four hours a day if need be, but no one expects me to sit in the sheriff's office. Everyone knows where to find me."

"From the train on my way here, I noticed a nice wide spot in the river. Is that a good place to raft?"

He frowned. "The Dells? Like you said, it's a wide spot in the river. Hikers and kayakers can set up camps down there. No vehicles, not even 4-wheel drives are allowed."

She had seen flashes of a tent in her visions, connected to the woman in the river.

"There was something else I caught in the papers before I saw the headlines about your ex-wife. A summer visitor was missing. Did you ever locate her?"

He shook his head. "Nope. Funny thing, we faxed everything we knew about her around the country. We didn't have much to go on but descriptions from a few people in town who noticed her. According to the computer, no one reported her missing."

"Nothing at the campsite?"

"Hikers found her empty tent and told me about it."

"What do you think happened?" She wanted to tell him about the body in the water, but she could not trust anyone, especially not him.

"She ran off with one of the other tourists, no doubt."

"Just left her camping gear behind?"

"Reckon she thought she'd be back for it and it didn't work out. Wasn't a whole lot of value there, a couple of hundred bucks maybe. She had rented a kayak and didn't return it. She must not have arrived in a car. That would have made tracking her down simple, if she'd had a car registered anywhere."

A kayak. Could have been a raft, too. The killer had to get her to the middle of the stream. Sheriff Albarade must be familiar with every inch of the river.

"On the other hand, if she'd left behind a car along with her tent, you'd have had to assume she didn't just hike out with another camper," Kate said. Plus a car would have a registration, but she didn't go there.

A closed look shuttered his eyes and he shrugged.

Now was not the time or the place to confide in him, but she needed help. Could she track down this killer alone using the computer she looked upon as her adversary? Doubts assailed her and she felt an anxiety attack coming on. Kate needed to get back to her room and hide away for a while. She closed her eyes and took a deep breath, then stood and held out her hand.

"It was nice meeting you." Maybe at his touch, she would get a feeling of good or bad. He reached forward and grasped her hand in a strong grip. She liked the woodsy smell of him, mixed with some kind of after-shave, but she received no vibrations, good or bad.

"Sure you won't change your mind about taking me rafting?"

He looked very sure. "Too risky. Maybe if it was the beginning of summer, with others in the raft. Then everyone's green and they all look out for each other."

"Okay. Guess I'll go back to the hotel, write up some background for my story, and use my imagination for the rest. See you later." There had to be some way of getting past that amiable reserve that seemed so much a part of him.

Looking into his eyes, Kate wanted some intuition if he was the one. He was muscular, dark, and moved fluidly. Was her sixth sense warning her and she wasn't reading it? How to be sure? Her emotions and thoughts were on overload and she had to get back to her room to think things out. The cowbell clanged as she closed the door behind her and hurried toward the hotel.

It was time to pull some answers from her computer. A sinking feeling told her the man would not or could not stop killing.

CHAPTER 6

In the hotel room, Kate checked to make sure the batteries were still charging on her computer and then poured a glass of milk. She sat looking out onto the street. The town reminded her of an eccentric recluse, allowing humanity to ebb and flow around her, but keeping a secret core in the middle that no one could touch. It was a feeling she knew very well from her own experience.

Reluctantly, she moved the computer from the desk to the bed. She kicked off her shoes, piled the pillows behind her, and put the computer on her lap.

As soon as the lid opened, it clicked on and Kate toyed with the figures from her bookkeeping accounts for a while, knowing it might take time before she received a vision. That was so frustrating about second sight. Never hers to command, it came and went seemingly at will.

Her mother and grandmother had called it "the gift." Kate had never wanted to use it until she needed to find where the drunken hit and run driver had hidden Annie's body. After she told the police, who had been unbelieving but cautiously cooperative, they found the body where she said, and she buried Annie next to her father.

Kate's thoughts returned to Sheriff Albarade. Something about him attracted her in spite of the reservations she felt. He was strong, yet showed a deep vulnerability buried inside. Had the sheriff been an actual suspect in his ex-wife's murder? The newspaper said the authorities were checking out local leads. The meaning of that statement was vague at best. She could imagine what visitors might think of this calm, bucolic town if they discovered a serial killer on the loose. It wouldn't look good to have the sheriff exposed as a suspect unless they were very sure he was the killer.

Kate shivered, thinking of how people could appear normal on the outside and yet harbor such monstrous propensities to do harm hidden inside. Was Albarade one of those people? Or was the stalker an outsider, moved on by now? Could he be waiting here for another victim? If the murderer was a tourist or from a surrounding town, he would be back. Only he knew his motivation, his reason for killing. And they always had a reason.

Kate leaned her head back against the pillows, staring at the screen. Her eyes narrowed, watching the sudden burst of colored lights as the screen saver took over, gyrating, pulsing, throbbing with color and weird forms, like a kaleidoscope that had fascinated her as a child. She couldn't look away.

The shapes changed and the color muted until she saw the image of the woman in the river merged with the woman in the old house. They looked so much alike it was uncanny. They could almost be the same person if she hadn't known better.

'*She is down there. Look for her.*'

The whispered voice in her mind floated around her shoulders, touching her ears and back of her neck like a soft, rolling fog. Kate moved her shoulders, trying to rid herself of the feeling.

"What do you want from me?" She said the words out loud. She didn't know how to communicate with this spirit. Could it read her thoughts or must she say the words? "What do you want from me?" she repeated.

No answer came. She touched the keys, at first tentatively, afraid to disturb the picture. 'What do you want from me?' she typed.

The picture shifted to the old house in the woods. This time she stood on the lawn in the front where the silhouetted figure had appeared. Fear tightened like a hard ball in her chest and she had to suck in air to breathe.

'*Can you see me?*' A voice, a man's voice whispered in her mind from the overgrowth of trees at the edge of the lawn. It was not the same voice that had asked her to look in the water.

Belatedly, she wondered if he could track her through the computer. If she could see him, could he see her? She pushed away the upsetting thought. Her fingers flew on the keys and she typed, *No, I can't see you.* Should she have admitted that? *Come out. Let me see you,* she typed.

A harsh laugh erupted from the monitor and then a long pause when she heard only crickets and an occasional frog from the distant woods.

Are you playing a game with me? she asked.

The laugh again. She tried to picture who the voice could belong to, what kind of person it would fit, but her psychic powers felt blocked. Blocked as effectively as if by a stone wall.

Did you call me, or was it the woman in the river? Kate thought that eventually she would ask a question he wanted to answer.

Jackpot.

'*She did. Not me.*'

Are you going to tell me why? she typed.

'*I don't have to tell you anything. You are the intruder here, not us.*'

Us. Did he mean the dead women? Was he including himself with the dead women? Kate took a deep breath. It was now or never. *Did you kill the women?*

Feeling his presence near, Kate drew up as small as possible into herself, fear causing her fingers to tremble so badly she didn't think she could have typed another word. What was reality and what was in her mind? It blended so completely she couldn't be certain he was not able to harm her. She touched her fingers to her throat, as if feeling that cold piece of wire bite into her neck, letting her life forces flow out around it.

'*That's right. You feel it, don't you? I kill with the greatest of ease. But you are not the one I'm looking for.*'

Looking for?

'*You can't trick me. Don't think you're safe. I can come for you when I want to.*'

Then why did you call me? Panic left a bitter taste on her tongue, as Kate felt the foreground with his faint image fading into the background of trees.

Please. Answer me.

'*I didn't call you. Remember that.*' Then he was gone. The brush and trees were no longer menacing. His malevolent energy had dissipated. Kate closed her eyes and fell into a deep sleep. When she awoke the next morning, daylight sifted through the curtains.

Before she forgot the details, Kate grabbed a pad found in the nightstand drawer and wrote what she remembered. She wanted to avoid touching the computer, which was back in its place on the dresser. Funny, she had no recollection of getting out of bed and putting it there.

She did not have much to write. The man spoke in a hoarse whisper. She could not place any special accent. He was looking for someone, a specific person. That was worth knowing. The figure said he could get to her any time. Was that just a bluff? How would she know?

Kate had no idea of where to start. Her first instincts were to tell someone about the woman in the river so they could dredge up her body. Whom could she tell?

The sheriff? Not yet.

The sheriff had said the victim in the house had been choked. He couldn't have meant that literally. It was a term the authorities had decided to release to the public. She wouldn't have thought of pulling a steel wire around someone's neck and tightening it until they were dead as choking, although technically it could be. The terminology did not fit. Garroted or ligature strangulation maybe, she didn't know for sure, but something was wrong. She knew the victim had not been choked by someone's hands wrapped around her throat.

One thing for sure, she needed to call Captain Murphy back in the city and ask him to check on Dillon Albarade.

Caution overtook what she had first thought was a good idea. If she called from the room, the old fashioned switchboard in the hotel would be able to monitor the call. Better to use a payphone out on the street. The less anyone knew about why she was here, the better. Not that she understood the answer to that one herself.

Kate pulled the blanket closer around her shoulders, suddenly feeling a chill. The murderer had actually spoken to her. Had he spoken out loud or through her mind? It didn't matter. She had made a breakthrough. He'd told her, '*I didn't call you.*' That could mean when the woman in the river called, he picked up on it. How had he done that? Was he a psychic? The idea caused a swift chill up and down her spine and frightened her more than anything she had seen or heard so far. If he had "the gift," he wasn't bluffing. He would find her.

Did he want to be caught? She had learned that some killers were desperate to stop killing and could not. Killing became like a drug, an empowerment they couldn't give up.

She had to get the sheriff out alone, to ply him with questions. First another trip to the library and then she must call Murphy.

Kate pulled on her gray slacks and slipped a fern-green turtle neck sweater over her head. If she stayed here long, she would have to go shopping. She dashed on a light coral lipstick, and ran a brush through her hair, which she thought looked pretty this way, shiny brown and curved around her square jaw line. For years, she had left it long and somewhat stringy, but she had it cut before leaving on her vacation. Everything had to be brand new, as new as she could make it.

She looked at her image critically. Not bad for the slightly-past-thirty generation. She was beginning to enjoy food again, too, and she had filled out a little bit in the right places.

She grabbed up her large, roomy purse and slung the straps over her shoulder, then turned for one last glance at the room. No cat to tell goodbye. Next trip she made, Rasputin was coming along, no matter what. She had seen people traveling with dogs and that seemed to work. Her cat was smarter than any old dog.

At the door to her room, her feet refused to move. Why couldn't she just stay here, safe and secure in this cozy room? Forces pulled at her to sit back down and stay put. Outside hid terrors never dreamed of.

Kate stepped out into the hall, her mouth dry. *I have been through this before and conquered it*, she told herself. *Move one foot at a time.* She patted her purse, which held a small tape recorder and a note pad. First stop would be the library to check if she could find anything more on the murdered Betsy Albarade. Any facts she could gather would help her know how to question the sheriff when the time came.

A chilly morning, sparkling sharp and clear, greeted Kate when she stepped out. She inhaled the strong scent of pines and imagined what it might be like, living in a little town like this.

Strangers nodded to her as Kate walked toward the little diner. She looked forward to a plate of fresh cinnamon bread. Once inside, disappointment claimed her when she looked around and didn't see the sheriff sitting at the counter.

The room felt warm and cozy with a large stone fireplace against the far wall, burning some kind of fragrant wood. She sat at the counter and nodded at the server who came her way with a cup and coffee pot. Kate held the thick white mug in her hands, letting her mind wander for a moment while soaking up the smells and sounds surrounding her. Customers spoke in subdued whispers, as if they too enjoyed the early morning tranquility.

A good way to start a morning, she decided, thinking of the blaring horns, ambulance or fire truck sirens, and brakes squealing on the city streets. She lived in the suburbs, so it wasn't that bad, but not as quiet as this.

"Hello there. Looks like you found the place again."

Kate almost spilled the coffee when her hand jerked. He was so quiet, so quick when he moved. It was uncanny. She swiveled the seat around to stare up at the sheriff.

He leaned over, one hand on the counter, looking into her eyes with an unnerving, penetrating look. It was as if he tried to see past her eyes, into her mind.

Her heart leaped into her throat. That could happen if he was the cat-like man in her computer. She didn't want it to be true, but now it seemed the most logical idea. She hadn't sensed a particular threat from this man, and yet his essence breathed an untamed masculinity that made her uncomfortable.

Where was her sixth sense, her psychic ability when she needed it? She wished there was some way to tame it, some way to make it do her bidding instead of the other way around.

She lowered her eyes from his probing look, and when he turned away, she watched him gracefully slide his long leg over the little stool. Her gaze traveled up his legs, his narrow waist, the wide buckle in his belt, the denim jacket covering what she now knew was a badge pinned on his chest.

"Hello there, yourself. You look pretty darn chipper for early in the morning," Kate said.

"Hah!" He snorted. "Call this early morning? I've been up since before daybreak. Got a call about some poachers. Game warden's on vacation so had to check it out. Never did find them, but they got the deer all right, saw the blood where they killed it."

"Does that happen often?" In her vision of the woman in the river, she had seen figures moving through the trees. At first, she thought of the stalker, but in thinking about it later, she had the impression of it being more than one person, short-er and bulkier than that of the man beneath the window of the old house. Hunters may have witnessed the murder. The thought excited her until she remembered that poachers were unlikely to tell of seeing anything in the woods.

"Poaching happens a lot more than we'd like. Some of the people living here before the state changed the laws, claim they have the right to hunt to feed their families."

"Haven't they heard of welfare or job programs? We all pay taxes to help people who need it."

He made a wry face. "Uh-uh. No one around here would be caught dead going on the dole. Hell, most of them regard unemployment as welfare and would never touch it. Nothing that smacks of standing in line waiting for charity is for these mavericks."

She thought about that. This was indeed a strange place, as if she had stepped back in time a hundred years. She wondered if the surrounding small towns were like Plenitude. How far would the townspeople go to protect one of their own?

"Are you c–certain it was deer b–blood?" she stammered before she could get the rest of the words completely out. "Someone killed in this town and you've never discovered who did it. Maybe he killed twice."

The waitress set a fresh cup of coffee in front of Dillon and refilled Kate's cup.

Dillon's eyes were unreadable beneath the lowered lids when he turned to face her. "Two killings? That's a strange thing for you to say. There was no reason to think of Betsy's killer as being anyone but a stranger passing through. She was unlucky enough to be in his path. Why would you think something like that?"

"Many reasons." She struggled for logical answers. "I used to know a cop. A detective. He told me about some of his cases. In the instances of serial killers, some of them…"

"What?" The word exploded from his lips and people in the diner turned toward them with questioning expressions. He broke off a piece of toast but laid it down again on the side of his plate before he spoke.

"What gives you the idea that killing Betsy was the work of a serial killer?" He had lowered his voice to a husky whisper and she noticed the patrons had politely turned back to their breakfasts.

Had she said too much? She didn't want to endanger herself, not until she could trust him.

"Well, then, if not a serial killer, you must have some idea of who did it and why."

A look of strain showed on his face. He leaned his elbows on the counter, holding the mug with both hands, as she had done moments before. His hands engulfed the large mug and only little bits of the white showed through. They were big, strong hands, surely strong enough to overpower slender women and pull a wire tightly around their necks.

He set down the mug and moved off the seat, pushing some bills on the counter between them. He took her arm in a grip that made her wince.

"Come on. Let's walk. I don't know why this should interest you, but I have nothing to hide. If you want to know—Betsy's death did create a scandal for her folks, a scandal we tried to hush up." He pushed open the door for her. Outside it had grown cold and blustery. "At first I was suspect. People around here don't get divorces and when they do, they don't stay friends like Betsy and I did."

"Did she ever see anyone? Have any other relationships?"

"She'd been seeing a fellow from the next valley. Not everyone knew that, but we talked about it. He's a good enough sort, but she could have done better."

They walked along at a good clip. She had to take two steps to his one to keep up with him.

"We questioned him, but he had a good alibi. I did, too. I was with an overnight rafting group."

Far from here? She wanted to ask the question. As an experienced woodsman in good physical shape, it might be easy for him to run through the woods after the campers went to sleep, sneak into town, do the deed and run back to the campsite.

"And you've never had an inkling of who did it? And why?"

He put a hand out to stop her and looked down into her face as they stood on the narrow sidewalk. Not many people walked by. Seedy looking businesses edged toward the fringe of brush and trees that indicated the edge of town. The paved road passed on and disappeared around a bend.

"That's what tortures me. We shut the case up because the mayor and his wife are in a rest home. She has Alzheimer's and he's trying to take care of her so he won't have to leave her alone there. He's not much better off, in his eighties. They had Betsy late in life and she was their pride and joy. They were not happy when she married me, let me tell you, but we worked it out at first. Too bad, it didn't stay worked out. Anyway, the case isn't closed, but what was the point of dredging it all through the papers and..."

"It must distress you that someone killed her and you don't know who or why."

"Hell yes! It boils the piss out of me."

He was walking so fast, she looked longingly when they passed the last bench.

"About these…" She had almost slipped up and said these killings. "About the murder of your ex-wife, you said you asked for outside help?"

"I didn't know what else to do. Still don't. With every passing month, I know he will get away with what he has done. The man was a goddamned spook. He didn't leave a clue. We don't even know how he got in. The doors and windows were all locked."

His angry words brought a picture flashing through her mind. The fleeting image of the cat-like figure climbing up the tree outside the window and leaping across to the roof and sliding down to enter the dormer window. Impossible. It was too far and humanly impossible. She had seen him do it. Wouldn't Dillon have a key?

"We called in help from Denver," he continued and she struggled out of her vision to pay attention. "Detectives from the attorney general's office went over the house and the property with everything they had. They spent a couple of weeks on it. Nothing."

Kate felt the wave of pain beneath his words. It was real and not put on, she sensed that much.

"Do you still want to go rafting?" he asked abruptly.

She stopped in her tracks. A feeling of danger surrounded his words, pulsing through her temples. He shoved his hands in his pockets and started to turn away, as if her answer was not important.

Why did he offer now? Why did he suddenly change his mind? He looked the type of man who would have short patience with rafting novices, especially women. Had he read something in her eyes or had she asked too many questions? He might suspect she was other than she pretended to be. Yet, the killer was psychic or at least had some semblance of para-normal energy, and that didn't fit with Dillon.

Would she come back from such a trip? Or would she lie out there in the water alongside the other woman, without any-one knowing where she was? Kate needed to call Captain Murphy and tell him what she had discovered so far. If she didn't call back, at least he would know where to start check-ing.

A gauzy haze slid between her and Dillon, blurring his image. If this was a warning, why couldn't she tell? "I'd like to go," she said.

'*Famous last words,*' came the echo inside her head.

CHAPTER 7

After Kate left the sheriff, she walked back toward the center of town. The first thing on her mind was to find a payphone and call Captain Murphy. The next, go to the library and start checking old newspapers again.

She found a payphone in the back of a magazine/book store, and no one stood close enough to eavesdrop. After dialing, panic hit. Suppose she sounded like a complete nut? Captain Murphy didn't have all that much patience with her at the best of times.

He sounded effusively friendly when he came on the line, probably because she was five or six states away from him.

"Good to hear from you, Kate. How's your vacation coming along?"

He had always called her Mrs. Macklin before. She was surprised he remembered her first name.

"Fine. Thank the boys again for chipping in for the laptop." *Yeah, thanks a bunch.* What would have happened if she had left it behind? Would the voice have found her anyway? Somehow, she doubted it. The electric static of the computer reacted with the energy field surrounding her psychic powers and formed the picture on the screen. Although that was not very scientific, she thought it happened that way. Who could explain such a thing? It just was.

"Could you check on a name for me? It's important or I wouldn't bother you."

A long, pregnant pause and then he cleared his throat. "Ah, Mrs. Macklin, you're not into another computer thing, are you?"

So. It was back to Mrs. Macklin. No matter, she was more comfortable with that coming from him. "I can't give you any details right now, Captain. But yes, I'm afraid that little rascal your department gave me is acting up like crazy. I've come across two unsolved murders, so far."

"Good God, woman!" He forgot his polite, suave facade and roared into the phone. "You had Detective Slater to protect and help you before. Don't go poking your nose into things that shouldn't concern you."

"I know, I know," she said and cut him off. "I'm not poking my nose anywhere."

"Then why did you say two murders? Those were your very words. Don't the authorities there know how to take care of things?"

She did not want to get into a deep conversation with Murphy. He was like a bulldog and wouldn't let go. Still, someone needed to know she was in Plenitude, in case of…in case of what? She did not want to go down that road.

Kate sighed. There was always a price to pay. She longed to tell him about the murdered woman in the old house and the body in the river, but he would hit the ceiling. Probably send out a detective, stir up everything with his big city ways so she would never learn anything. Someone wanted her to get to the bottom of the murders and that was her one and only plan, if you could call it anything so dignified as a plan.

"I'm sure the authorities know what they're doing, only they don't have a lot of that sort of thing going on up here. No one's been murdered in this area since the gold rush days."

"And you know more than they do? Is that the impression I'm getting? Stop me if I'm wrong." His voice raised an octave, grating on her nerves more than usual. In spite of that, talking to him gave her a sense of comfort.

"Really, forget it. I'm sure the local authorities have everything under control. I just want to check on one of them. Name's Dillon Albarade. Could spell it d'Albarade."

"Is this the suspect by any chance?"

His voice said he would be packed and out of the office if she said yes.

"No. Of course not. He's the sheriff here. I just want a handle on his background."

"Okay. I can check it out for you. Does this mean you are seeing those crazy vision things again? We should have never given you that laptop to take with you."

You didn't think the visions were so crazy when they helped solve a case, she wanted to say. "No, no, of course not," she lied. She was getting used to telling lies and that bothered her. "I met this charming man and wondered about him. You can't be too careful. I didn't think you'd mind." There she went again.

"That's smart." His voice changed. He sounded a little deflated, annoyed. "I don't mind at all. Give me a telephone where I can reach you."

"That's no good. I'm in Plenitude, Colorado, staying in the hotel with a switchboard. It's a small town and everyone knows everything about everyone. I can call you back tomorrow or the next day, if it wouldn't be too much bother."

"Sure. But you be careful." He went into his Uncle Murphy mode, only he was not much older than she was so it had never been too effective. In his own way, Captain Murphy was not unattractive. It was only that he had suffered when she compared him with Slater. Murphy was sensitive and articulate, a university graduate in his chosen field, and dreadfully ordinary.

Kate gave him her address. She needed to have someone know where she was if she didn't turn up at home eventually. What would happen to her cat at the boarding kennel?

What made her think of that?

After hanging up, she left the bookstore and headed toward the library, sailing past the man at the information desk. By now, she knew where to go.

In the back of the library, she immersed herself with the microfilm, starting with the date she had left off, and began reading the papers again. Two weeks after the headlines of Elizabeth Bartlett's death, she found a little box in the middle of the paper toward the bottom. It read, *The sheriff's office checked out a few local suspects in the slaying, but the death was attributed to person or persons unknown. The crime is listed as unsolved and the investigation will continue.*

Searching forward on the film to a week later turned up a smaller blurb in the paper stating that the mysterious tourist was officially listed as a missing person but would likely turn up safe and sound in her own home state. The folksy attitude of the editor annoyed Kate. In all fairness, though, if the sheriff had no name to work with, if the woman had not registered in a hotel, but camped out, how could any resident be expected to know who she was? It was only by a little digging, talking to people on the street, that Albarade had managed to work up a description.

A sinking feeling told her she had reached the end, and there was no need to look any farther. Now she had to choose whether to believe the sheriff. Was he really stalled in his investigation? Was this a guilty man hiding a terrible secret?

Maybe it wasn't a serial killer at work here, but her runaway imagination. Could the sheriff have become angry at his ex-wife, perhaps because of her new relationship, and killed her? That would make the woman in the river a stranger. Suppose the woman in the river had been killed years ago and it was just a coincidence that both women were murdered in this little town.

Kate sat on a bench on the library lawn. The street was peaceful, bucolic, a country street in the center of a country town. People walked down the sidewalks and as a diversion, she tried to pick out the locals, to see if she could tell them from the tourists. There weren't many visitors left.

The peaceful setting warred with her sinister, complex thoughts. The key. She needed a key to open the first door to the puzzle. The first key could be the stalking shadow that spoke to her in the computer, the same one who invaded the yard of the old house. If the sheriff did it, why would he skulk around in his ex-wife's yard? Was he waiting for something to happen in the house before he entered? Waiting for the lights to go out, for her to come home? Kate had a strong sense that the killer was waiting for something.

Chances were the woman in the river was connected to the murder in the old house. The method of killing seemed the same. Either there was a psychopathic killer hiding out as the local sheriff or a cunning predator who had invaded Plenitude.

Whoever it was had killed two women and escaped. *Nearly* escaped, until the woman in the river had called out for help.

The call had brought the killer back, too. What an eerie feeling, wondering if she hadn't come this way, if she'd never decided to take this vacation, what then? Would the woman have lain in the water until she disintegrated, un-mourned and unburied?

The water was cold and dark, swift moving and not stagnant. Perhaps that held the body together so it hadn't fallen apart, so that Kate could see her as a whole person. Someone would have to dredge the river, but that couldn't happen until she could convince someone the woman was there, until she trusted someone enough to tell them.

Kate rose from the bench, suddenly chilled by the late afternoon wind coming off the mountain. Time to return to the hotel. The idea appealed to her so much that it scared her. Safe, tucked away in a small room. Safe only until she turned on the computer again, which she had to do.

What if it warned her about the rafting trip with Dillon Albarade?

CHAPTER 8

In the hotel room, Kate sat on the big chair at the window, not wanting to touch the computer. Was the town conspiring to protect their sheriff or the dead girl's family? Or was it simply that no one knew anything?

Should she go on a rafting trip with Dillon? That thought stopped her. When did he become Dillon instead of the sheriff? He hadn't mentioned if anyone was going with them, but there might be a last minute party of rafters, he as much as suggested that. With a group of people, surely nothing could happen to her. *Not necessarily*, a small voice chided. It would be a simple matter for a river-wise man to contrive a commotion in the raft and in the confusion, push her overboard.

She paced the room. Something didn't fit here. Something wasn't right, but it was impossible to put her finger on it. The computer drew her inexorably forward. She flipped on the switch. Immediately the spreadsheets came up with the last bookkeeping job she had worked on. All of her customers knew she was taking a vacation. She had worked ahead as much as she could, allowing for the time off.

Her fingers hovered over the keys, not knowing how to start her visions. She closed off the bookkeeping part of the program, entered the word processor and began typing questions.

Who are you? Why do you kill? Why did you call me here? What do you want from me?

She typed the words repeatedly until they filled the screen. Little jabs of electricity tingled at her fingertips and, looking up, she saw the words had disintegrated as if blown apart by a bomb. When the screen cleared, the river appeared with rushing, tossing water but no sound came through. It was like watching the TV with the sound off. The now familiar figure edged away from the tree line on shore, but not so clear as to let her make out anything. She could tell he was tall and moved with a feline grace.

She had to keep reminding herself that she was sitting in a hotel room and not out on the river.

'*You are getting closer to the center. You know how I got in the house.*'

The words flowed across the screen. So quickly, it might have been her imagination.

She rubbed icy fingers together, forcing the blood back in them in order to type.

I saw you leap from the tree to the roof, but I still don't believe you did that. Impossible. Her hands moved over the keys, putting the words on the screen as fast as she could, afraid to lose the connection.

'*I did it, believe. I can fly through the air, that's nothing for me. I don't understand how you saw it.*'

How do you get in my head? How do you know my visions?

Did she just hear that derisive laugh of his or was that, too, a part of her imagination?

'You don't expect me to answer that, do you? I did not bring you here. She did, the one in the river. She wants to be found. I hadn't counted on that.'

But you know I am here, you know my thoughts. Some of them. How?

No answer. He only answered what he wanted. Clever of him.

Why do you kill? How many have you killed?

A long pause came and she feared he wouldn't answer.

'I told you, I am looking for someone. When I find her, she will be the last. I don't remember how many I've killed, that is not important. They all deserved to die, they look like her. They are bitches, too, I can tell. When I kill them, I am killing her but when I've finished it, with each one, I know I haven't found her yet.'

Kate watched the ghostly form move restlessly back and forth just inside the perimeter of the trees. If only he would edge out a bit. Could she force his hand?

Kate took a deep breath and started to type.

What if you are lying to me—lying to yourself? You enjoy the killing. Admit it. Are you truly searching for someone special, or do you just enjoy the hunt and the kill?

That harsh laugh again.

'You are a worthy adversary, but never forget, that is what you are to me, the enemy. I will tolerate you as long as it amuses me. I have never had this with anyone else, it's intriguing. Nevertheless, beware of annoying me. I know where to find you.'

He was playing a game with her. He somehow locked on to her visions, to her thoughts. He had to be psychic, too. Was it on the same level as her ability? Stronger? That idea felt so frightening, her thoughts skittered away from it. Her heart beat faster until it was hard to breathe, her chest felt tight. He knew everything she thought. She didn't have to type it out on the keyboard.

Kate waited, but he had vanished into the dark trees.

When she backed out of the word processing program, the spreadsheet returned to the screen. Kate shut off the computer and moved back to the chair by the window.

Her skin felt clammy with a chill that went all through her. Her hands trembled until she had to clasp them together to hold still. Never could she have imagined someone able to challenge her with psychic powers. Her first instinct was to turn and run. That method had always worked for her in the past. Except once she involved herself in a puzzle, once she immersed her being into helping someone who called upon her, she could not turn back.

What next? The only hint of a key to the deaths started with the woman in the water. She had to be dredged up. The way to do that was to convince the sheriff. If he were guilty of killing the women, then he would have to kill her to stop the questions. The man in her computer didn't *feel* like the sheriff. But he could be very clever at trying to outsmart her, playing his sick game.

The phone rang, startling in the quiet room with the hum of the refrigerator as the only sound. No one knew to call her here.

"Mrs. Macklin? Kate?"

She sighed. He was not supposed to call the hotel. She hoped the switchboard was on automatic. An odd little burst of pleasure hit her to hear Captain Murphy's voice. He was so blessedly ordinary, so remarkably normal.

"Hello, Captain. This is after work for you, isn't it?" She smiled at the sound of him clearing his throat. He seemed nervous, which was unlike him.

"Umm. It was easier to call you from home. Did I pick a bad time?"

Kate felt comforted by his small talk. He was good at putting people at ease—when he chose to.

"No, of course not. I didn't want you to call at the hotel. How did you find me?"

"Ha! Simple deductions. You said you were in Plenitude, Colorado, a very small town according to the computer atlas. You also said you were staying at *the* hotel. From that I took it to mean there was probably only one hotel in town."

"Oh, my, I'm impressed, Captain." She really was. She'd had the idea of staying hidden away until it was necessary to get in touch with him.

"You can call me Murphy if you'd like. Most do behind my back."

She laughed. He had a sense of humor. That came as a surprise. Slater had despised him so much there hadn't been room to see anything but the man's faults.

"Okay, Murphy." Suddenly she did not want to hear anything about Dillon Albarade.

"I know you said you'd call me, but the tone in your voice worried me."

She wanted to tell him how sweet that sounded, but didn't. "What did you learn?"

"In a second. First, I want to hear about you. Been worried about you and that computer."

"I'm going on a rafting trip." That ought to set him back on his pressed boxer shorts.

She had this funny image about men, since she began venturing outside again. It popped into her thoughts first to take away some of the fear of strangers. Men in authoritative positions frightened her the most and, to get past this hurdle, she imagined what kind of underwear they wore. Her husband had been boxers, Dillon was surely jockey, same as Slater, and here was charming, pompous Murphy in pressed, probably Egyptian cotton boxer shorts.

Kate giggled into her hand, turning the phone away so he wouldn't catch the sound.

Too late.

"What was that? Did I hear you laughing?"

"Excuse me, had a cough coming on."

"Kate? Did you say rafting? That doesn't sound like something you'd do."

How would he know? He was right, though. It had been her goal for so many years to blend into the background so that no one noticed her. When you weren't noticed, not so many bad things happened to you.

"Listen up, I've got news."

"I think I should go out and use the payphone down the street. Did an old-sounding man answer the phone when you called?"

"No. Not at all. It was one of those robot recordings."

"Well, okay, guess Ralph stepped out. Go ahead, what have you got?"

Her thoughts fragmented off into meeting Dillon for breakfast this morning. She had begun to look forward to their little conversations.

"What?" She had missed part of his monologue. "Excuse me?"

"I said," he growled, his patience short, for some reason, "Dillon d'Albarade was in Viet Nam. He went over after the war as part of the peacekeeping team. Mop-ups, they called them, a tough bunch."

"He never mentioned that. Of course, we haven't spoken all that much." He'd had time to tell her about his grandfather and his mother and recite a Welsh poem to her, though.

"Most of them don't talk about it."

Murphy obviously hadn't gone to Nam.

"That's very interesting, but I was inquiring if he'd been in trouble or anything like that."

"I just mention the Viet Nam thing because the special unit that he served in was strictly covert. Still is, but being a police captain gives me a little leverage here and there."

Kate imagined him preening just a bit, touching the near-bald spot on the top of his head and rearranging the reddish blond hair to cover it.

"I still don't see that this is anything I need to know."

"It can mean something or nothing. It just means that you have to take care in your dealings with this man. Everything is not always as it seems. They were taught that black is black and white is white with no gray areas. These highly trained guerrillas were a law unto themselves, sent in to track down the worst war criminals who would never see justice and clean the slate."

"Good Lord! Are you sure of this? The end justifies the means sort of mindset?"

"Exactly. As a cop, it goes against everything I believe in, but still, I can see the underlying justice in the idea."

"So the mop-up committee went in like a bunch of Rambos to get the job done by punishing the unpunished?"

"You got it."

Kate was silent, thinking about what it meant to her to know this about Dillon. Before she heard this, her immediate thought had been how bad she felt going behind his back, rifling into what he apparently wanted kept secret.

This new facet to the sheriff made him the perfect assassin. She had the greatest urge to hang up the phone and run back to bed, pull the covers over her head like she used to do when she stayed home alone.

"Okay. Anything else?" She took pride that her voice sounded normal.

"No, pretty much routine. Besides his stint in Viet Nam, he has lived in Plenitude all his life. I can fax you this information if you like."

"No, Murphy, you don't need to do that. I'd better hang up now, though. Can't tell how long the desk clerk will be gone."

"I'll remember the switchboard next time."

Kate wondered if there need be a next time.

"You didn't tell me what you're up to, Kate. Sounds like you may be getting in over your head. Again."

He was the only one who knew the half of what happened in her last situation. She had often wondered how much he put on his official report. "No, it's okay. Look, I'll try to call you back as soon as I can, to keep in touch, if you want me to."

"Hell, yes!" he blurted and then stammered like a schoolboy caught writing dirty words on the blackboard. "Of c–course I want you to. I'd just l–like to know what you're into that you n–need information about the local sheriff."

"It's personal. Can't talk now, Murphy. I'll call from a phone booth sometime this week. Could be I'll have something to tell you by then or maybe this is all one big ugly dream."

"But, Kate—"

"Thanks a lot for your trouble. Bye." She hung up briskly, to let him know she was finished, at least for now.

What did this latest wrinkle about Viet Nam mean? Even without this knowledge, she knew Dillon had the strength to overpower the women. When she saw the two women, on her astral projections, as she had learned to call her mind-travels, neither looked to be small and dainty. The one in the water was a hiker and camper, traveling alone, and apparently used to taking care of herself. They could not have been pushovers. Yet, there was no sign of a struggle in the old house. Had he caught Betsy in her sleep? Kate wished that were so, but didn't think it happened that way. With a stab of insight, she knew the killer needed his victims to see him as they died.

Kate imagined the wire tightening around their throats, cutting into the flesh. She touched her fingers to her own neck, trying not to feel the pain. She did not want to feel the pain. Slowly, slowly the wire tightened. Did he do it from the back? Surprise them? No, he wanted to see their terror. He needed to see himself mirrored in their eyes. That was probably when he realized he hadn't killed the right person, but he had to finish it.

Dillon was capable of such violence. It was plain in his past, in his government service. From what he told her about his childhood, he could have had mixed feelings toward his mother. He could have loved her for her gentle nature and at the same time despised her weakness that let her father ruin their lives. He must have seen her running away as abandonment. His mother left him behind with his grandfather, a man he hated.

Certainly, Dillon believed the old man ordered his father's death. He hated his grandfather so much he would not accept the valuable ranch and acreage that he left behind.

Did Dillon Albarade hate enough to kill the ones who tried to get close to him? There was still the outside possibility that he had known the tourist. She could have come into his shop to rent the kayak and they could have even gone out together.

Oh, God, and here she was blindly shooting into his circle like an unguided missile.

❧❧❧

The following evening Dillon called from his shop saying he had time to take her rafting in the morning, early. "Early morning is the best time for you to see birds and wild life that disappear after the day wears on."

It sounded sensible and Kate agreed, but didn't sleep half the night because of her troublesome thoughts. Dreams came to her, dreams of lying in the still water, looking upward, no one to help her, no one to mourn her, no one to bury her. She woke, bathed in a cold sweat and couldn't sleep any more. By the time she heard the wakeup call from the night clerk, she was dressed and ready to go.

Right on time, Dillon pulled up in front of the hotel in his four-wheel-drive. It was a good sign that he wasn't hiding anything or he might have asked her to meet him somewhere.

He leaped out of his side to open her door, a gesture that seemed incongruous in the light of her worries the night before. He looked so damnably handsome, wearing a Stetson and a fleece-lined denim vest. The hunter-green plaid shirt under his vest made his eyes look deep, jungle green. His baseball cap lay between them on the seat.

Was he trying to impress her with the cowboy gear? If so, it was working.

"Hi. Guess you couldn't round up any more rafter business."

"Morning. Hop in. Looks like you're the last of my season."

Kate looked in the back seat at the rolled up sleeping bags and lanterns. A warning zinged through her and she swallowed, unable to speak. She climbed in and fastened her seat belt with shaking hands. "Are you planning a camping trip? I don't know if I can afford more than a one day trip."

He shrugged. "We never spoke of a fee, no need to now. I have to haul in the canoes and raft and stow them in the shed for winter. I'd be going anyway and company's always welcome."

"It's just that I don't see why you need so much equipment."

"Have to warm up after the rafting. Need somewhere to sit and dry out. That's why I told you to bring the extra clothing. River spray soaks right through your clothes, and it's damned cold."

She felt warmth toward him without wanting to. "Do you provide all your guests with such individual attention?"

He grinned. "Maybe. Maybe not. I usually handle a trip on the water pretty much like this. I build a fire and furnish blankets to wrap up in. I grill fish or steak over the campfire. Don't worry about a thing, it's all part of the job description."

Her lips curved in a tiny smile, thinking of the inappropriateness of frugality when she might not live to see tomorrow.

The car was warm and cozy, like the inside of a tomb. She felt the need to break the silence. "How many times do you take people out during the summer?"

"It varies from season to season. I choose my clients. This will be my last river ride until next summer, that's why I asked you to come along. I'll store my gear in the sheds and lock them up for the season."

"Oh." The dawn was just spreading pinkish tentacles of light across the curving highway, touching between the trees skirting the road. The thick row of trees along the edge and leading down the bank toward the river stayed in eerie darkness. Occasionally she caught a glimpse of the river off to the side. "Where are we going, exactly?"

Dillon didn't answer, just took a right from the highway onto a narrow road that traversed above the river. They traveled a few miles and so far, there had been no other traffic on the little road.

He gave her jeans, thick wool shirt, and down jacket an approving look. She had pulled her hair back away from her face in a ponytail. She wore hiking boots she bought yesterday at a shoe store for what she considered an exorbitant fee. She would have to work all year at her bookkeeping jobs just to pay for this vacation.

"I've got the kapok vests, you needn't worry about that," he said.

What was he talking about? "Kapok vests?"

"Life preservers." He glanced at her a long moment and she caught up the slack.

"Oh, of course, I know life preservers, just hadn't heard that term kapok recently. Every place has different terminology, I suppose." How dumb of her, not to know what a kapok vest was. She should have read up on rafting while she was in the library. But then she was supposed to be covering a trip for her newspaper, wasn't she? That didn't mean she had to know all the details.

He would spot a phony if she tried to make out she knew too much about water sports. As it was, she had fibbed in telling him that she and Mac had rafted.

"I'm not going to take you on white water," he said. "Too dangerous first time out. We'll just mosey down the river at a good pace."

"We're camping at the Dells, aren't we?" A flare of excitement mixed with dread sped through her. That was why she brought her computer.

He shot her a quick look. "How'd you guess?"

Her pulses raced at his question. Was it innocent or calculated? She took a deep breath. "It wasn't exactly a guess. I'm psychic." She tried for lightness in her voice. "It runs in my family. My Scottish grandmother was psychic. I'm the last of the line, looks like." She watched his eyes, to see if he flinched. If he was psychic, too, he might show some surprise at least.

He cleared his throat, as if the conversation made him uncomfortable.

"Are you?" she asked abruptly.

He turned to look at her, his dark eyebrow raised quizzically.

"Am I what?"

"Are you psychic?"

He laughed. She felt relieved that the laugh was not familiar, although the laugh from the killer was muffled within her thoughts, sort of whispered, so she couldn't be perfectly sure.

"Hell, no. Wouldn't want to be. Don't think I even believe in it, though I try to keep an open mind about things in general."

Kate waited for normal questions about how her psychic abilities worked, but none came. That was odd. It could mean that he didn't want her to pry—if he *was* psychic. Surreptitiously, she reached her fingers toward his hats lying on the seat between them. She clutched the brim of the Stetson first, closing her eyes. Nothing. No sensations came through with the Stetson or the baseball cap. She had never been able to work in that way, in what psychics called psychometrics. When they touched an object belonging to someone, they received vibrations, visions. It had never worked for her.

Had he blocked her out? Experienced psychics could slam up blocks to keep out intruders. She had never tried that either. The more Kate learned about the subject, the more her reluctant acceptance of "the gift" developed into something she no longer feared.

"Thank you for bringing me along," she said, turning in the seat to look at his stern profile. When he made no comment, she let it go, but the troublesome apprehension returned.

Dillon switched on the radio to a country western station. The fan in the heater hummed just below the sound of the music. She closed her eyes and rested her head back against the seat. He braked suddenly and before she knew what was going on, he opened the car door and raced around to the front of the vehicle.

They had stopped in a little pull-off area. Kate touched the can of mace in her pocket. Was this where he was going to approach her?

Dillon stuck his head in the open window. It was the first time she realized that she was cold.

"Sorry. Took the Bronco in for a lube job yesterday and Amos must have left the plug loose on the radiator. The car's running hot."

She could see steam boiling out of the front, under the raised hood. What she knew about cars she could carve on a wooden pencil, but this seemed remarkably convenient.

"I think I have an extra plug in the back. Have to let it cool. Do you have a cell phone?"

The question sounded odd to her. Did he want her to have one? "No. Never got used to the idea of someone calling me any time they wanted."

"It wouldn't do much good anyway, Plentitude is in a sort of a valley and when you climb this little incline on the side road, what with the trees and all, nothing gets through."

Kate felt the trees lining the narrow road closing in on her. No sounds of traffic, even though he said the main highway was almost parallel with this cut off road. Nothing sounded in the stillness but the rush of water from far away. There probably was not a gas station closer than Plentitude, but she didn't ask, afraid of the answer.

He left the hood up and slid back under the wheel.

"Too bad we can't have the heater on," she said for lack of anything else to say.

He laughed. "Ah, I can see you know all about cars. No water, no heater, that's the way it works." He reached toward the back seat. "Here, let me get a blanket to wrap around you."

"No! I mean, that's okay. I'm perfectly fine." She was not going to wrap herself up like a sausage in a bun. If he was the killer, salivating for a new victim, he was going to have to work at it. The fact that she didn't fit the description of the two dead women was of little consolation. The man who tuned into her thoughts knew what she looked like.

They sat in silence. The new day brought a bit of warmth from the sun, but very little of the rays made their way down through the trees.

"Are you here on a vacation?" he asked.

He obviously was not good at small talk or he was trying to catch her in a lie. She had already told him she was doing a piece on rafting for a Sunday supplement.

"Working vacation, I guess you'd call it."

"Where you from?"

"New York. Ever been there?"

"Nope. Wouldn't want to go, either. I got everything I need right here."

"How wonderful." She had begun a sarcastic answer but it turned into the truth. It *was* wonderful if you knew where you belonged with such certainty.

The minutes stretched past an hour. What was he waiting for? If he was going to make a move, why dally until another car could possibly come this way? Surely, someone would drive by eventually.

As if in answer to her thoughts, he said, "Not many people use this old road in the off-season. There's a cutoff that the locals know and prefer."

Great.

He got out and peered under the hood. Maybe she should get out, too, let him know she was concerned. Kate shivered as she crawled out of the car and stood in the front. How had he disappeared so fast? She looked down and saw him lying on his back, his long, denim-covered legs spread apart, pants tight around his hips. He was under the car, but not all of him. Oh, no, not all of him.

In spite of her fears and suspicions, she felt an audacious wave of desire. There was something erotic about a man lying flat on his back, helpless. Kate turned away when he slid out.

"I'll go for water. I won't be long."

It took at least a half hour before he returned up the steep incline with two gas cans filled with water.

"I thought you'd abandoned me."

"Nope. This is the highest crest of the road and river. When we leave here it's all downhill."

"Wouldn't you know that'd be the way?" she said.

Dillon poured the water in slowly and paused often to look beneath the car.

"Doesn't seem to leak. Amos just forgot to tighten the radiator petcock."

He wiped his hands clean on a rag from the back of the car and walked toward her.

Her fingers, numb with cold, tightened on the mace container in her pocket.

Dillon leaned forward and reached out his hand. She flinched as he pulled a large, orange leaf out of her hair and waved it lightly across her nose.

"Say, you're a mite jumpy."

That was an understatement. She wasn't sure if her clenched hand would release the mace can until she warmed up a bit. She managed a grin. "We about ready to go?"

He nodded, opened the car door for her and, when she sat down, walked to the front of the car and slammed down the hood.

They traveled the rest of the way in silence until he slowed and braked to a stop at another cutoff on the side of the road.

"Here we are. I keep most of the gear down there in a locked shed. I'll make a couple of trips with our stuff. Wait here for me so I can help you. It's a steep path."

It was warmer now. The sun shone fully on their wide place off the road, a scenery pull-off from the looks of it. The river leaped and careened down the canyon and Kate felt misgivings rise up sour in her throat. She watched Dillon's broad back, receding down the stone steps, and began gathering up sleeping bags and blankets. She might be a city woman, but she was not some hothouse flower he had to pamper every step of the way.

Part way down the path, she ran into him coming up. The blankets were blocking half her sight and running into him was like hitting a brick wall. She tilted back and he reached out to grab her arms, his hands rough and hard even through her jacket.

"What's this all about?"

"I can help. You don't have to do it all."

"It's my job, but hey, I can use the help. Follow the trail, but be careful. You'll see where to pile the stuff. Wait there, this should be the last trip."

"My, aren't we bossy?" she muttered, watching her step as he suggested. She threw the armload on the beach and looked around. The river didn't seem as loud down here as it had from up on the canyon road.

Standing on the windy beach, looking out over the dark restless water, she felt little fingers of cold begin to play against her skin. They were totally alone. She pulled the little black mace container out of her pocket, took off the safety latch, and poked it back into place. She would not go down without a fight.

Then she sat down on a fallen log and waited for him.

What would happen when they arrived at the Dells? By then, would intuition come to let her know if she could trust Dillon? A warning by then could be too late. He said he wasn't psychic and the killer definitely was, but Dillon could be lying. She had certainly told enough lies since she came here.

Her life was on the line if she guessed wrong. Suddenly Kate had such a desire, such a tremendous need to live. She had so many things left to do. She had wasted so much of her life in grief compounded by her fear of strangers. She didn't want anyone to take what she had left away from her. But, neither did the two women who had died so brutally.

It was a chance she had to take. She could not turn her back on the others to come, the others who deserved to live and wouldn't if this madman was not stopped.

Filled with fear and wanting so badly to run and hide somewhere, Kate managed to steady her trembling body and waited for Dillon to come down the trail.

CHAPTER 9

When Dillon returned with the last of the provisions, he put them down and sat next to her on the log. "That's the lot," he said.

"Looks like you intend to stay out a week."

He took off his baseball cap and slapped it against his thigh as if shaking out dust. She was beginning to see that as a sign he was considering his answer.

"I stow my excess stuff in this aluminum building until next season, is all. Thought I might as well bring it down on my last few trips."

"How long will this trip take?"

He leaned forward to look at her. His eyes, green as the trees surrounding them, stared into hers and it seemed as if he could not avoid the issue any longer.

"I usually make this last outing alone. I enjoy the solitude after so many tours with summer visitors."

"Why did you bring me along then?"

He grinned, a little boy grin in a face that had been through the end of time and back. "You intrigue me. I wanted to get to know you."

"Me?" Her voice squeaked up an octave, embarrassing her. Until the word intrigue hit her. Was that a word the killer had used? No, he'd said, '*You amuse me.*'

"Yeah. You're different from anyone I have ever met. You looked prim and proper, kind of stiff when we first met. You may be a city woman, but you seem suited for this country. I like the way you look, have from the first time I saw you in the cafe."

Was he putting her on? She thought of herself as terminally plain. Too thin, small boobs, long legs, brown hair, even features. Her only unique attribute was her wide, spare jaw line, giving her a bold, tenacious look that she had seen on popular models in women's magazines. Yet, that was just a look, not her.

When his words sank in, the warm trickle of perspiration started to seep into her layers of clothing, even though it was still chilly. The wind blew sharp off the river. If he was the killer, then he was psychic and would know that she was going to track him down, no matter what. Maybe that was what intrigued him.

He reached to touch her hands, clenched together in her lap, as if in answer to her unasked question. His touch made her shiver. Kate pulled away and stood to look at the river. She should sense danger if he was the killer. She was afraid, but of what? Of physical danger or her feelings about this compelling man? If he was drawn to her, it was time to admit she had the same reaction to him.

Dillon unfolded his long legs to walk over next to her. "Are you cold? Or are you afraid of me?"

Kate laughed, a nervous little laugh she was not proud of. "I don't know. Both, I guess," she answered truthfully. "How do we begin our trip?" It was her turn to stall.

"We'll have to hike upstream a ways. The river leaves the road and the best starting place is up there. This point is too rocky. I store the raft and my canoes here at the end of the season, but keep them up river for use during the season."

"And the Dells are down that way?" she pointed downstream.

"Yep. We'll raft, towing the canoes, and by the time we get to the Dells, you will probably be mighty weary of the trip. Then, depending on the time, we can camp there for the night or hike back here to the car. Beyond the Dells is severe white water."

"Sounds like a lot of trouble just to take a little ride on the river," she commented.

"Some hate it, others can't get enough. From the time you get out there to the time you quit, you're wet and cold and feel like you'll never dry out."

"Then why..."

"Why do people do it?" He shrugged. "Because it's there, I reckon. It's a challenge, only not as strenuous as mountain climbing or as dangerous as skydiving. We've never lost a customer yet."

Yet? Not a definite comfort. "Will my laptop be okay? I keep it with me to make notes." She hated to take a chance, bringing it along. Maybe the killer had discovered by now how she got into his head. It would be easy to destroy both her and the computer at one time. Still, she had to be at the Dells with her computer, praying it would tell her what she needed to know about the killer and the woman in the river.

"Sure thing. All our equipment will be under tarps. Unless we capsize and then I can't guarantee. But that's highly improbable unless a strong wind comes up."

Unless we capsize? Was that a warning? The car was above them in the parking lot. She could still retreat and ask him to take her back to town. If she did that, he would never come out here with her again. She had to get him and her computer to the Dells.

"That's good enough for me. How can I help?"

In a few minutes, they were on their way, hiking up the trail at a slight angle from the road. He wore a backpack with his sleeping bag rolled up and tied to it. She carried a lightweight backpack, plus her computer wrapped in plastic, and a smaller sleeping bag. Her load wasn't heavy, not nearly as bulky and heavy as what Dillon carried, but still, after they walked halfway into the afternoon, she felt weighted down and tired. It was slow slogging through the woods, sometimes down to the beach, and then up again when the trail changed.

When she lagged, he stopped and turned around. "Sorry, I keep forgetting you're a city girl. You keep up pretty good, though."

Kate took a deep breath and bent over to put her hands on her knees, resting her back and shoulders. "I'm not used to walking this much," she admitted. "But I enjoy it, maybe that makes the difference."

His eyes crinkled at the corners with his grin. "It's not far now, just around that bend." He pointed ahead.

When they finally made it, the river had straightened out, become less choppy, almost calm, and the wind had died away. A large rubber raft and a smaller one were pulled up on the shore with a long line that looped around a tree.

"Aren't you afraid someone will steal your raft between expeditions? It looks expensive."

"Nope. There isn't much theft around here. We all know each other. An occasional tourist might be tempted, but this is a special place that few outsiders know how to get to." He pointed upward. "You can't get back to the road from here, anyway."

Great news. She was down here alone with a possible serial killer and no way out. Where was that damn psychic stuff when she needed it?

Dillon tossed the gear in the small raft, covered it with a plastic tarp with a thick rope threaded through a huge grommet, and tied everything together to the side of the raft. There was a canoe at the edge of the water that he hooked to the back of the raft rigging.

"Here, let me help you with this." He held one of the kapok vests he had been talking about earlier.

She straightened out her arms and he slipped the vest on her and adjusted the collar. His hands felt warm and a little rough against her skin. She imagined he lingered overly long near her neck before he reached down to tie it in front.

"Can I help you with yours?"

He shook his head. "No. Thanks anyway. I'm used to doing it."

When he geared up to his satisfaction, he helped her on board, untied the mooring line, threw it in the craft, and then pushed off with an oar.

At first, Kate felt icy terror when they crested, splashed, and sailed over and through waves on the river. It was such a helpless feeling. She had no control over her situation. It was all up to Dillon and she had no way of being sure just how much control he had.

"I thought you said we wouldn't be in white water?" Kate forced her voice into a high-pitched shriek to make herself heard over the water.

His grin was wide. "Lady, this isn't white water by a mile. Just a little narrows to navigate until we get to the center." His shoulders moved with effortless grace as he manipulated the oars, sliding the small craft around rocks that surfaced suddenly, keeping away from the shoreline.

After Kate's first panic, she began to enjoy herself, tilting her face into the spray, smelling the rich, loamy river, tasting the icy water on her lips, inhaling the odor of pines that permeated the air.

Once he spared a look back at her and his rich laughter exploded against the walls of the narrow canyon of rocks and trees.

It was just dangerous enough to get her blood soaring. Every nerve ending in her body tingled and she began to feel a dimly remembered warmth spreading through her stomach and warming her breasts as she watched his movements. What was the matter with her? Was the danger turning her on? Or was it the sight of this rugged, powerful man in front of her, making all the right moves with his tight Levis and muscular arms and shoulders? He had slipped out of his jacket, disdaining the kapok affair he made her wear. The sun slanted down on his dark hair curling damply on his neck at the edge of his collar.

What a terrible waste it would be if he were the killer. But then, she knew all about that kind of waste, didn't she? The old hurts of her life flooded back unexpectedly, coming in waves that overwhelmed her. She felt engulfed in sorrow for what had disappeared from her world.

She must not forget that if he was the killer, he had nothing but contempt for other people's lives. She tried to imagine his big hands pulling on a wire that terminated a living, breathing person, but her mind refused to picture it. Nothing in her psychic capacity was sending off any vibes either for or against Dillon.

She couldn't wait to get to her computer as soon as they stopped.

"Dells—up ahead," he shouted above the rushing noise of the water.

Kate held her breath. Now was the time for him to make a move, if he was going to. She had nothing to defend herself with, but will and caution and the tiny little mace container. But she was determined she wouldn't make it easy for him.

The canyon walls had gradually disappeared. The river widened and the water spread out, choppy but more even. The raft gave one last leap across a small wave and eased up, to settle on the still water. This section of the river was more like a gigantic lake, where the swiftness along the edges subsided calmly. It looked dark and deep. Trees closed in all around until only the center of the water was afire with sunlight.

Dillon worked the oars to move closer to shore and leaped out, snagging the line, and loping up the bank to tie it onto the nearest tree.

She was thankful her sudden lust for him was gone. It had been the combined excitement of the heady movement in the swift moving water, the sensation of imminent danger, the spectacle of the outdoors, and the unusualness of her situation, she told herself.

As Dillon lifted her out, he held her close to his chest a moment longer than he needed to. Kate tensed, waiting for his next move. He set her down easy, just above the lapping water line.

While he built a fire, Kate unpacked the raft and spread out the tarp to dry. She was chilled to the bone and as wet as she had ever been from a shower. Maybe that was why the erotic feeling left so abruptly.

"Want to share that smile with me?" He stopped laying out the kindling for the fire on the beach and looked up at her. "What are you thinking?"

"Ah...nothing, just a fleeting thought." She felt herself blush. "What can I do to help?"

"We got a late start, no need to hurry back. We'll camp here tonight. It'll be dark by the time we get back to the shed and I don't want a poacher mistaking us for a deer rambling through the woods."

"Does that happen?"

"Some of them shoot first and look later. I've seen cows and dogs and almost everything you could name shot up and left to rot or thrown into the river."

Thrown into the river.

"That's awful. Can't someone stop them?"

He shrugged. "It's the way it's always been here. Why don't you get into something dry? It was on the list."

"Yes, and a very detailed list it was, too." She waited while he untied the heap of possessions and extracted her backpack.

"Ah...where do I..."

He lifted his head in that slight tilt, a grin splashing across his tanned face, his eyes crinkling at the corners. With the fire crackling and blazing up behind him, in silhouette, he looked surrealistic, not of this earth.

He looked shadowy.

She shivered and rubbed her arms.

"See? You're already chilled. Pick a spot over there, just beyond the trees." He motioned toward the edge of the woods. "No need to go too far away."

He didn't have to worry about that. It was late afternoon and the sun sank out of sight early in the mountains, earlier in the forest. It would be dusk soon and then dark. She moved back into the woods far enough so she could still see the campfire. It didn't take long to shuck out of her cold, wet clothes and pull on a fresh pair of jeans and a warm flannel shirt. She would have to wear the same jacket, she hadn't thought of bringing an extra.

"Here, take mine," he said when he saw her emerge from the woods. "I've another inside the bedroll. I always take a spare. Someone is bound to forget."

"Thanks." She shrugged gratefully into his fleece lined denim jacket, savoring the smell of him left behind—woodsy, coffee, smoke from the fire. Man smells.

He laid out their bedrolls on the beach, a circumspect distance from each other, but not too far. Then he started to make supper.

"Need some help?" She didn't want to move, she was so cozy, but it was only polite to ask.

"Thanks. It's under control."

When he had the meal ready, they pulled closer to the fire. After they ate the plate full of bacon, hash browns, and scrambled eggs, they sat a while, looking up at the canopy of trees. Stars peeked through like tiny twinkling grains of salt scattered with a giant shaker.

"Do you like the city, Kate Macklin?"

"Yes. It's all I know. When I came here, I thought how comfortable, how serene, and peaceful it was and then..."

"And then you found out about Betsy. Hell, that is one murder. Your city has hundreds. Why would that bother you so much?"

"It's not just that. In the city, you learn to adapt to a spirit of impersonality. Outsiders think of that as cold and hard, but it's a method of survival. There is just too much going on that would overcome you if you didn't insulate yourself. You have a lot of that closed feeling here, in this little town. It makes me uncomfortable."

"You don't think Colorado is beautiful? The mountains, the trees—the whole state is magnificent."

She liked the way he let his defenses down when he spoke of something he admired.

"It is beautiful. The people are nice, too, for the most part. Who knows? I may grow to love it here."

"I hope so."

They sat in silence near the comfort of the fire, and she sensed he didn't want to talk. The night was dark, the stars distant in their brilliance. The smell of pines, the tangy smell of water, and the burning coals lent a mystic air to the night. An owl hooted in the distance, a soft, gentle sound and always in the background a gentle lapping of water near the shore. Birds nestled in the thick trees making little rustling noises.

By the time they were ready for sleep, the fire had died down to orange coals, the night grew damp and chilly with the start of a light wind rushing through the trees.

Kate decided not to change into the flannel pajamas she had brought. It would be easier to sleep in her clothing, especially since she should be prepared. Prepared for what? Did she still believe Dillon could be the killer? She needed to get to the computer in the worst way.

Finally, Dillon got up to cover most of the fire, leaving a few coals burning for light. If they had to get up during the night, he explained. There was no moon and, except for the stars, it was the darkest night she had ever seen.

"Good night, Kate," he said, and she said good night back.

A few minutes later she heard his breathing change like when a person sleeps. She held her hand over the flashlight when she retrieved her computer, opened the lid, grateful to have remembered to charge the batteries.

At first, the bookkeeping program came on and she moved through the spreadsheets, impatiently. The scene on her monitor began shifting. The sensation of coldness surrounded her, the familiar crinkling ice at the back of her neck. She saw the woman in the river again.

'*Close. You are so close. I am down there.*'

The words didn't come from the killer. Kate felt it was the woman in the river talking into her ear. The voice in her mind was so low and whispering. It had no gender, but she also felt no threat.

Can you tell me what happened? She typed on the keyboard, clumsily, by the light of the dying embers. She didn't want to use the flashlight batteries up. She might need it later.

Gradually the scene changed and golden fog swirled as Kate concentrated on the little screen. When the soft haze cleared away, she saw the forest, this forest. A small tent stood in the clearing with a lantern hanging to shed light through the sides.

She was inside the woman, seeing with her eyes, feeling her emotions. Kate struggled to break the thread between herself and the computer screen. She did not want to watch her die. She didn't want to know how it felt at the last agonizing moment.

Inexorably, Kate was drawn farther into the scene, her psyche blending with the woman. There was no escape. She couldn't break away.

The woman was changing her clothes, getting ready for bed. Even out in the wilderness, she was modest, slipping an overlarge T-shirt over her head. She wrestled with the buttons of the flannel shirt and dropped it, then the bra, next she shoved down her jeans and left her panties on, kicking the jeans over against the tent wall. She was modest, but not neat.

As she began brushing her long, dark hair, she heard the snap of a twig, sounding loud even above the constant noise of the river. She started to turn toward the tent flap, but before she could move, something thin, cold, and hard snaked around her neck, tightening. A bone-hard knee pushed into her back, against her spine, holding her erect, when she otherwise would have crumpled in fright and pain.

There never was a sound between them, even when she was almost unconscious. The terrible wire bit into her soft flesh, choking off air and yet he squeezed tighter.

For a brief instant, he relaxed his hold and took his knee away from her back. She gasped, hoping, praying he was going to stop. He turned her around, almost gently and let her look into his eyes.

The eyes of death.

She tried to focus. He looked blurry. Her mind cried out. She didn't want to die. Now it hurt, it hurt so bad. Now she wanted it to end, she wanted it over with. She was resigned. Ropy muscles in his neck popped up with the effort as he strained to finish it.

Then all was black. The computer screen was empty, dark, blending with the night, but the monitor made crackling noises.

Kate knew there was more. Her heart was beating so loud she thought Dillon must be able to hear it.

The scene shifted to the picture she had received on the train, a picture of the same woman, just murdered, only now she was in the river.

The thin silver wire marred the white neck, part of the woman's shirt was torn and for the first time, Kate saw a strip of flesh gone on the inside of the woman's arm, above her elbow joint, excised precisely, carefully so as not to mar the surface of her skin.

The same mark found on Betsy Albarade.

The view of the woman in the river faded away and Kate saw the camping tent, almost where she sat now. She sensed the canvas walls surrounding her and watched a gracefully moving dark figure holding a purse, looking through it, his fingers touching paper money, which he passed over. He pulled out a driver's license, staring down at it a long time as if soaking up the details about the woman he had just killed.

Kate struggled to see what was printed on the license, but the killer moved away, pocketing the license and what appeared to be credit cards. Outside the tent, he put some large, heavy rocks in the purse and flung it out into the river.

Kate watched the splash as it sank. She concentrated on her computer screen, needing to see more, needing to see the face of the killer. During her extreme concentration, as if he recognized her presence, the killer turned toward the screen to face her. She knew he couldn't see her, this had happened in the past, but that was no consolation. Although darkness shrouded his face, the eyes, dark and penetrating stared at her, pinning her to the spot.

Dillon had green eyes. But they could look dark at times.

She leaped to her feet and hit the dirt running for the woods. If the man lying next to her did this, she had to put as much distance between them as she could. In her blind terror, how she would get out of the woods, find her way back to Plenitude, occupied but a second in her thoughts. Get away, get away her heart pounded. A thick red haze formed in front of her eyes, she was so frightened.

She crashed through the brush and heard the sound of someone behind her. She made a bee-line for the water, past thinking straight, she wanted to get away from him. If the raft was there where he had left it, she could push it off into the water. He would have no way to follow then.

A hard hand grasped her ankle just as she toppled over at the edge of the river, a fraction short of hitting face first in the water.

Kate was past terror now. Sorrow overwhelmed her, making her bones turn soft, immovable. She would join the woman in the river, and lie here forever, with no one to know.

"For God's sake, Kate! What the hell's got into you?" Dillon pulled her backward, his hand on her ankle. He had taken a dive to reach her before she touched the water.

He hugged her close, wiping her hair away from her face. She struggled in his grip, trying to get loose, hitting him with her fists.

Her body felt drenched in sweat in spite of the cold night air. Her chest still burned from unaccustomed running. Her neck throbbed in sympathy for the woman she had seen die. She touched her tongue to her lips, expecting to taste the warm liquid of her own blood.

"Shh. Quiet, woman, quiet now, everything's okay." His low deep voice penetrated her terror. Her heart slowed its drumbeat in her chest. Easier breathing returned gradually so that her throat relaxed and she quit struggling.

Dillon explored her face with gentle fingers, brushing away the grit and small stones, wiping her hair back from her face. She leaned into his shoulder with complete surrender. Only then did he tilt her head back and touch his lips gently to hers at first and then with a need that matched her own. The kiss seemed to go on forever. He was the first to pull away, shaking his head.

"I've needed to kiss you since the first time I laid eyes on you," he admitted.

Me, too, she wanted to add, but didn't. There was too much between them yet. He could have killed her on the spot. Those eyes, those terrible eyes staring out of the computer, the man those eyes belonged to would have killed her. But they weren't Dillon's eyes.

"I've been so wrong," she murmured into his chest as he picked her up to carry her back to their campfire.

Blessedly, he refrained from asking her questions while he rubbed her hands between his and wrapped her in more blankets. They sat close to the flames he'd built up again and she leaned far enough away to watch the firelight slant off the planes of his cheekbones. How could she have thought he was the killer? There were so many inconsistencies in the way Dillon walked, his mannerisms, his attitude, his eyes. Not the eyes of the killer.

"I guess you want to know why…" Her voice was shaky and she swallowed past the tightness.

"When you want to talk." He pulled her close, nestling her in the crook of his shoulder.

The killer, although she hadn't seen his face, had none of Dillon's brawn and density. The killer was thinner, wiry and muscular, like a ballet dancer.

"I woke to see you typing on your computer. All of a sudden you leaped out of the bedroll like a scared rabbit."

"You chased me," she accused.

"Damn straight. As soon as you veered toward the water, I knew I had to stop you. That water is so cold, you'd have died of hypothermia before I could get you back to town."

"I need to tell you the truth of why I came here." It was time to tell him everything she knew. It was time to be honest with him. She had to have an insider break through the town's distrust, to drag the river for the body.

The body of the woman she had watched die and had come to bury.

CHAPTER 10

They sat in front of the crackling fire. Kate wrapped her arms around her knees, her hands clenched so tight they hurt. She wanted to say it right, she might not get a second chance. Dillon waited for her to speak, his eyes unreadable.

Kate touched her hand to her neck, as if she felt the cold bite of the wire into her flesh. Did it take long to die that way? Was there a lot of pain? She knew the answers. She had just come back from the hell the woman had endured.

She pointed over the sleeping blanket to her laptop. "I see things in my computer," Kate began, not sure where to start. When Dillon didn't respond, she hurried on. "I saw my daughter, Annie, lying dead in the street, struck by a drunken driver. I saw the man loading her body into his car. I knew he would throw her somewhere she'd never be found."

"Oh, God, Kate." Dillon raised his hands as if telling her he didn't know what to say.

She pushed on. It had been a while since she had let the memory outside to air and she needed to finish the story. Maybe her pain would heal now.

"It came to me on the computer. I saw where he hid Annie. Under a viaduct in a place the highway workers and equipment dumped the used cement and dirt. She never would have been found. My daughter called out to me. She wanted me to find and bury her next to her father. That's why the woman in the river called to me."

Kate sensed Dillon's confusion. She waited for his interruption. It was hard to tell what was going on in his head. When he didn't interrupt, she continued.

"I was traveling on the train through Colorado on a vacation when I saw this woman in the river." Kate set the computer down and got to her feet, pointing. "There. She is lying down there. A voice told me she was."

"Let me see if I've got this straight. You aren't a newspaper reporter sent here to do a rafting story, are you? I didn't believe that for a minute."

"Why not?"

"You don't have that edge most reporters have, you know, story at any price."

"That's a wide generalization, but no, I'm not a reporter."

"You saw a woman in the river that no one else knows is there and you stopped off to investigate. For God's sake, why?"

"That's one reason why I'm taking the first vacation of my life. I had to get away. Actually, I wasn't sure if her death had happened yet and thought maybe I could prevent it."

"You've done this before?"

"Yes." Her voice was low.

He bent his head closer to hear. "Ah, I see. You look into your computer instead of a crystal ball. Makes perfect sense to me."

Kate sighed. This was not going to be easy, but at least it was far from the reaction she expected—outright disbelief. She could understand cautious skepticism.

"I know it's tough to accept, believe me, I've had problems with it myself."

"Any idea who the woman is in the river, or why she's there?"

Good questions to let her know he had an open mind. "No. I don't know who she is. You and the town know as much about her as I do. She is—was—a traveler, a summer tourist. She had a tent just where we're sitting."

Kate had his full attention. He straightened, his eyes pensive, his body taut, as if he was holding his breath.

"How could you know that?"

"It had a little battery light hanging just there," she pointed over her head. "It was still lit when he went inside. There was a purse. He filled it with rocks and threw it in the river after removing anything identifying her."

"You've been checking the library files, but even so, there's nothing in the paper about where the tent stood. And you are right, it was here." He pointed his thumb downward to the ground where they sat. "And the woman was gone."

"I told you, I see things."

"What else did you see?"

You don't really want to know, she thought, remembering the old house and the body of his ex-wife on the bed.

"She called to me. Someone called to me. This woman was killed in a cold-hearted fury, a wire wrapped around her neck."

He leaped to his feet and pulled her up roughly to face him. "What the hell's going on here? What do you know about the wire?"

Kate was silent, but looking into his eyes, she saw honest puzzlement and anger.

"We checked it out and figured the woman was a missing person who just took off for parts unknown," he continued. "You're getting her confused with Betsy." After he had said the words, she knew he was shocked at admitting so much. The part about the wire must be information they were holding back.

"You're hurting my arm." She pulled away from him. She was five-foot-eight, and he loomed over her.

"Ah, I'm sorry." He moved backward to put a little distance between them.

"That's not all," she plunged on. "I saw your ex-wife in that old house. She was killed the same way. Police call it ligature strangulation."

The look in his eyes was one of stunned bewilderment. He could not have faked it. It was then her final doubts about him disappeared forever.

Dillon turned away for a moment, looking out over the water. She walked forward to stand at his side. They didn't speak for a long time. When he looked at her, his expression was grim, his mouth a straight line with lips flattened in a grimace.

"That was privileged information. We told the reporters that Betsy was choked to death, but we never mentioned the murder weapon. You couldn't possibly know that unless..."

"Unless I was there? Exactly. I was there. I didn't want to be. It scared the hell out of me, but I had no choice. I saw other things, too."

He bent his head to look into her eyes, as if that would let him understand what he was hearing.

"Here, on the inside of her arm..." Kate raised her own arm and pushed back the long sleeve to expose the tender white flesh on the inside. "There was a little strip of skin removed. No blood, so the killer excised it after she died. Carefully, as if he didn't want to mar the skin too much or disfigure her."

"Sonofabitch! I don't believe what I'm hearing." Dillon grabbed her shoulders, pressing his fingers in until she winced. "You *saw* all this? On your computer?"

"Yes, yes I did. You can call Captain Dennis Murphy in New York at the Tenth Street Precinct, if you want verification. He knows all about my visions."

"Sit. I'll get us some coffee. I need time to digest this."

She watched him stride toward the fire, bend in a fluid movement, and pour the dark liquid. That graceful carriage of his, which she'd noticed from the beginning, was what had kept her thinking he was that shadow at the foot of the window. Now his grace proved not to be furtive, just something masculine to admire.

"I think of the woman in the river as Lenore. I've never said the name out loud before, but she should have a name."

He stopped pouring the second cup and looked at her. "Lenore?"

"From Edgar Allen Poe's *The Raven*. Remember that old poem? 'Sorrow for the lost Lenore, the rare and radiant maiden whom the angels named Lenore, nameless here forevermore.' I didn't want to keep calling her the woman in the river."

When they sat down side by side, Dillon covered her hand with his. "This had to be hard on you. It must be hell to be saddled with this so-called gift."

Her hand felt warm and cozy, engulfed in his and she didn't move away. He *believed* her.

"I hated the pictures when they first started," she admitted. "Problem is, I don't get to see exactly what I want to see. There is a selective vision taking place, something that is beyond my capacity to control. It's as if fate or destiny has to be fulfilled and I am not allowed to stop it. Yet, at some point it's okay that I step in. Believe me, it's not something I'd wish on my worst enemy."

"Did you go inside Betsy's house?" His voice echoed his doubts, but he was intent, waiting for the answer.

"I didn't go in the steps of the killer or the victim that time, thank God. I went in there afterwards. He had just...finished. She was lying on the bed as if asleep, with her long hair strewn out over the pillow."

"The bastard cut some off, must have taken it and the piece of skin with him for twisted souvenirs." He growled out the words, as if barely able to say them.

"Like the credit cards and driver's license from the woman in the river." A flash of something important, something she could not put her finger on, sped through her thoughts. She tried to slow the burst of ideas, but had no control over it.

Later. She could only hope it would return later.

"I saw the killer's shadow at the edge of the trees in front of the house. He was looking up, as if he knew I was there. I call him the Catman. He does amazing things."

"Tell me about the woman at the bottom of the river. Lenore," Dillon prompted, after a few moments of silence.

It was clear that he wanted to get the sight of his dead ex-wife out of his head.

Kate listened to the crickets. Occasionally she heard a crash of brush from some small animal rushing through the woods.

"It could be dangerous," she finally said.

"Does that mean you're in danger? Does he know about you?" The frown between Dillon's eyes told her he did not like that idea.

Good question. "I think he may be aware of my presence in a way." She hedged a little not wanting him to know everything, especially about the killer being psychic. "I don't think he knows where I am or who I am. He just knows someone is watching him."

Dillon's hands tightened on hers. "You can back away, go home, and leave. I would give anything to find the bastard that killed Betsy, but you have no stake in this. It's not worth another life."

"I'd be lying if I told you he doesn't terrify me. I don't have a good fix on him yet, but he is a psychopath. I get the feeling he wasn't always evil, but he's got to be stopped."

"Few people are born evil, Kate. It's a learned thing."

Did he get that idea from his Viet Nam duty?"

"You're probably right. He isn't interested in killing me. Not yet anyway. I feel that very strongly. He is playing a game, taunting me to find him. A detective back in the city, an old friend, said that the psychotic killers sometimes beg to be caught. You just have to find the key."

"Maybe the key is the woman in the river."

"Exactly! I have felt that all along. I get the strong hunch that the killer messed up by killing two women in the same town. I doubt he has ever done that before. His strength lies in striking in an unsuspecting area and moving out quickly, leaving no trace of why he chose his victim. That way there's no link between him and any other murders he might have committed."

"There's something else you may not know," Dillon said.

"What's that?"

Kate pulled her hand away to slap at a mosquito and immediately wished she hadn't. It had felt so warm, so protected inside his clasp.

"You're right. There was a wire involved in the murder, but when we found Betsy, he had taken it with him. You saw something that wasn't there."

"That was my vision." She rubbed her arms with her hands, trying to stave off the numbing cold, which permeated her clothing.

Dillon reached forward and stirred the fire so that it flared up.

"I'm not cold. It's terrifying to think the killer may have been in the room while I looked at the body." But she had seen him below, looking up at the windows at the same time. Did he know she was there? They had to be on separate planes of time and reality.

"I want to hear more about the dead woman." Dillon's voice was steady, a deep, comfortable sound that made her tangled thoughts smooth out to a little more normalcy.

"He killed her in the same manner, strangled her with a wire. I didn't see her arm until today, but the skin was removed the same way."

"She had long hair?"

"Yes. Long, dark hair. I saw it streaming around her head like seaweed."

"Curious. It begins to make a kind of sense. Both women were about the same age, same coloring, and same hair. I noticed that when the composite was made to put in the paper."

"Didn't you go out with the tourist at one time?" She thought the question might be out of line.

He laughed, a short bark that startled birds roosting overhead. "No. She came into my shop several times, looking at camping equipment, wanting to know about camping at the Dells. I told her if she could hike down there, she was allowed to camp. No vehicles," he said by way of explanation.

At Kate's questioning look, he continued. "That's it. I did not date her, not once. The townspeople tend to gossip. The cops from Denver tried to work up a connection between Betsy and the missing woman and me, but they couldn't make it stick. It was crap."

"That's what kept me from confiding in you in the beginning," Kate admitted. "I thought there was a connection between you and the women and it made sense that if you were a psychopathic killer, you'd—"

"You thought *I* was the killer?" He looked at her in astonishment. "Why the hell would you come down here with me if you thought that? Woman, that's plain stupid."

Kate laughed. "I know."

"I hope to God you don't make these snap judgments often. If you're going to keep doing this thing with your computer, looking for stray bodies here and there, it only takes one time to make the wrong choice."

Dillon sounded worried. Kate felt elated that he would be concerned about her welfare. "Can you drag the river? We need to find the body."

"I can, but that holds a two-edged sword over my head. If we don't find her, the town's people will laugh me out of office. If we do, Denver will come back on me full force, wondering how I knew where to look for her."

"You could tell them I told you."

"Jesus! That is the worst idea yet. The people here are generous and good for the most part, but their way of thinking is sort of inbred, never changes. They make Washington Republicans sound like the most progressive liberals of our times. They would run us both out of town."

"You've got a way with words, Sheriff."

For a moment they were just a man and a woman, sitting side by side, enjoying each other's company.

The moment didn't last long.

"Are you going to look for her?" Kate prompted.

"I have to, don't I? Everything you have told me so far has been right on the money, and I would be foolish to ignore the lead. It's just going to be very tricky."

"I don't think we have to worry about the killer right now. He has this hit and run style. I sense that he never re-visits where he has killed. Or if he does, he would never kill again in that same place."

"You mean you think he's killed more than these two?"

"I'm afraid so. Like a cat, he stalks his victim. He's able to move around freely. I don't know how, but he'll never get caught at this rate."

"That's a bad scenario."

"There's more. He told me he's looking for someone." Oops, she hadn't meant to bring that out yet.

"What? Are you saying you talked to him? Did you see him? You said he didn't know you. What are you holding back?" His voice was harsh, a voice he might use to question a criminal, a police voice. The coziness between them had vanished.

Kate swallowed past a dry throat. "I just hadn't gotten around to telling you everything yet." She tried to placate him with a steady, calm tone. No need to admit that the voice said he knew where to find her anytime he wanted. For one thing, the killer was probably bluffing so far. It would be the excuse Dillon needed to send her packing for home. She wasn't free to go yet. Not until she had helped the woman in the river.

His arms folded across his chest, his brow wrinkled with impatience. "I'm waiting."

"I see a figure sometimes. Once we tuned in on each other. I was typing on the computer and he seemed to be whispering, or maybe it was some kind of telepathy. He said he was looking for someone."

"Looking for someone?"

"Well, it's obvious, isn't it? Lenore and Betsy are quite a bit alike in many respects. Both were attractive, with long, dark hair, both about the same age, same build. You said that yourself."

He rubbed his mustache. "I could fax other sheriff stations, find out if there are any missing or homicides involving women of their description."

"Yes!" He was finally getting into it. She knew he believed her, against his will, but still believed.

"There may have been witnesses to the murder of the woman in the river, or at least to the rifling of her belongings."

He looked at her with interest, waiting.

"In my vision, he was rifling through her things, but I thought I caught sight of shadows at the edge of the woods. It could have been poachers."

He grunted. "I'll check it out."

"There's something else," she began with hesitation, wondering how much of her visions he could or would absorb.

"I don't like the sound of that."

"The killer isn't going to stop until he's found the person he's searching for. He said so."

She clamped her hand to the back of her neck and stifled the scream that arose inside her, wanting out. The back of her neck warmed, the little hairs lifted, as if someone had just breathed against her skin.

The killer may have transferred through time and space as she did with her own psychic abilities. That was a frightening thought.

She could tell Dillon didn't hear the wild, hysterical laughter ringing through the silent wood that turned her blood cold. The laughter continued until she wanted to put her hands over her ears, but she was afraid Dillon might think she was completely bizarre. The shrieking cacophony gradually lessened, siphoning off toward the water where it subsided into a sibilant cackle somewhere in the middle of the river. A deadly reminder of the body that lay there at the bottom.

The Catman had been listening to them. He knew *everything*.

CHAPTER 11

Dillon strode back and forth in front of the campfire, hands clasped behind his back, deep in thought, kicking at stones in his way. Kate didn't interrupt his concentration. She had enough concerns to conquer on her own. The killer knew where she was. He knew how to find her.

Abruptly, as if coming to a decision, Dillon stopped pacing. "We'd better get some sleep. Big day tomorrow."

He pulled his sleeping bag closer to hers. It wasn't long after they had crawled inside their sleeping bags when she heard his even breathing and knew neither of them would sleep. There was too much to think about. He had his own demons to deal with. That must have been hell to find Betsy, sprawled dead across the bed they had once shared.

Occasionally during the night, he asked her a question and she would answer, otherwise only the sound of the river blended with the persistent hooting of the owl and the crackle of embers.

Kate dozed off sometime between night and morning, that mysterious hour when souls choose to depart their bodies,

when mothers give birth. She woke up screaming, fighting
through her nightmare. In the dream, the Catman shape shifted
between Detective Slater, Dillon, and a sinister stranger. The
shadow moved closer, closer, lithe and graceful as a panther,
his eyes glittering in the reflection of the dying campfire.

His hands were outstretched—reaching—until he drew
closer and she saw him gripping short wooden pegs. He held
them about a foot apart in his hands, wire wrapped around each
wood and taut between.

In a panic, she struggled to wake up. Part of her needed to
see his face, part of her feared to look upon the visage of death.
Screaming, she sat up, bathed in sweat, tears pouring from eyes
clenched tight with not wanting to see.

"Kate! What is it, Kate?" Dillon rolled to her side, grabbing her shaking shoulders.

For a moment, she fought him with every bit of strength
she had, but he held on tight, ducking his head against her rain-
ing blows until he could grasp her hands and hold them.

"Kate! Kate! Wake up!"

His low-pitched, soothing voice finally penetrated the
panic. Her terror receded gradually, ebbing away, leaving tentacles of menace behind. It had been so real, the dream.

Dillon leaned her back against the soft material of the bedroll and gently brushed the hair away from her forehead.

"You need cool water. I'll put some on a towel to hold to
your face."

"No! Don't go!" She held on tight, afraid if she let him go
even for a moment, the dream would return.

Dillon stretched out his long body next to hers, shielding
her, holding her close against his chest. His chin rested gently
against the top of her head. She felt his heart beating.

"Oh, Lordy, that was the worst yet." She heard her voice tremble, as if it came from a distance.

"Dreams can be rough."

He must have endured nightmares in his lifetime, but she realized men never liked to expose them to the light of day.

"I don't think it was a dream. He was here, the Catman. He can astral travel like I do." She tried to steady her pulses, keep the flutter from her voice. "It was a warning. He's bored with the game he chose to play with me and I'm getting too close."

Dillon rocked her in his arms, against his chest. It felt good.

"There is something I have gleaned from all this," she said.

"What's that?"

Kate took pleasure in the sound of his deep voice above her head, stirring the top of her hair with puffs of warm breath.

"The killer has a lot in common with you. That's what confused me from the start. He is dark. I sense that. He's also tall, like you, and graceful, but not as big as you. He's leaner, wiry."

She pulled away a little and twisted to face him, wanting to watch his expression. "I know how he got inside the house. Inside Betsy's house."

His expression solemn, Dillon shifted his shoulder to nestle her head closer. "Yeah, we couldn't figure that out. She always locked her doors and windows. That old house spooked even her, I think."

Kate almost regretted bringing up his ex-wife. That had to be extremely painful, thinking of her dying alone and in so much agony.

"He leaped from that tree over to the roof. That window wasn't locked."

Dillon pushed her away a space to stare into her eyes. "Impossible!"

She shook her head. "I saw him do it. He bragged about doing it. With the greatest of ease, he said. That was how he described his killing, too."

"My God, he'd have to be an Olympic jumper or a damn fine athlete."

"It's a start."

"If you're right about everything, you've given us good leads. We'll leave here soon as it's light and head back to town. I'll get my deputy and volunteers to drag the bottom."

Kate winced, thinking of curved barbs tearing into soft flesh.

As if he understood, he said, "It's not a sight many people can stomach, pulling a dead body up from the water. She might not even be here, if he didn't weigh her down. The current is strongest toward the top, but there's a constant undertow effect."

"She's down there." Kate echoed the voice that rang in her head. The voice from her computer that started this quest.

He grunted his assent and gave her a quick hug. "We may as well start packing our gear. Looks like we won't be sleeping anymore tonight."

But he didn't leave her. They stayed close together, snuggled down in her sleeping bag. She felt his erection against her body and at the same moment, he moved away, pushing out of the covers, disentangling his legs.

"I'd better go."

She touched his arm. "It's okay, Dillon. For a moment there, I needed you, too."

He knelt, bending his knees and hunkered down to look into her eyes. "Any other time, Katie, any other time." His voice held promise and regret.

She lay back to watch him maneuver around the campsite, after he came back from washing his face and doing whatever needed doing, just out of sight at the edge of the water.

A good, strong, kind man, was this Dillon Albarade. She almost wished he had not been quite so strong at this particular instant. She tried to remember the last time she had sex but the idea was too obscure to hold on to. By now, she had probably forgotten how all the parts came together. Funny how the threat of dying horribly, being stalked by an invisible psychopath who said he could reach out to her any time he wanted, made her realize how much she'd missed making love.

Kate laughed out loud at her outrageous thoughts.

Dillon turned to look at her, a dark brow curved upward in question, his mouth twitching at the corners as if he was ready to share a good laugh.

Forget it, she was not about to tell him her thoughts.

"Mmm, the coffee smells good," she answered. "Think I'll do what you did, run to the river and wash my face, brush my teeth."

"Good idea. I'll start cooking the bacon. Nothing clears a confused mind like early morning bacon and eggs in the outdoors."

She smiled. "You were born a hundred years too late. I picture you as one of those mountain men, rugged and ready to take on grizzly bears by the dozen."

His eyes crinkled at the corners when he grinned. "Reckon that's pretty close. I've always felt out of place."

Maybe it's because you haven't met the right partner to go through life with, she wanted to say. But that would have been too forward for her, at almost any point in a relationship, but especially in the beginning. Besides, she didn't quite understand how that idea popped into her head. It had no place in her life. No one belonged in her life ever again. It was too hurtful.

Alone, at the edge of the river, Kate looked out over the widening part. The bank at the other side was steep, enclosing the water with a large buttress of land jutting outward, protecting the semi-circle so that part of the water was still, out of the mainstream of the current. The dark forest crept all the way up, casting a shadow over that side of the wide river, shrouding the water in darkness. The sound of the rushing river filled her ears and she had the strong feeling of someone creeping up behind her, but it was like being in a vacuum, she couldn't hear anything but the river.

Sensing the presence of danger, her mouth dried and her heart sped up. She swerved to look—at empty air. Only the wispy plume of smoke from the campfire rising over the high bank separated her from Dillon.

Had she imagined the rustling movement at the edge of the trees on the bank, the slight tremble of footsteps on the soft sand behind her? This was getting bad. Her visions had always stayed safely within the confines of the computer before. Kate finished her ablutions quickly and hurried back to the security of the camp.

After Dillon stowed away the raft high up on the shore, they packed quickly and headed toward the storage shed. The hike up to the car didn't seem to take as long as it did coming down nor did it seem like the same trail. It only took hours instead of half a morning and an afternoon. Especially since they walked quickly, wanting to get back to town. Dillon walked behind her, making her feel safe, covering her back. He must have seen the haunted look in her eyes when she came back from the river.

Since leaving the Dells, she did not sense any more threat. Whatever it had been, its essence stayed there. Waiting for her to return.

CHAPTER 12

Kate sensed the excitement in the air since returning from her outing with Dillon. Word must have sped around about the river dragging. She would bet only the locals knew about it. It had become easier to separate the natives from visitors by now. Local men wore jeans, washed and faded, and flannel shirts topped by sheepskin vests. It was sort of a uniform for them. The women were harder to judge, but the locals didn't wear skin-tight Calvin Klein jeans and gobs of Indian jewelry like the visitors.

She had several good nights of sleep. The computer didn't intrude, or if it tried to, she was not conscious of it. Each morning she awoke, ravenous with hunger for the first time since she could remember. In the back of her mind, anxiety niggled, a fear of the future that months ago would have had her scurrying to get behind closed doors. It was different now. She was still afraid, but willing to meet it head on. Someone had to stop this killer. He was enjoying his work too much.

Kate watched the awakening of the town, a quiet, morning with a street empty of people. So serene and peaceful. What was the town hiding? Was that all in her imagination? Was it nothing more ominous than the simple matter of dollars and cents, and the town keeping a murder quiet for the tourists?

It proved to be an easy job, choosing something from her pitifully small wardrobe. It never mattered much before, but now she liked the way Dillon looked at her. The gray wool pantsuit matched her eyes and softened her angular body. She wrapped a pink silk scarf around her neck and tucked it down in the collar.

She brushed out her fine hair, fixing it at the nape of her neck with a silver barrette purchased at a trading post down the street. She liked the look of the woman facing her in the mirror—nothing flashy, but definitely a new and improved version.

Kate went downstairs, hoping to slip out the front door of the hotel without Ralph catching her. She knew the desk clerk would have questions and she had evaded his curiosity so far.

"Morning, Mrs. Macklin. Good day out there, cold, but clear." He took pride in his weather reports, as if it were part of his job description.

"Good morning. Yes, it looks fine." She attempted to hurry past.

"You got a visitor," He pointed toward the lobby filled with chairs and couches. Sarah Jenkins waved from the bowels of an overstuffed chair. Her tiny frame looked swallowed by fabric.

"Hello, my dear," she chirped. "Do you have time for a visit?"

"Of course." Kate rushed forward and bent to hug her. It was nice to see Sarah again. "Don't get up, please."

They settled down to visit with Ralph staying within earshot.

"Are you enjoying our town?" Sarah asked. Her little bird-like eyes sharp with curiosity.

"A lovely village." Kate wished Ralph would move on. There were some questions she wanted to ask about Betsy and Dillon.

Finally, after a few boring generalizations, Ralph interrupted. "I've got to go out for a minute. Watch the place for me?"

Both Kate and Sarah nodded.

As soon as he shut the front door, Kate moved closer to Sarah. "There's something I'd like to know, if you could tell me."

Sarah smiled, waiting.

"I've met the sheriff, Dillon Albarade. He seems like a nice man."

"Oh my yes, Dillon is a real gentleman. The ladies in town love him to death, but he doesn't pay 'em any mind."

"Do you think he's still in love with his dead wife, Betsy?"

Sarah shook her head vehemently. "Oh my no. Those two didn't get on from the beginning. None of us could imagine why they married in the first place."

"I read the newspaper account of her death. The article listed her as Elizabeth Bartlett."

"She never liked Dillon's foreign name, used hers from the start. Told everyone it was because she was an artist and wanted to keep her own name. In my day women didn't think of such nonsense."

"Still, it had to be a shock when she was murdered."

"Yes, it was. To all of us. They even thought Dillon might have had something to do with it for a while."

"No!" Kate hoped she sounded properly shocked.

Sarah arranged her dress precisely around her skinny legs. The material was navy blue and clean but well worn. In all probability, Sarah Jenkins couldn't find the quality of clothes like those that she used to wear in the good old days so she held on to her ancient garments.

"For a time it looked like they were going to haul him away to Denver, but they didn't."

"Not enough evidence? Did anyone from town think he'd done it?"

"Well, maybe some. There are those who don't take to Dillon. Some say he is arrogant and cocky. But isn't he good looking though?"

Sarah leaned back and laughed with such enthusiasm that Kate couldn't help but join in.

"Why did Betsy stay out there in that old house all alone?"

Sarah's lips drew into a line of disapproval. "We all thought that was one of her nuttier ideas, to live in her childhood home. The whole family moved into town so Betsy could go to school. Betsy was like a flower child. Her father was mayor here for decades and they had her when they were already old. A menopause baby, she was. They doted on her, spoiled her rotten."

"That's too bad," Kate said, trying to get in a word just to be sure the conversation kept going.

"Soon as she and Dillon divorced, she moved out there to paint and do her sculpting. She did sell some of it, I heard. Took it to Denver to a gallery."

Sarah leaned back. Kate felt her probing look.

"You seem mighty interested in our town history," she commented.

Time for another fib. It made Kate uneasy, but what else could she do? The truth was not going to work. "I'm doing an article for a magazine on rafting in Colorado and when I met Albarade at his shop, I just got interested," she said.

Sarah patted her purse, a bright red shiny vinyl that looked out of place with her demure, old fashioned clothing and her black grandma boots. Yet, it seemed just the right accessory for the little woman.

"Would you like to go out for a cup of tea or coffee?" Kate offered.

"Oh no, child. I have shopping to do. Besides, I want to get away before that tiresome Ralph gets back. He never shuts up."

Kate turned away to hide her smile. It was a case of the pot calling the kettle black. She helped Sarah out of the chair and walked her to the door. "Gosh, I don't remember if I shut off the iron. I had better go back upstairs. Thanks for the visit, Sarah."

Sarah reached on her tiptoes to touch her dry, wrinkled cheek to Kate's.

When Kate came down the stairs, Ralph had returned.

"Hear the sheriff's going to drag the river. Never been done in my recollection. Just hope the weather holds. Feels like rain," He rubbed his elbows inside his plaid flannel sleeves, a skeptical look on his face.

How did Ralph know everything? Maybe he had a special computer, too. What made Ralph think she would know the sheriff well enough to care one way or another? It was a very watchful town. The idea gave Kate the creeps. In the city, you would have to be dying in the street before anyone would notice and maybe call 911.

"I don't know. Excuse me, I have an appointment and I'm late." She didn't want to say too much, not knowing what Dillon had told his deputy. That must have been how the word got out, since she could not imagine Dillon spreading it around. Gossip would start soon if it hadn't already, now that people had seen them together.

The short walk to the diner was invigorating. Kate inhaled the scent of pines, the rich earthy smell that seemed to envelop the little town, and wondered briefly how it would be to stay here, forever. She laughed out loud, shaking her head to rid herself of the outrageous idea.

When she entered the diner, Dillon was there. She threaded her way beyond the tables toward him.

"'Morning. You look good enough to eat for breakfast." His expression was open, unguarded and filled with approval.

She liked that in a man. She smiled back at him. "Hi. It *is* a good morning."

He had his Stetson perched on his knee. That meant he was starting out his day as sheriff.

"I waited for you."

She saw that he had been drinking coffee and she thanked the waitress for coming to fill her cup.

"I'll have what you're having," she said.

He raised a skeptical eyebrow, and ordered the bacon, eggs and hash browns with a side of sourdough hotcakes.

She poured homemade blackberry syrup on her stack of pancakes and they ate in companionable silence. When her plate held only one last small bite, she leaned back and sighed with contentment, rubbing her stomach ruefully.

"If I keep this up, I'll have to buy a new wardrobe."

He looked her up and down in a frank, teasing way. "You look good to me, Kate, but a few extra pounds couldn't hurt.

First time I saw you, you reminded me of a greyhound, lean and all sharp angles. You've a softer look about you now." His voice had dropped to a hoarse whisper, knowing people nearby were curious.

She blushed at his compliment. Surely, she couldn't have changed that quickly, but maybe she had in his eyes. That was a comforting thought.

He left some bills on the counter for their meals and stood up. "Ready to go? Sure you don't want seconds?" He grinned.

"Yes, I'm sure." Her first instinct was to jab him playfully in the ribs, but she refrained, knowing everyone was looking.

He greeted several men as they passed in the doorway.

Outside, the rush of cold air struck her after the over-heated interior of the diner.

"Bracing? I like fall," he said, clamping his hat down with one hand and holding her elbow with the other.

"Sure is. I like it, too."

"It gets better. Winter's my favorite time."

"Why's that? In the city, the snow comes, nice and clean and white. Then it melts into dirty slush and freezes again, yuck!"

"Ah, it's not like that here. The first snow will come, any week now. It stays on the ground until spring. By the time it gets dingy and worn out, another snowfall cleans everything up. Winter is dependable, always the same, while summers can get crazy sometimes."

"Crazy?"

"Well, what I mean is, sometimes we have a hot summer, gets into the '90s. Creeks and water holes dry up and cattle die. Sometimes we get fierce winds and dust storms that come from over the mountains. It's unpredictable."

"I've been wanting to ask. Is there a proper time to wear your cowboy hat and a proper time to wear the baseball cap?"

He grinned. "Hadn't thought of it before, but now that you mention it, there's something to habit. This here's my sheriff's hat, ma'am," he spoke in an exaggerated drawl. "The baseball cap is for work in the shop."

She laughed. He was a good person. Strong and resilient like the mountains surrounding the town. The high Colorado sun and dry air had weathered his warm brown skin to a tan that Hollywood actors would have given their birthright for. His shoulders, wide beneath the denim jacket, looked like a line backer's.

He steered her to a bench just down from the diner, and they sat, watching the slow-moving traffic.

"It'll snow soon," he predicted.

"I hope you get the body out before then."

He cleared his throat, but didn't reply.

"Since you're wearing your cowboy hat, does that mean you're sheriff now? You haven't changed your mind about looking for Lenore, have you?"

"No. We'll start the dragging this week."

She felt surprised at the suddenness of his decision. "Good." Kate longed to ask Dillon about the information Murphy had dug up about his Viet Nam days, but knew he would never understand why she checked on him behind his back. He probably hadn't taken her seriously when she told him how frightened she'd been of his resemblance to the killer with his dark grace, his easy way of moving.

"I need to go with you," she said.

He shrugged. "You should. It won't be easy though. If we find something it could haunt you for a long time," he warned. If we don't find anything…"

"Your job's on the line, isn't it?"

"Right. The town doesn't have a big budget and this will take extra manpower, overtime, and equipment. Once we start, we will have to keep it up until we are ready to quit. You can't dredge a while and stop or you lose your place."

That made sense. "What will you tell them about me? What are you going to say motivated you to drag there? It's going to look awfully suspicious when you find her."

He kicked a booted toe into a clump of grass at the edge of the sidewalk. "I don't want to involve you any more than I have to. The deputies will want to know why you're at the site. I called your Captain Murphy. Not to check you out," he added hastily, holding up his hand in a conciliatory gesture. "I needed to know how the police handled your...ah...gift during their investigation."

"And did you gain any insight?" She smiled inwardly at the near-pun, and wondered what Murphy thought when Dillon called.

"I sure as hell did. The captain said they tried to keep you out of it, so the newspapers couldn't catch on. He said you didn't want publicity or anything like that."

"Oh, God, no! That would be the worst thing imaginable. I value my privacy more than you know."

"He told me that. He warned me if we caused you harm he would hold me personally responsible. He sounded like he meant it."

"Murphy? Are we talking about the same man?" She felt warmed to think he showed such concern about her welfare. He had always acted uncomfortable around her. "Dillon, about Betsy. You say authorities cleared her boyfriend? Did you know him? What does he look like? If he is dark and athletic, that might be a good start."

"He had an alibi. He's blond, kind of short and chubby, works at an all-night diner up at the next village."

That shot one theory to heck and back. She pointed to the sky. "It looks dark enough to rain or snow this afternoon. I had better let you get back to work. You may need to go to the river early."

"We don't have to do it today, it's waited this long."

"No! You've got to do it soon! I think he is going to keep killing until someone stops him. We may get some kind of clue from the body. Maybe that was one of the reasons why Lenore wanted us to find her."

Dillon looked startled. "You haven't told me everything you've seen. I'd like to hear it."

"It's kind of erratic in my mind right now."

"You knew about Betsy and her old house."

"Yes. Yes I did. Will you pick me up when you're ready to go back to the Dells?"

He held her hand briefly. "You bet."

Kate watched him walk away, shoulders hunched into the wind, holding his hat on with one hand. A big man, he moved with a sturdy grace. She thought of all he had been through in his lifetime. Would he ever find what he wanted from life?

Would she? First, you had to know what you wanted.

CHAPTER 13

Kate slipped into the hotel side door and ran up the stairs rather than take the noisy elevator. Filled to repletion from the unusually large breakfast, she felt sleepy. Maybe a nap would be in keeping in case Dillon decided to go to the Dells today.

She kicked off her shoes, stripped out of her clothes, and snuggled under the covers, naked. The sheets felt deliciously cold on her body but she soon warmed up beneath the blankets. The room was cool, but she didn't bother to turn on the old fashioned heater. As she dozed off, she heard the click of her computer keyboard. Click, click, like someone typing. She rolled over and sat on the edge of the bed, looking at the beast on the dresser. A strong desire to look came over her. A deeply buried need that made her clutch her pillow in front of her as a shield. Was she becoming addicted to the danger? To the thrill of communicating with the killer, playing out his sick game?

Addiction was not good, but she had come a long way and should be able to quit when she wanted to. As if in answer to her turmoil, a golden glow emanated from the crack of the closed computer top.

Something, someone had turned it on. Kate stood reluctantly, not wanting to move forward, but knowing she had to. When she reached to touch it, the computer felt icy cold, as if immersed in frigid water.

Unable to deny her need any longer, she grabbed a towel from the stack on top of the dresser and wrapped it around her. She pulled up a chair, and sat down to open the case. Words piled across the screen. She waited, knowing they would eventually make proper sentences.

'You can't have her back. Leave her alone.'

Did he mean the woman in the river? She held her hands together, fighting the urge to type questions, hoping this time, he would get careless and say something revealing.

Nothing on the keyboard moved, but letters flooded the screen, colors pulsed, red and orange, angry, brutal colors that hurt her eyes, invaded her space.

'How did you find me? Who are you?'

Elation flooded her, elation mixed with relief. He knew where she was, that was clear from his contact at the Dells the other night. He was able to do that because of her weakness from being in the shoes of the slain woman. He didn't know who she was. Not yet. His threat to come for her had been a bluff.

She sighed, suddenly weary and drained of energy. Instinctively she knew it was bad for her, to let her defenses down. Turning off the computer wouldn't work. She reached to yank out the cord and slam the cover down, but the words whispered in her ears stopped her. A warm lethargy took hold of her and her hand flopped down in her lap.

'*Beautiful one, sweet, gentle, beautiful one, we are both on a long journey—a quest to find our soul mates. What else could we be? Do you not see we have to meet? You found me, I found you. Do you know how impossible that is? It has to be fate. Let me show you how it started.*'

The soft, erotic murmur in her mind licked at her ear, wrapped sensuously around her neck, touching lightly against her breasts. She gasped, frozen in time and space.

A scene came over the computer and she watched, fascinated and unable to move.

ⅇⅉⅇⅉ

Nicholas slept soundly when suddenly he felt warm all over. He had a painfully hard erection and put his hand down to touch long, silky hair, like a dark cloud over his stomach. He sat up, startled completely awake.

"What the hell are you doing?" He looked at the woman poised between his legs, looking up at him.

"Shh, Nikki, relax. I'm horny, is all. I need this. You know you want it." He leaned forward and she placed his hand on her melon shaped breast, dragging his hand down her gently rounded stomach. So smooth, so soft.

She was stark naked.

He stared at the dark triangle that intersected her shapely, muscular legs. He wanted to pull away, oh god, he should pull away, but he couldn't, not if he died right on the spot. His strong, tensile fingers curled around her nipple, caressing it gently. She whimpered and continued to kiss him in ways he had barely dreamed of.

"Oh, Nikki, you're so goddamned good-looking, someday the girls will be all over you. Come on, there's nothing wrong with this. No one will know. I want to be your first. I want to teach you."

She turned gracefully and began crawling slowly upward along his body, her mouth leaving trails of white-hot kisses behind.

Suddenly he felt a wave of desire that consumed him like a raging fire. As she straddled him and pushed herself closer into his flesh, she leaned forward, her long hair tangled in his fingers. He had always loved her hair.

He groaned, came too fast the first time, and tried to pull away in shame, but she soothed him and made him do it again.

"I know, Nikki, you're so young, but you'll learn. Fifteen is a good age. I learned a lot earlier." Her voice tinged with bitterness. "I wanted to be the one to teach you."

When it was over, Nicholas Masaarate sat up and looked at his sister sleeping so peacefully next to him on the narrow cot. He touched her hair, carefully so he wouldn't wake her.

Nothing would ever be the same for him again.

∽∂∾∂

Kate closed her eyes, slammed down the computer lid and jerked the cord out. What had she just seen? And why? What did the forbidden sex between a young boy and his sister have to do with the killings?

The voice she had heard before whispered seductively in her ear, disturbing the hair at the side of her neck. She must not listen! The voice in her head was like a soothing, compelling caress covering every inch of her body, leaving no portion untouched. The words felt like satin, sliding exquisitely over her skin, moving into her most intimate parts, invading her secret recesses so tenderly subtle that her nerve ends responded, pulsing, throbbing rhythmically. Her breasts swelled, her nipples hardened.

A feeling of total euphoria urged her to the brink of rapture. She bit her lip, arched her back, lifting almost out of the chair, her neck tilted back, she was close to surrender.

Surrender. The warning came like a shot through the haze of her desire, her hunger to finish what had been started. She longed to know release more than anything, but not more than life itself. She forced her eyes open and leaped up to run toward the bathroom, slamming the door behind her.

Kneeling down in front of the toilet, she let the nausea come, and leaned against the smooth coldness of the bathtub to gulp great breaths of air. Her skin, her body, her soul felt invaded, plundered, violated.

Yet, she still craved release.

CHAPTER 14

Kate awoke, lying in the bed, naked but wrapped in her housecoat. How strange. The room was dark and the drapes pulled. A figure sat sprawled in the over-stuffed armchair by the bed.

Her mouth was dry, her head ached unmercifully and her body felt as if someone had dragged her behind a car for miles.

"Who's there?" She sat up and flopped back down again. The blood surged to her head in a roar and dizziness overcame her.

In a second, the figure from the chair lurched toward her.

"Don't be scared, Katie. It's me."

Ah, Dillon. She didn't have the strength to feel relief. "What happened?"

Did she have some kind of trance or spell? It felt eerie, as if her memory wiped out from the time she left Dillon out on the street.

"Damned if I know. I called your room to tell you we were ready to go, and no one answered. I called Ralph at the desk. He said he saw you go up, but you didn't come down again. I came right over and he let me in. That's when I found you in the bathroom. Like you had been ready to take a shower or bath and fainted. Scared the hell out of me."

"That's weird. I don't remember going inside the room. I was talking to you on the bench out there and..."

He sat on the edge of her bed. She touched his hand. "Did you go to the river?"

"Lord no, Kate. I wouldn't leave you behind. I didn't know if someone attacked you or what. I brought the doc up here. He said you had something like a weak spell, he called it. Your pulse was down to nothing, your blood pressure low, but not life-threatening. He said you needed rest. You slept hours."

"And you stayed here?"

Dillon nodded. "Yep. I can't begin the river project without you. I want you there to show me where to start dragging. I'm going to make enough of a fool out of myself as it is. I need your help to do it proper," he said with a tired grin.

Dillon had sat in that lumpy, uncomfortable chair for hours, waiting for her to wake up. That single unselfish act immersed her in comfort, wrapping around to protect her. Protect her against what? If only she could remember.

"I feel like I'm the one who's been dragged through the river. This has never happened to me before. I barely have the strength to raise my hand." She lifted her hand to demonstrate and he caught it up, holding it to his cheek. She felt the coarse beginning of a beard. His woodsy, man-scent started an uneasy stirring in the pit of her stomach.

She touched her lips to his hand.

He leaned forward and kissed her, hard.

She gave him back the feelings she had been holding in for so long.

He began to unbutton her housecoat while she pulled open the pearly snaps of his shirt. His hands were clumsy, yet strong and powerful. She needed him with terrible urgency.

"Hurry, Dillon. Lie down beside me," she whispered hoarsely.

In a moment, he had shucked off his boots, pants and everything else. She squirmed out of her wrap, wanting to be finished undressing at the same time he was. At first, she was awkward. It had been so long, what if she forgot how? The exquisite need for him overcame her shyness and when he was ready, he turned to her waiting arms.

She had not forgotten a thing.

ℰↃℰↃ

They leaned back against the pillows in bed, suddenly reserved and awkward. Reality intruded and Kate knew they had to think of other things.

"Thank you for staying with me."

"Want to tell me what happened?"

She shook her head. It wouldn't be a good idea to let him know a ghostly apparition in her head had primed her for lovemaking. Some of the remembrance of what she had seen on the computer and heard inside her head just before she blacked out gradually dribbled back.

"I had to be sure you would be all right when you woke up." He pulled her close to kiss her lightly. She touched the back of his head, liking the way his thick hair felt between her fingers.

He swung his legs off the bed.

"I'd better go. Daylight will come soon enough, have to get our gear ready for the diving."

She threw the covers off, but he sat down beside her, putting them back over her. "Stay put, sleep some more. By the time daylight comes, you will be raring to go. If not, we can postpone it until you are ready. We'll wait for you."

"Thanks. Not many people would have believed me. I shouldn't have waited so long to come to you with my story about her—Lenore."

"Ah, I don't know how much I believe, truthfully. I know that you don't lie and you believe it. The bastard who killed Betsy needs to be put away. I won't rest until we get him and I will do just about anything to make it happen. I hate to believe it's connected to other killings, though."

His loyalty to his ex-wife touched Kate. His chin thrust out, making his jaw line more square, and his lips narrowed into a straight line when he spoke. She was glad not to be on the wrong side of him.

ᘒᘓᘒᘓ

Toward morning, Kate thought she heard the same insistent clicking noise from the direction of her computer, sounding like a keyboard, someone typing. A nightmarish feeling of apprehension crept over her. In her present condition, sleepy, with the awareness of Dillon's lovemaking still lingering, a strong force within warned her not to investigate.

Kate pulled the sheet and blanket over her head and waited until the noise stopped. When it finally did, she reached for a book and read until she dropped off to sleep again.

By the time the morning sun shone through the window, she awoke restored. The sex with Dillon had been good. She stretched and ran her hands over her ribs, down her hips, remembering the feel of his hands on her body. How would they behave in front of people? She didn't know how she felt about Dillon. She hoped their making love wouldn't compromise the reason she was here. The objective was to find the woman in the river and to stop the killer.

She would have to overcome the after-effects of whatever had laid her low. Probably a touch of stomach flu, she thought, brushing her teeth and stepping into the shower. How could she lose track of so many hours?

Kate dried off, dressed in jeans and a sweatshirt, and threw her jacket on the bed. When she was ready, she called Dillon. Strange, she knew where he hung out, how to reach him at his shop, but had no idea where he lived. They agreed to meet at the diner.

He had chosen a booth instead of his usual perch on a stool at the counter, which surprised her. They ate breakfast in silence, the flow of conversation surging around them, insulating them from any awkwardness they might have felt after their intimacy.

"You all right? You sure look a lot better than yesterday, before…"

She smiled at his hesitancy and felt the same shyness. "It's been a long time for me," she whispered.

He cleared his throat, plainly uncomfortable speaking of emotions. "I know. Long time for me, too, and it was good for both of us." He reached across his plate and ran his fingers across her hand.

"I can't wait to get out there."

"Better not eat too much," he advised.

Her eyebrow rose in question. He was usually coaxing her to eat.

"This will be rough, I'm not going to kid you. When a body lies in icy water like that river, for—let's see, it had to be since July—that's when she disappeared, well, seeing it is not something you'll ever forget." He glanced around at the patrons in the diner as if just remembering where they were.

A tall, thin man pushed open the diner door. When he made his way toward them, everyone greeted him. Dillon introduced him as Deputy Jerry Wallace. The customers in the restaurant pretended to eat and talk as usual, but Kate felt their curiosity. If they only knew the half of it, wouldn't that make them choke on their biscuits?

They waited for the deputy to finish his coffee. Dillon tossed some bills on the table and they braced themselves for the wind as they exited the cafe.

On the way to the Dells, with the deputy sitting in the back seat, they were quiet. The same country western station played softly on the radio.

Dillon's hands were tight on the wheel. "I tried to keep this low key, but everyone in town will know about it one way or another by tomorrow."

"I figured that. The patrons in the cafe were watching us. Ralph from the hotel knows already."

Dillon slanted a look behind, aimed at the deputy. "Jerry, next time I tell you we're going to do something, keep it under your hat."

The young man blustered. "Ah, boss, I..."

Kate looked around to see the deputy's face redden and turned quickly to hide her smile, but Dillon caught it and grinned, too.

"In spite of what you think you saw in your...ah...vision, if we find her, it'll be bad. It's tough on us all." Dillon's voice was low and she didn't think it would carry to the back seat over the sound of the radio.

"I pictured her as a whole person. What if she's in pieces?"

"Hard to say what condition she's in. The current could have swept the body downstream. The killer had to weigh her down good, otherwise she'd have floated up by now, someone would have seen the body."

"Big, jagged stones from up there," she pointed to the mountainside that crept downward in places to the river.

"What?"

"He used large stones." She had caught a flash when she saw the tent. "He wired them to her body."

"If he was smart enough to use wire, that could hold her forever, rope would eventually deteriorate. If he used wire, that meant he was carrying it around, waiting to use it."

"I don't think this murder was planned," Kate said. "But the other one, with your—with Betsy—that was deliberate and premeditated."

Dillon's hands tightened on the wheel, the knuckles turned white. "God, I wish you could tell me what else he's done. Do you suppose this was the start?"

"I'd like to think so, but I'm afraid not. I haven't caught visions of any others but something very strong—a hunch—tells me he's killed over and over again."

"How the hell does he do it without leaving clues, without tripping up?"

"He did trip, this time. Lenore wanted someone to care enough to bury her, so she called out to me when I passed by on the train. Otherwise no one would have known about her and everyone would have thought Betsy's murder was done by some transient passing through, looking for money for booze or dope."

"You're forgetting I was the main suspect for a while. I'd like to get that cleared away, once and for all."

"It must have been hard, being suspected of murdering someone you once loved."

"You'll never know the half of it." He slanted a look at her before looking ahead at the road again. "The Denver officials aren't satisfied as to my innocence. I can't blame them, with Betsy's doors and windows all locked, makes it look like an inside job."

"The top window in her bedroom couldn't have been locked," Kate reminded him.

"Sure, but who...oh, that's right, you said someone you call the Catman leaped across the trees to the window. I'll believe that when I see it." Dillon slowed, pulled onto a parking area and started to turn off the motor.

Kate stayed his hand. "When we came out here alone? Did you really have car trouble?"

He looked momentarily surprised and then his husky laugh made her smile too. "Wish I could take credit for a nefarious scheme to be alone with you longer, but in all honesty, yes, the radiator leaked water out."

They climbed out of the car. The air was still and cold.

"Kate, there's something you should know. Even if...ah...when we find her, she could be in such bad shape that we might not make an identification. I mean you need a picture, fingerprints, dental examination—something to send to other places. It all might be gone."

"I've thought of that. It could be of no importance to her. Maybe she doesn't have anyone else in her life. She just wants to be buried. She hates it in the water." Kate rubbed her arms, cold beneath the heavy clothing. She was so close to this woman, as if her every thought was clear. It was not a comfortable feeling.

She took Dillon's grunt for acceptance. "Hey, you didn't say anything about there being another way to get down to the water. How come we had to trudge all morning through the woods to get to the rafting place?"

Dillon grinned. "You're psychic. Figure it out."

A current of pleasure ran up her spine and she turned away so he wouldn't see her smile.

A sheriff's car pulled up behind them, and four men got out. Dillon introduced her to the men and soon they loaded their gear and headed down the trail.

"I thought you were going to drag for her. I see some men carrying diving equipment."

"Two of us are certified divers. We'll try dragging first. If the bottom's too rocky where you think she is, grappling hooks won't work there."

He had served as a diver in Viet Nam. The flash of that truth came to her. Why didn't he want anyone to know about that part of his life? Could it have been that rough?

The men who had come from the other car joked and laughed, but the closer Kate got to the rushing water, the more apprehensive she became. What if she was causing a lot of trouble for Dillon? What if she misjudged the message or the place, or what if Lenore had slipped downriver, forever out of reach? So many questions. So much at stake.

Kate lifted her chin and straightened her shoulders. Whatever the outcome, she had taken the chance, done her best to interpret her visions. That was all she could do. Her only other alternative was to have kept quiet and continued her vacation. That was the old Kate.

At the bottom of the trail, the men set the equipment down, all business now, joking gone. She caught them glancing in her direction from time to time, as if wondering about her, wondering why the normally hard-headed sheriff would listen to a kooky broad who descended on them from out of nowhere. She didn't have to be a psychic to know what they thought.

The men dragged in shifts without stopping. Moving along, anchoring the boat and then maneuvering forward a few more feet. Some debris came up but since it was a secluded place with only hikers allowed, they didn't find much refuse. Dillon did discover where the poachers had been when they dredged up weighted antlers several times. This was a perfect place for deer and elk to come to drink at dusk.

After several hours of meticulous work, one of the volunteers shouted to those waiting on shore.

"We got something, Sheriff! Sure as hell, we do." His voice rose excitedly and little ripples ran up the hairs on the back of Kate's neck.

"Slow and steady, boys, bring it in careful like," Dillon shouted over the water.

Bring *it* in. Not her, not the body, not the woman she had named Lenore, but *it*. That's what the killer had relegated his prey to, an object, an it. Somehow, this outraged Kate more than anything up until now. She didn't blame Dillon for his choice of words, a defense mechanism to distance himself from the victim.

While they waited, he walked back to the supplies lying on the ground and chose a small rolled towel. He went to the shore, knelt, and immersed the cloth in cold river water, wrung it out, and handed it to Kate.

"What's that for?"

"Tie it across your nose and mouth when we bring the body up. It's not a perfect solution, but it helps."

"Will it be that bad? She's been in the cold water a long time, you'd think it would be like a frozen body."

"Don't kid yourself. It is the worst smell in the world. The cold water makes a kind of soap out of the fatty tissues in the body."

"We hauled a floater out of a lake up around Denver," one of the men standing nearby commented. "Jee-zus! I washed my nose out with everything but battery acid for weeks afterwards and still smelled it."

Each man had come prepared with dry rags in his back pocket.

"Isn't a coroner usually present?" she asked.

Dillon looked into her eyes, as if trying to convince her. "Kate, you have to understand, this is really off the wall to us. I can't call in a coroner or medical examiner from Denver, just on the say so of a—a psychic vision."

"It makes sense. You'd have to have a valid reason to search for a body before you call in a public official and so far you just have my intuition."

"I didn't suppose you were aware of investigative procedure, but then you had that case that you and Murphy worked on."

"I picked up a little of the terminology from listening."

"Sounds like." He let it go.

They watched as two men pulled up something and slid it on wide black plastic.

"It's a dog, Sheriff," one of the men called out to him.

"Hell! That means you and I have to dive, Jake." Dillon's look singled out a man standing with several others nearby.

The man shrugged, as if expecting it, and Dillon motioned them to bring in the boat. He and Jake separated their gear and shucked off their clothes. Kate was beginning to wonder about their lack of modesty when she saw that they had dressed prepared to dive if they had to. Both Dillon and Jake wore form-clinging body suits beneath their clothes.

Dillon laughed at her expression. Maybe he did it to ease the tension. "Had you going for a minute, didn't we? These are dive skins."

Jake spoke up for the first time when they began to pull on the wet suits. "I hate the clammy feel of the rubber stuff next to my skin."

"Will you be warm enough? What if you get chilled down there, won't that cause problems?" What had she set in motion to involve these men in danger?

Dillon looked out over the water. "It's around forty feet deep in that still area, like a little lake off to the side. Our downtime will be about an hour, then we'll have to surface and warm up before we try again." He spoke to the men, as well as to her. She knew this must be the first time for them.

Dillon and Jake resembled men from outer space. "Isn't it cold?" she asked. "That suit seems so thin and tight."

"It'll leak a little water, here and there. But as soon as the water hits your body, it heats to match body temperature."

"What's that other suit you laid out and didn't put on?" She was stalling, but couldn't help it. She had a bad feeling about this.

Dillon walked over to the parcel and held it up for her inspection. "It's a dry suit. Seals around your neck so no water ever gets inside. You can wear sweats or street clothes under here and nothing leaks in."

"Isn't that better to wear?"

He shook his head. "More maneuverability with these light weights. They fit like a second skin."

The men in the boat returned to shore.

"What'd you do with the dog?" someone asked.

"What'd you want us to do with it? Stunk like hell, we threw it back."

Dillon made a face. "Reckon we'd better stay away from that corner of the river, eh Jake?"

Jake laughed. He seemed to enjoy the drama.

Kate thought everyone but Dillon was enjoying the day outside with none of them believing for a minute they would find a body.

She touched Dillon's arm and pulled him aside. "Lenore's in a deep pocket with a bit of rock overhang." The flash just came to her in an instant, but she was getting better at catching them without needing the computer.

He looked at her speculatively for a long heartbeat and nodded. "We won't need a tie-off rope between us, Jake, there's not much current where the body may be." He pulled on his hood. The scuba tanks lay on the shore, ready to be strapped on.

"We won't need the Hookah either," he called out to one of the men standing waiting by the pile of equipment. As if knowing she wanted to be a part of this and to not be ignored, he said, "That's like an air compressor with hoses. Both Jake and I could hook up to it, but I don't think we'll be down that long."

She watched as they made final preparations, fastening on their flashlights, strapping on their tanks.

"Keep the body bag and the two lift bags close to the side of the boat so one of us can come up to get them if need be."

Kate knew then that, although he trusted her, he didn't actually believe they would find anything. He just had to be sure.

The boat moved out with the men inside. When they were in position, Dillon and Jake put their mouthpieces on, adjusted the lights fastened to their heads and splashed overboard.

They were gone a long time. Kate tried her best to concentrate, to visualize if they needed help, but nothing came. Even if they were in trouble, none of the men would dare go down without wet suits. Dillon had said only he and Jake were professional divers.

At first, Kate sat on the bank. The afternoon had warmed a little but now turned chilly. When dusk came, they would have to stop and she wasn't sure they could return tomorrow. She couldn't blame Dillon if he said forget it. It was a big leap of faith, and he was so locked into logic. His whole training as sheriff and in Viet Nam had been for procedure.

The minutes ticked by. She wished someone had stayed on shore with her so she could ask questions. How long would their oxygen last? Would the extreme cold penetrate even the rubber suits after a certain time? He had said they had an hour of safe time, but what happened after that? She should have asked Dillon those questions before, but hadn't thought of them then.

Kate paced the beach. She'd never felt so helpless. Some of the men in the boat were smoking, some talking low, but no laughter now. It had been a long time. She could tell by the worried frowns on some of the men that this was not a good sign.

Finally, a sleek dark head broke the surface near the boat and a gloved hand came out in a signal. The nearest man in the boat handed over the package containing the body bag and the lift bags. After that, the men jumped to attention, getting the bottom of the boat ready, moving all the gear out of the way. They dipped their cloths into the river and wrung them out.

Relief flooded over her when she recognized Dillon's wide shoulders emerge from the dark water. He and Jake shoved a plastic-wrapped object carefully up to the waiting men who quickly tied the cloths around their noses and mouths.

A somber group headed back to the shore. When they got close, Kate smelled the putrid, rancid odor of the body, like nothing she had ever smelled. She gagged and tied the wet rag around her face as the men had done.

Dillon waved her back. She still had the picture in her mind of the young woman with long flowing hair, a nice-looking woman except for the wide staring eyes and the slice of blood around her neck.

Deliberately disobeying Dillon's command, she waited until they had maneuvered the plastic wrap onto shore and walked slowly forward. She stood next to Dillon when they pulled back the sheet of plastic, and was unprepared for what she saw.

The thing lying in front of them was no longer human. Had it ever been? She stared at the monstrosity. This once vibrant, happy woman was now bloated and covered in yellow wax. The killer must have stripped off her clothing to make it easier to tie her down. That way no telltale bits of material would rot off and wash up on shore.

Dillon and Jake had cut the wires from the weights when they brought her up, but her flesh puffed around the wire embedded in her flesh. The killer most likely tied the large rock around her middle, the rock she had seen in her vision. That part was so bloated, it was hard to tell, and Kate couldn't bear to look at it any longer. The soft, yellow, spongy tissue of the face seemed to be falling apart. The air was cool, but many degrees warmer than the water.

There was no noose around her neck. But Kate had definitely seen that in her visions. The hair, falling out in patches so that bare scalp showed through, was long and scraggly. It would possibly show that he had cut a chunk out of it for a trophy.

Sick to her stomach, Kate backed up, away from the scene. Pitiful, pathetic Lenore. Several of the men ran towards the trees and she knew they were vomiting. One of the men zipped the body bag closed.

Dillon and Jake had gone behind the trees to change out of their wet suits and dive skins.

"I need two men to go back for the county truck. There's no way we can put the body in the trunk of a car." Two men volunteered and Dillon motioned them to go ahead. "No talking to anyone, hear? We have to organize what we want to say to the press and the townspeople to avoid a panic. They might put the two killings together right away, both same M.O., both women killed around the same time." He glanced at Kate to verify this.

She nodded.

Dillon turned back to the men. "And bring the car back, we don't have to ride crowded all together in one vehicle and a truck."

He didn't want anyone riding with them. He probably had more questions to ask her. When the two men left, the others walked away from the body, their voices low murmurs, talking quietly.

"I want to talk to you," Dillon said, taking Kate's arm and pulling her toward the opposite end of the beach. He indicated an outcropping of rocks and they sat, looking out over the water for a long moment without speaking.

She touched his shoulder. "That was hard for you, Dillon."

He flinched and smoothed his moustache to hide his agitation. "I've seen a lot of bad stuff in my day, but oh, God, Kate, I don't know what to say. I honestly did not believe you. It's only fair to admit that."

"Why did you come out here?"

"Like I said, I'd do anything to catch Betsy's killer. After I talked to Captain Murphy, I realized there was a possibility you were right. He believed in you. I'm glad I took the chance."

"I know she's bloated—but even if they don't find the wire buried in her flesh, I saw it wrapped around her neck. He might have removed it as he did from Betsy, but something let me see the wire as if it was still there. Can an autopsy show he killed her that way?"

"Maybe. The hypoid bone is probably broken or seriously bent. That happens in a strangulation."

"What will you tell them about how you found the body? Can you say something popped to the surface and you investigated?"

"That's thin, but it could work. The deputies know different, or at least they suspect something odd with you being here. I don't think they would mention you when I ask them not to. Unless…I mean…you deserve all the credit."

"Good Lord, no!" Kate's shoulder touched his side and he put an arm around her. "That's the last thing I want. People staring at me as if I'm some kind of a freak, poking into my life. Oh, no, Dillon, don't let it out if you can help it."

"There's still Denver's notion that I might be involved with Betsy's murder, and now this body with the same M.O. It's going to be dicey for a while. The autopsy will show if the larynx and throat cartilages have been broken."

"I don't envy the people who have to do the autopsy." She shuddered. "What a terrible smell."

"It's worse than just putrid flesh. It's that business with the soapy substance. After a year or so in the water, nothing's left but the soap."

"She had stuff in her mouth and nose," Kate said. "Did the killer do that?"

Would she ever get that sight out of her mind?

"No. The way he tied and weighted her down, her face dragged against the bottom some, that's what filled the cavities with rock and debris."

"The cold hearted bastard. He's got to be stopped."

"I got a feeling that's going to put you in jeopardy." Dillon took her hand and held it a moment, as if he needed to establish some contact.

"I'll be truthful with you, I'm afraid my link with him is the only way we may catch him."

Dillon leaped to his feet, pulling her with him.

Out of the corner of her eye, she saw the men look their way, curious, but he was oblivious to their stares.

"I can't have that!"

"He...ah...he came to me only a couple of times the way I travel through space in my mind. He doesn't know who I am and I don't think he knows how to find me—yet." She pulled Dillon back down to the rocks and the men turned away, talking among themselves again.

"Hellfire, you didn't tell me that before. Does he talk to you? What does he say? Can you see him?"

"No. Just shadows so far. I've tried to put it together…do a profile. I know he is dark, swarthy, muscular, and yet not solid like you. He's like an extraordinary athlete, honed to knife sharpness."

"Any idea why he kills?"

The scene in her computer of the forbidden love between sister and brother had to be one of the keys, but she didn't know how to put it together yet and wanted to avoid conjuring up the thoughts of how the killer invaded her space. "I've asked him, by typing words into the computer, but he laughs at me. He says he's looking for someone and when he finds her she will be punished and he'll stop killing her."

"He thinks these women he's murdering are the same as the one he's looking for?"

Kate shook her head, pushing back the hair from her neck where it had come unbound from the barrette. She was sweating in spite of the chilly wind off the river. Just thinking of the killer did that to her. It could mean he was getting close.

"No. He knows they aren't her, but not until after he kills them. He can't stop himself until it's over though. Then he knows it isn't her, but he feels no remorse for killing an innocent woman. They shouldn't have looked like her, tried to fool him."

"God, what a sicko. I've never run into anything like this before. We don't have that stuff going on up here."

"Don't kid yourself. Serial killers are loose all over. There could be a couple of thousand psychopaths roaming the country, hunting and stalking their victims. It's almost an epidemic. Most of them will never be caught." She'd done a lot of research on the subject. The information stuck in her brain even though she had hoped never to have to think about it again.

His eyes narrowed, his mouth thinned, and he looked as if he didn't know what to say.

"I know. It's scary. Solitary killers have roamed the highways for years, picking on prostitutes, runaways, and women in trouble—the crimes mostly unsolvable."

"What if this sight of yours overwhelms you eventually? This is the second time you've involved yourself with a crazy killer. How much do you think you are able to take?

"I've given it a lot of thought. I guess the answer is, I will take as much as I have to. From the very first when I discovered "the gift," I fought it. I didn't want to be a freak. I didn't want to know other people's thoughts or feelings any more than I wanted them to know mine."

"What changed?"

"The need to find my daughter's body started it. I had a premonition at the time of my husband's accident, but failed to act on it. I felt something really awful at the time a car hit Annie, but forced it away. By the time the vision came to me so I could locate Annie's body, I was ready to accept it."

"It could inundate you someday," he warned again.

"I know. I hope to learn how to block out some of the images when I want to." She had the feeling the Catman was better at blocking than she was. She motioned toward the black plastic-wrapped body. "The woman in the river called to me so clearly. She wanted to be buried. She needed to be found."

"Now that's over, will you leave?"

"It's not over. He has to go on killing." A flash of an older man lying dead on a hard-packed earthen floor intruded. A figure above him tilted his head back to laugh. She shivered.

"Here, take my jacket," he began, pulling his arm out of the sleeve.

She stopped him. "No, I'm not cold. It was a feeling that he has to come back here. It's as if he left something valuable behind." That idea was new, and the first time it had entered her thoughts. He needed to return to Plenitude for some reason. "It may be the only mistake he's made by killing two women in the same town. He feels angry and humiliated knowing this. I brought it to his attention and he has to do something to change it."

"There's one way he could change the past and that's by eliminating you, the evidence of his mistake."

That was smart of Dillon. She didn't pursue that line of reasoning, fearing he would make more of it than he should. "He may be stalking someone right now. He isn't ready to stop killing. He gets off on the fear and terror of his victim before he kills. It feeds his sickness, his emptiness."

Kate knew he would return. Like an unsatisfied lover who can never leave, he would come back for her. All she had to do was wait.

CHAPTER 15

It took several hours for the truck to arrive to pick up the body. While they waited, the men sat near the shoreline, talking in low tones.

"Have you told them what my role is in this?" she finally asked Dillon.

They sat on an outcropping of rock on the other side of the beach.

"No. I had to say something, so I said you were a reporter and had known the missing woman. That was a mistake."

"How so?"

"Don't you suppose the papers from Denver and other points of Colorado are going to want in on this? A double homicide within the same time frame in a little town like Plenitude is news. They'll dig around and find out about you."

"You had to tell them something."

"Why don't you pack up and go home? No sense in subjecting you to this. You were honest with me about your fear of going out in public. This might bring some of it back."

"I wonder if we ever get over our fears entirely."

"I think you should leave."

Kate shook her head, stood and paced the beach. "I can't. Don't you see? I am the only one who can find out who he is. What he is. Maybe I won't be able to do it, but can you think of anything else to try?"

"You mean set yourself up as bait?"

"I don't think it will come to that. He doesn't know who I am. When and if I lock on to his whereabouts, or his identity, he may know then. I hope to be ahead of him."

What a frightening thought. Something niggled deep within her memory, a provocative, erotic and terrifying memory that she couldn't quite grasp. It had to do with this killer she called the Catman. One thing she was certain of, he would have no more compunction about cutting off her life than he had the others, even if she didn't fit the description of the one he searched for.

Kate tried not to look toward the object lying wrapped in plastic, alone on the beach, but she couldn't stop herself. There lay a once vital young woman, left without dignity, with only ugliness to mark her passing and now a nameless grave.

"He didn't want me to find her in the water. He will be angry. If you can hold on to my privacy, I can try to track him. Otherwise, he'll have only to read the papers to locate me."

"Oh, God, you're right." Dillon stood next to her as they looked out over the water. "It's obscene that Betsy and this woman were slaughtered by the same man, right under our noses. It made more sense that a transient who needed money killed Betsy and got scared before he could find anything to steal."

"I know. This makes it more impersonal in a way. Tragic that she just happened to resemble someone he hates."

A horn honked from above them on the road, breaking the calm of the woods. Birds flew in noisy panic from nearby trees.

"They're back with the truck." Dillon gave her one last look of concern and motioned to the men. One by one, they dipped their rags and towels into the river again and tied them around their faces before bending to the plastic-wrapped body lying downwind on the beach.

Kate followed, wondering what she would do next.

The three vehicles made up a little caravan as they headed back into town. On a corner just before the hotel, Dillon stopped the car.

"Better get out here, Kate. I've got a feeling the whole town's going to turn out for this, like a three-ring circus."

She had put her hand on the door handle, preparing to step out, when something in his words sent a flash through her vision and she gasped. That happened occasionally, away from the computer, but not often. It was like the zigzag of a lightning streak across her eyeballs, a memory, a split-second image triggered by his words. She tried to remember what he had said, so she could think about it later.

"You all right, Kate?" Dillon put his hand on her arm. "I can drive into the alley behind the hotel, let you in that way if you don't want to walk."

"Oh, no, it's fine, right here." She didn't want any more conversation to interfere with her thoughts. She had to get up to the room, turn on the computer and find out what that flash meant. Something told her it was important.

Kate watched the small procession drive toward the center of town. A peaceful feeling settled around her shoulders that had nothing to do with the violence the killer had inflicted upon his victim. It had to do with answering the call of the woman, of Lenore. Her identity might never be known, but she wouldn't be left alone in the water, rotting away into nothingness.

Kate hurried to the hotel. Once she reached her room, she kicked off her shoes and poured milk in a pan to warm. She needed a cup of cocoa. At the bathroom sink, she splashed water on her face in an effort to get rid of the smell that lingered. A shower would feel marvelous, but she wanted to turn on the computer.

What was it in Dillon's words that triggered the lightning flash of vision? Anxiety tightened her neck muscles and she reached back to rub under her hair. At this very moment, the killer could be stalking his next victim.

Propping up the pillows on the bed, Kate lay on top of the bedspread and set the computer on her lap, waiting impatiently for the two-minute lapse when the screen saver came on with the pulsing light show. The screen saver was an accident she was eternally grateful to have.

Using her older computer at home, she had to work at her books until her eyes were ready to close and she became sleepy before the visions came. With this new laptop came the screen saver program, which worked like a form of hypnosis on her if she stared at it long enough. It saved a lot of time and energy, but wasn't much help keeping up with her bookkeeping jobs. She had done a lot of extra work the old way.

The lights on the screen flashed and jammed, danced and jiggled, and then began a steady pulse. She stared, keeping her thoughts at bay as best she could. All except Dillon's last words. She tried to concentrate on them.

"Better get out here, Kate. I've got a feeling the whole town's going to turn out for this, like a three-ring circus." She repeated the words, both in her mind and out loud.

A blurry picture came onto the screen, slowly emerging in place until it made sense. It showed a young woman, her brunette hair in a single long braid down her back, walking along the highway. She had a backpack slung over her shoulder, a plastic jug of water fastened to her belt. A traveler.

Kate recognized the woman in the river. Lenore.

She seemed so happy, so contented. Scenes flashed by, like a soundless TV movie, scenes of her journeys, hiking and hitching rides. Everyone was kind to her. No one tried to harm her. She was doing what she wanted to do. Nothing entered the scenes about her past, or whom she belonged to. That seemed not to be important to her.

Just as suddenly as they started, the scenes stopped and the flashing in the screen saver disappeared. Kate waited a while, and when nothing unusual showed on the monitor, she put the laptop back on the dresser.

What did the vision mean? She had learned long ago not to ignore any of them. The revelations came for a reason.

When she pulled the drapes aside to look out, there seemed to be more activity than usual on the street, but the sheriff's office was beyond her line of vision.

Kate sat on the edge of the bed, and closed her eyes to bring up the scenes she had just witnessed. The peaceful feeling surrounded her again, the feeling she had on the sidewalk just before she came upstairs. It had nothing to do with Dillon's words. It had everything to do with the body in the river.

The woman had wanted Kate to know she had been happy doing what she wanted, traveling around, seeking adventure in the outdoors. There was no sense of anger at her fate, no feeling of distress that her identity might never be proven. It was like a thank you, but not yet a goodbye. Would the goodbye come when Lenore was put in the ground at last? Or when her killer was caught?

Kate continued to concentrate on the scene of the joyful woman, to avoid the remembrance of the bloated corpse dragged out of the river.

Activity on the computer interrupted the tranquility of the moment. Between the gyrating colors of the screen saver appeared flashes of a large, colorful tent. A circus tent, with long poles holding up the center, the corners and sides tied down. A few scruffy looking elephants were tied by their legs to short stakes and tigers lay in cages, tails swishing.

'*With the greatest of ease.*' The line from the killer came whispering in her ear. Another line flashed so quickly she almost missed it.

'*I killed him first.*'

The scene shifted back to the screen saver.

Kate pulled out a yellow pad she'd bought from the grocery store and began writing, not wanting to trust her memory, not wanting to key it in on the word processor. If the Catman could talk to her on the screen, he might be able to read what she had written on the screen.

She spent the rest of the day in her room, munching on odds and ends from the little refrigerator. Her curiosity nearly drove her outside, but she knew Dillon would come to talk or meet her somewhere when he had something to tell her.

Toward evening, she heard a knock on her door, but before she could put her hand on the knob, he called out.

"It's me, Dillon. Brought some hamburgers, thought you might be hungry."

"Oh, boy, talk about psychic." She let him in and closed the door behind him. "Did Ralph see you?"

Dillon shook his head. "He was at the diner when I drove by." He leaned forward and kissed her. A sweet, gentle kiss that made no demands.

He hadn't tried for intimacy with her since finding the body. She knew her powers made him exceedingly nervous and that might be something he couldn't deal with over the long haul.

"You look tired," she said.

He had lines around his eyes she hadn't noticed before. "It hasn't been easy. I had to notify the big boys from Denver, along with the medical examiner, or it would have looked suspicious. As it is…"

"Are they picking on you? I should think they'd have been properly grateful that you found the body."

He grinned sheepishly. "You've a way with words, Kate, that's for sure. No, they didn't exactly pick on me, but they also weren't properly grateful at my finding her. They wanted to know how the hell I did it."

Of course. It had to come down to that, didn't it.

"They started questioning me again about Betsy, trying to make a connection."

"You'll have to tell them about me, Dillon."

He snorted. "Fat chance! What makes you think they will believe you? It'll cause more confusion and they won't back off from me until they're ready to."

"You said you had an alibi."

"Yeah. They punched holes in it right away last time. Claimed I could have sneaked back here, killed Betsy, and returned unnoticed to my rafting group."

There wasn't much she could say to that, having had the same idea until she knew he couldn't be the Catman. "Did the medical examiner have anything to add? Do you think he'll be able to make an identification?"

Dillon shook his head. "Don't think so. Not much to go on. Bone structure is still there, they could work up a police composite from the skull. No fingerprints. The minnows and other fish saw to that."

She winced. "Teeth? Don't they identify bodies by teeth?"

"Sometimes. Hers seemed to be perfect. Not even a filling."

"I saw her as she was before she died. I could tell the police what she looked like. It's just that I can't draw worth a darn."

"No! I don't want you involved. I described her like you told me and I remembered a little from renting her the tent. Maybe we can work something up. I'm sorry, Kate, but I doubt she'll ever be identified."

"I don't think it matters. She kind of thanked me today, and I was hoping she would say goodbye, but she didn't. She may be waiting until we bury her."

Dillon cracked his knuckles, and the hamburger on the paper plate lay ignored, the fries congealing. "That gives me the creeps, honest to God. I have to believe you, but I don't have to like it. It isn't natural. You're seeing things that don't exist—in the proper time frame, at least."

"I know. Sometimes I feel the same way, but this time the vision felt positive. I watched her traveling from state to state on this great adventure. Good God, Dillon, she hitchhiked with strangers and nothing happened to her until she got into this quiet, peaceful glen of a place where she met her killer. That says something about fate, doesn't it?"

He rubbed his arms through the flannel shirt, as if he had chill bumps. "Yeah. Hell of a world we live in."

She decided not to say anything about the circus scenes on her computer yet. Not until something came of them. They were too disjointed and pointless and he seemed to want the subject of her visions closed.

They finished the soft drinks he brought and she put out a package of chocolate chip cookies for dessert.

"You realize you're compromising us if Ralph catches you here eating with me?" She hoped a little light-hearted teasing would get his mind off his problems at least for a minute.

It seemed to work. He laughed outright and reached to touch her cheek. "Ah, Kate, you're a wonder, and right, of course. I might have to marry you, make an honest woman out of you."

She liked the sound of his laugh. "Do they still do that?"

"Around here they do." He pointed to the computer. The screen saver flashed rainbows of color onto the screen. "That's nice. The one I use at the sheriff's office just goes blank after two or three minutes."

She looked at the screen and did a double take. The picture of the circus tent had returned, blinking on and off at intervals between the gyrating kaleidoscope of colors. She swallowed nervously. Had he seen it?

She had to ask the question.

"Do you mind looking at the monitor a few seconds? See anything you can recognize?"

He turned his full attention to the computer screen where she saw the animals and the tent several more times. He continued to stare and then turned to her, shrugging.

"What am I supposed to see? Colors, shapes, that's all there is, isn't it?"

So much for that experiment. It was still her own psychic powers bringing out pictures no one else could see. It was scary but comforting in a strange way, to know they were meant for her alone.

Dillon shoved the chair back and shrugged into his jacket. Holding his hat in one hand, he took her hand in the other.

Her heart went out to him, the big, honest cop who was going to take a lot of heat before he climbed out of the fire. She looked down at his hands, hands that at one time she thought might have exacted vengeance on two human beings.

"Got to go, Kate. The group from Denver will be back in the morning. Do yourself and me a big favor, and stay in for a few days. Any restaurant in town will deliver."

"Sure. I know all about that." She recalled the hours, days, months and years spent inside her home, afraid of human contact. She thought of the debilitating fear as a virus, feeding on itself, expanding inside her brain and body, growing bigger, gorging on her terror with every passing day that she gave in to it.

Did she want to start hiding all over again? That wasn't right either, and it had little to do with self-control. She hadn't actively started hiding when Annie died. She had merely sat back and allowed the numbing fear to gradually take over. When she buried Annie, solitude became her crutch.

In the morning, when she heard Ralph plop the usual morning *Sentinel* at her door and she saw the front page, it didn't take a second to make up her mind.

Three-inch headlines spilled across the newspaper. *Sheriff Under Cloud. Denver State Police Question How He Knew Where To Look For The Body In The River.*

She scanned the article, which posed the questions, how did Albarade know where to look for the body, and why had he waited from July, when she went missing, until now to look for it?

Kate tore off her housecoat and pajamas, cursing as a button flew across the carpet. She had brought one power jacket, as the sales clerk called it that went with a pair of black slacks. She smoothed it out on the hanger and smiled. Lipstick red—she had never worn anything in her life but pastels. It was important to make a strong impression at the very first. A familiar pulse throbbed in her neck, which she recognized as an intense stress signal.

This was Dillon's town, and he was in trouble. She couldn't sit back and let him destroy his life to protect her. If she gave in—if she hid away—the fear would come crashing back to conquer her. This time she refused to sit back and wait for it.

CHAPTER 16

Kate hesitated briefly at the front door of the station and then pushed forward. If she waffled too long, she would run away.

Dillon's chair hit the wall as he rolled the seat back from behind his desk when she entered. His mouth tensed in a straight line, his eyes betraying alarm.

"Kate! What the hell?"

The room contained three strangers dressed in look-alike suits, as if they and the material were all cut from the same bolt of cloth. Dillon stood out, wearing tight jeans, wide buckled belt, plaid shirt, and denim fleece-lined vest. In his cowboy boots, he stood taller than any of the trio.

She smiled, feeling so proud of him.

"I thought you might need some help. I wanted to be here."

Dillon looked at the men. "Excuse us, fellas," he said. "We need to talk." He took her arm none too gently, and pulled her back into the jail area, slamming the door behind them.

"I thought I told you…" His expression was fierce, his eyebrows descended almost into his eyes, his mustache quivered with outrage.

"Told me?"

"Okay, asked you—asked you not to get involved."

She put a hand on his arm. "This isn't just for you, Dillon. I am not going to hide. If they don't dig out the truth about how you found the body, they'll make your life miserable."

"I can take it, if you're safe," he persisted stubbornly.

"Thanks. I reject the thought of crouching in my room, fending off the outside world and my responsibilities. I want to, more than anything, and that is the truth, but if I hide, I'm not free to look for him. Don't you want to find the killer?"

"God yes. You know I do."

"Then we tell them what we know. Maybe they can make more sense of it than we can. The feds have computer files, and they can look for the special Modus Operandi of this killer. How many killers murder with steel wires? How many killers chop off bits of their victim's hair and cut a slice out of her arm? If he has killed before, it has to be noted somewhere. It's the only way to do it."

He ran his hand through his hair. "Damn, they won't believe you. I didn't, remember."

"I remember. However, I have Captain Murphy on my side. All they have to do is send someone to interview him. A straighter arrow you have never seen. He has to be impressive. He can show them the file on the work I did for them."

"Did you ever stop to think his department might have destroyed that part of it? How will it look years later when someone goes through and finds out they were dealing on a daily basis with a psychic? Don't you imagine they might have thought of that?"

She leaned against the wall. In the semi-gloom of a crackling fluorescent light, it was apparent the cells were empty. Not even the obligatory town drunk or a weekend bar fighter to mar the serenity of Plenitude. How did a double homicide find its way here?

"Well? Would they delete their files and records about your work?" he demanded.

She shook her head. "Nope. Murphy is a by-the-book cop. He was the first one willing to listen to me. He believed in me."

"For both our sakes, I hope you're right. With what you know and the fact that we've been seen around town together, they may think we're in cahoots. Who knows how their minds work?"

She had thought of that, too.

When they went back into the room, the three men were standing as they had been before. Two were talking low, the other gazing at the wanted posters on the walls as if he'd never seen any before.

"Ah—gentlemen, I'd like to introduce you to Ms. Katharine Macklin of New York."

They nodded politely with identical solemn expressions. "I'm Captain Peter Hawkins." One of the men detached himself from the others, moving forward. He gestured toward the other two men. "Detective Morrow and Detective Spivak."

She hid her smile behind her palm. Captain Murphy would have fit in with them so well. All three men had to be wearing silk boxer shorts in beige or gray.

"How do you want to start, Kate?" Dillon asked.

One of the men gestured toward a chair. "Won't you have a seat, Ms. Macklin?"

"No, thanks, I'll stand. Make yourselves comfortable. This may take a while."

Kate began by telling them about her psychic ability. She went on to say how she located her daughter and met Captain Murphy and how they worked together to solve a case before she left on her vacation. She exaggerated about the working together part. The captain hadn't been that much help, but at least he never stood in her way.

Kate paused to glance at Dillon. He grinned encouragement. The detective's expressions were politely non-committal.

"Would you like a cup of coffee, Ms. Macklin?" One of the men pointed toward the coffee area in the corner. Dillon had made a fresh pot.

"No, not now, but don't wait for me, help yourselves." They didn't move. She thought she'd better continue before they fell asleep on their feet. They looked that bland or bored.

"Anyone mind if we tape this?" Hawkins nodded to Spivak who opened a brief case and took out a small tape recorder.

She looked at Dillon, who shrugged.

"No, we don't mind," she said.

She started talking of her trip to Colorado and the vision she received when she passed The Dells. She told about trying to find answers to her questions and then meeting the sheriff.

"So that's about it." She stopped pacing in front of them and looked at each in turn. Right, silk boxers, she repeated, trying to get a grip on her overwhelming feeling of invasion. They were staring at her if she were some bug under scrutiny.

"Sheriff Albarade is telling the truth. He had nothing to do with the murder of his ex-wife and Le—the woman in the river. I saw the killer face to face. I mean, he was shadowy, I'll admit—" She saw him through a dying woman's eyes, blurred and outlined in brilliant red. "I could probably describe him to you. I keep notes, too."

Deliberately, with every eye on her, she went to the coffee pot to pour a cup. Her hand shook but she hid it with her back to them. Their collective stares were becoming almost too much to bear. Dillon had warned her. If they troubled the unshakable, sturdy sheriff, how did she think she stood a chance of facing them down, making them listen to her? Well, she couldn't let Dillon twist in the wind alone, could she? Meanwhile the real killer was going about his gruesome work.

"Ah...Ms. Macklin," one of the men began.

She turned to face him. "Yes?" About time someone had a question.

"Did he...ah...when he spoke to you, did he tell you why he did this to two strangers?"

"First, he didn't actually talk to me. It was more like words typed on the computer. And yes, as a matter of fact, he *did* tell me why he killed them. He is looking for someone. Someone who looks like these women. He's done more, I don't know how many. It sounded as though he's moving about the country committing these atrocities."

She watched the men while they seemed to digest this. The one in charge, Peter Hawkins, pushed away from his place against the wall and glared at her. The man using a tape recorder snapped it off as if with an unseen signal.

"This is a pile of shit! You're wasting our time," Hawkins exploded.

At last, a crack in their composure. It was a start. Dillon didn't take it that way.

"Hey, watch your mouth. I've talked to Captain Murphy in New York. He will back her up. All she said is a matter of record."

Hawkins looked glum. "Okay. Say this is all on the up and up and she's no flake, why would he pick on this town to kill two women?" He nodded to the agent to start the tape again.

"Outside of the fact they resemble someone he's after," Detective Morrow spoke for the first time, his voice dripping with sarcasm.

"Look." Kate took a big swig of Dillon's cowboy coffee and nearly spit it out. No wonder he spent so much time at the diner. It tasted and smelled like she'd imagine burnt asphalt to taste and smell. "You called me a flake. Go ahead, put me down as some nut case and ignore me. The killer will get away with what he's doing. You'll spend time re-hashing your old investigation of the sheriff and discover that his alibi is holding and that he didn't know the tourist. There's no connection between them. And you'll end up right where you are now, holding that bag of shit you just spoke of."

Dillon turned toward the window to hide his grin.

Hawkins mumbled something, looking uncomfortable.

The man closest to the coffee pot poured himself a cup, which must have been some sort of signal. The other two did the same. Cream and sugar, of course, she sneered. On the other hand, maybe it was the only way to drink Dillon's coffee. They may have been smarter than they looked.

"You can check with NCAVC at FBI headquarters in Quantico," she said. "Ask them to feed the information I've given you into the computer, see if it comes up with a match."

Hah! She'd finally gotten their attention. Dillon looked pleased at her catching them off guard. Not many civilians were familiar with the FBI profiling system.

"How do you know about NCAVC?" one of the men asked.

"I went through all this before with the case that I mentioned back in New York. The National Center for Analysis of Violent Crime is no secret. There's a way this killer is moving around, doing his thing, and not being documented. We need to isolate the link between victims and the place of their deaths. Locate where he's hit, and you make a connection between the victims and the killer."

"Yes, ma'am. Good thinking. That's our job, isn't it?"

She hated condescending pats on the head worse than if they had continued to dismiss her.

"Next time you see all this on your computer, can we have a look?" Spivak drawled.

Morrow chortled and swallowed the sound when Hawkins frowned at him.

She wouldn't allow them to bait her. That was what they wanted to see, a hysterical, out of control woman. She felt like jerking both their ties until their eyes popped. At this point, she wanted nothing more than to slam out of that room and never see them again.

"That won't work." She kept her voice even. "I experimented on the sheriff. He was in my room when I saw something on my computer. All he saw was the screen saver."

Dillon's eyes were thoughtful. She would hear about that when they were alone.

"Maybe I can help you," Kate said sweetly. "Sort of start the ball rolling." She couldn't resist showing off just a bit for Dillon.

"Yes, ma'am," Hawkins said politely, not trying to hide a yawn behind his palm.

Kate took a deep breath. "I'd say the killer's probably not psychotic—he knows right from wrong. He's a psychopath, a man without a conscience and maybe schizophrenic, with a mission he is compelled to fulfill. He fits the profile of being an organized killer to a T, except when he killed the woman in the river. That was his mistake. He has to have control or power over his victim. I believe he thinks this person is the one he is looking for until the last moment, and then it's too late. He knows it isn't her, but he has to finish it. Am I going too fast for you, gentlemen?"

There was a collective shake of heads. She had their attention. She took a deep breath and began again, closing her eyes in an effort to remember what she had jotted down on her yellow pad.

"The killer makes no effort to hide his victim. That's why I say the woman in the river was a spur of the moment impulse, probably his first and last of that sort of mistake. He had to hide her. He is probably fanatically structured and never breaks his rule of one murder per town. Then he moves on."

The men straightened, looking at her with sharpened interest.

"Go on, please." A grudging respect sounded in Hawkins' voice.

Detective Slater would have been proud of her.

"I don't know if he has a comfort zone, but if he does, he won't stray far from it. The comfort zone obviously isn't a physical place, such as a city or town or even a state, or you would have heard about his killings before. They'd be stacked up in a holding pattern in your computers."

Kate waited for them to interrupt, but they were at attention. Dillon looked stunned.

She took a deep breath and continued. "There was probably some abuse or a serious relationship problem in his background, something to feed this love/hate emotion he has for his intended victim, even though it doesn't appear to be sexual. Maybe it's a family member he's killing over and over."

Kate had always been a closet psychologist. When she developed the agoraphobia, she had had tons of abnormal psychology books delivered to her house from the library bookmobile. She read them from cover to cover.

She toyed with the idea of telling them about the flashes of circus scenes but decided against it. It could mean nothing more than interference from some source, although she had never run into that problem before. Something told her she had to check that out on her own before she mentioned the circus. It could discredit everything she was building up here and set things moving in the wrong direction.

"He's dark, not foreign, though, I don't think. He's about the sheriff's height, forty pounds lighter maybe, wiry and strong, clean shaven, no facial hair that I could see."

Hawkins had his mouth open as if to say something, but clamped it shut.

"There's something else you should know. He's coming back here. He has a reason to return. It's like he forgot something."

"He might come back for Kate." Dillon finally spoke into the silence that surrounded her last words.

The detectives looked puzzled. Kate was surprised.

"That's right. He has no power over Kate as he does his victims. Maybe he can't accept that. She knows about his one lapse of control, when he killed the woman in the river. It's possible he can't handle loose ends and she's definitely one."

Kate tended to think of Dillon in terms of his environment, small town sheriff, not much going on here. But this showed he had been giving it a lot of thought.

"Maybe you should be in protective custody," Hawkins suggested.

They weren't snickering now, they were serious. Their doubts had dissipated, and she felt a new, positive force in the room.

Dillon must have felt it, too. "I thought of that. We don't have the manpower to keep a twenty-four hour watch on her, but—"

Kate didn't want anyone watching her. "That would never work. Did I mention he's psychic, too?"

By the incredulous looks on their faces, she guessed she had forgotten to bring that up.

"Do you mean he knows—he would know about any investigation of him?"

Her smile was rueful. "I'm not certain about that aspect. I haven't pinned down how psychic he is, or what form it takes, but he is tuned into me. He's playing a game with me now, so far as it amuses him."

"Doesn't that scare you?" Hawkins asked.

"Damn right it does. But I can't let him know that."

"Just how does this ah...psychic business work?" one of the men asked, no hint of mockery in his voice.

"I don't know everything about it, although I've studied it quite a bit. I inherited my so-called gift from Scottish ancestors. He could have learned his from—" She almost said a circus. Circuses have fortunetellers, and maybe not all of them are fakes.

They were waiting to hear what else she had to say about the killer being psychic.

"The killer could have inherited his ability or it could be learned. It works that way, too, if a person is receptive. A sensitive, some call it."

"Can you read our minds?" one of the men asked.

You'd better hope I can't, she wanted to say. "No. That's clairvoyance or telepathy. I block that out. I'm not into that sort of thing. I do astral projection, that is where a psychic's soul or spirit makes a journey through time and space to witness something. That's what I did to see Betsy Albarade. I have distant viewing where I walk in another person's footsteps, see things through his eyes, sometimes the killer's, and sometimes the victim's. I've tried psychometrics, where a psychic is supposed to hold an object belonging to the subject and get into his mind, but that doesn't work for me."

"I see." Hawkins looked as if he just sucked on a lime without a Margarita chaser.

Dillon spoke again. "Kate knew about the wire he used on his victims. We let the paper assume she'd been manually strangled."

His wife's violent death still distressed him. It had to be hard, constantly reminded as he was of that terrible murder scene.

"She also knew about the little patch of flesh he stripped from Betsy's inner arm. She told me it was the same with the woman in the river. We never let that out about Betsy's arm. Kate knew the victims had long hair, with a chunk cut off. The killer probably took the hair and the piece of flesh as trophies."

The man with the tape recorder stopped his machine to turn over the tape. Two dogs barked down the street, the sound funneling into the silent room.

Hawkins set down the paper cup he was holding and jammed his hands into his pants pockets. "I guess the best thing to do is wait for the completed autopsy results. Meantime we'll check our files, see if we can come up with anything." He looked at Kate and Dillon, but neither had anything else to say.

"Does this have to be in the news?" Kate asked. "I'd like to be left out of it."

"The killer will know exactly where to come looking for her. She thinks he's bluffing yet and isn't sure where she is," Dillon said.

Hawkins held up his hand. "Hey, we don't want this out any more than you do. It wouldn't look so hot, having the Denver office dependent on a psychic when we have the finest computer network in the world." His men snickered nervously, as if unsure whether he meant it as a joke or not. "What about your newspaper? I understand you have one here in town," Hawkins asked.

"Don't worry about that. The editor and I have known each other all our lives. We can get together on how much to let out. I'll have to promise him a scoop on the big papers, if he cooperates, but he will."

Dillon walked them to the door. "Keep in touch, let us know what's going on, okay?" His voice was casual. "In a pig's rear end you will," he muttered as he turned away and closed the door on the last man.

"You don't think they'll keep in touch?" Kate asked.

"Oh, hell yes. They think I'm guilty and you're a fruitcake and probably suspect we could be in it together. They'll definitely keep in touch."

"You mean all that talking and they weren't convinced? I think you're wrong. They were listening."

She couldn't blame him for being skeptical of the outsiders. They had given him a hard time when they should have allowed him to grieve for Betsy.

"I know I was impressed. You knew a hell of a lot more than they did. When they call your Captain Murphy, or the likely scenario is that they will send someone to talk to him, that might change their minds. Until then, we'll be watched."

What's new, she wanted to ask, but didn't. She was just jumpy.

"Come on, I'll walk you back to the hotel."

"Dillon, can you get Lenore's body back here when they're done with her?" Kate felt natural about her having a lovely name like Lenore instead of everyone referring to her as the woman in the river.

Dillon looked down at her, one eyebrow raised questioningly.

"I think she'd like to be buried here, in Plenitude," Kate said.

He took her arm in a sort of proprietary grip that didn't feel half bad.

"I could arrange that." He looked up at the sky. "Looks like it might snow sooner than we expected."

'*I will come for you when the first snow falls.*'

Kate faltered, almost stumbled and Dillon held her arm tighter, turning to look at her. "Are you okay? You're white as a sheet."

The voice came like a silken threat, crinkling across the back of her neck and into her mind. She had heard that seductive voice before when she blanked out in her hotel room.

The walk to the hotel and up to the safety of her room seemed to take forever.

CHAPTER 17

That night Kate had no problems with the computer. The fact that she covered it with a pillow and took an over-the-counter sleeping pill didn't hurt either. She awoke the next morning full of questions. After dressing and taking a few hurried moments to fix her face and brush her hair, she rushed to the diner to meet Dillon.

It was cozy, for a short time, sitting side by side as if no one else existed in the world. Still, there was that nagging voice in her ear about the first snowfall.

Dillon ordered for them and they sipped on the coffee while they waited. She hadn't realized how hungry she was until the waitress set the platters in front of them.

"When did you say you expect the first snowfall?" she asked between bites of toast.

He thought a moment. "Best thing you could do is ask Ralph."

She waited for his accompanying grin, but he must have been serious about Ralph's capabilities with the weather information. "I've avoided that man for so long, I'm ashamed to confront him," she admitted.

"Ralph's okay. A mite nosy and enjoys his gossip, but he's harmless. We could get our first snow in a couple of weeks, maybe less. The storm fronts come down from Canada and so far, signs point to an early winter. We've already had several nights of frost. Why? Is that a signal you have to leave?"

He had been trying to get her to go away since he discovered her involvement with the murders. It sounded as if he'd changed his mind. She couldn't tell him about that brief flash of message. She had no reason to trust her receptors yet. Dillon would get all bent out of shape and paranoid.

Kate put her hand on his arm, ignoring the stares of the patrons. "Dillon, do you suppose you could take me to Betsy's house? I would like to poke around a bit alone. See if I come up with anything."

"Sure, I could do that. Still got the key."

"I know. Her father built the house when he first came to Plenitude. Some of the furniture is very old and beautiful." She recognized his look. He was considering what she just said. He knew she had never been inside using his key.

"Betsy left the property to me. I thought I might turn it over to the historical society."

"You don't want it? Do you always make a habit of turning down property given to you?"

"Looks like. When this was a mining town back at the beginning, Betsy's father and mother came from Missouri to make their fortune. He was a cabinetmaker until his arthritis crippled his hands. The people elected him mayor for years. No one ever ran against him."

"How did you meet Betsy?"

"We knew each other in high school. A one-room school, everyone for miles around went to it. After high school, she left for a while, took up painting and sculpting."

"Must have been hard for her to fit in here again."

"It was. When she came back, we dated off and on. She was president of the local historical society for a couple of years. She wanted me to sign over grandfather's ranch to them. It was the first cattle ranch in the area."

"You said you and Betsy came from opposite sides of the tracks. Why do you say that?"

He grimaced. "It's hard to explain to…"

An outsider? There was that word again.

"My grandfather didn't speak English too well. He came over from Wales, bringing his wife and daughter. He never mixed, and refused to let his family mix. Funny how he thought the townspeople were riff-raff and they thought of him as a backward foreigner for all those years."

"You'd think your grandfather would have had more empathy for your father then."

"Oh, no. Not on your life. The Basque were brown-skinned sheep lovers and not to be trusted within an inch of the place. I'm glad things are changing. Kids now won't have to put up with that crap."

"That's progress. Good progress. Can we go out to Betsy's today?" Kate was beginning to feel pressured. She couldn't sit back and wait for the killer to come after her. She had to locate him first. The best place to start with her computer was at Betsy house.

They finished their meal and while Dillon paid, Kate took their jackets from the rack by the door and waited. They walked slowly down the street, but it wasn't long before Dillon let her know it disturbed him to have her visiting the house alone.

"I'll have to stay with you, Kate. That's the only way I'll let you in."

"That's absurd. There's nothing to harm me in that old empty house."

"You ever get freaked out by a place? I know it's dumb, but that house has always bothered me. It's so quiet. Especially at night. There's a kind of unearthly quality to the place. I never understood how Betsy could stay out there alone."

Kate thought of Betsy rattling around the big house, oblivious to the man outside stalking her at night. The hunter watching his prey through the open windows, waiting.

"It's okay, Dillon. You're welcome to stay. I just need to look around, to see if I can pick anything up."

Dillon drove down a road heading out of town. Gradually the road narrowed. The trees alongside made a graceful canopy overhead while beneath it stayed dark and dismal. She shivered, thinking how scary the place had to be at night. The pavement stopped abruptly, when the road turned to graded gravel, and after that, hard packed dirt.

"Has to be hard to get in and out of here during snow or rain," she said.

"That's for sure. Of course, everyone in town knew Betsy. The snowplow came out soon after a blizzard. The rain was something else. She could be isolated for days. I reckon she liked it. She got a lot of work done."

They pulled up in front of the house on the circular drive and sat a moment after he turned off the ignition. The nape of her neck prickled and cold chills washed over her. The place was exactly as she had seen it on her computer. The old fashioned gables, the weathered-wood exterior, the long windows staring out like unseeing eyes, she had seen it all. She glanced up at the shingled roof, which brought an uneasy flash of *deja vu*.

Around the perimeter of the house, trees and brush encroached to a point and then stopped abruptly as a lawn took over with ankle-high grass mixed with wild flowers.

"Where are her paintings?" Kate asked.

Dillon sighed. "I have most of them at the shop. She did abstracts, never did understand them. Some of her sculptures are still in the garden."

"That's the garden over there, isn't it?" Kate pointed toward the corner of the house.

His lips turned up in a faint smile. "Betsy was good at a lot of things, but gardening wasn't one of them. She started what she thought would be a rose garden so she could look down on it from her little balcony. After she dragged in every interesting rock in the county, it turned out to be a rock garden."

"I've seen some pretty nice rock gardens."

"Not like this one. I helped her bring in a couple of the bigger boulders. I'm telling you, by the time she got the garden the way she wanted it, there wasn't room for plants. I brought her a rose bush, covered with blood-red roses. Damn thing's probably dead."

He smiled at the remembrance and Kate felt such pity— pity that Betsy died so young, before she completed her life.

"Did she enjoy her garden, after all?"

Dillon looked at Kate with an odd expression. "I'm sure she did. Betsy was what in the 'sixties would have been called a flower child. Impulsive, generous, capricious, she was a joy and a challenge. She wore her friends out eventually, as she did me."

"She stayed with her painting and sculpting?"

"Yeah, that was her anchor. Maybe that was one reason she loved this old place. Claimed the light was perfect nearly all day and she brought her canvases out to paint. I scattered her ashes just over there by that waist-high boulder in her garden."

"I'm sure she would have wanted that." Kate tapped the computer lid, anxious to start looking around.

"You don't go anywhere without that computer, do you?"

It was true. Was the computer going to take the place of her dependencies she had thought were conquered? A good question without an answer. Perhaps one never totally conquers a habit or a need—something just takes its place.

He was waiting for her answer, as if it was important for him to know.

"I don't know if I'll use the computer, but thought I'd better have it along." She was sure it wasn't the answer he wanted. He didn't like her visioning, yet he had to work with it if he ever had a hope of solving the murders.

They waited in silence a few more seconds. Kate figured he was thinking back to Betsy's last days. Going over so many times, how he could have stopped her terrible ordeal. Guilt, too, was a dependency.

"Ready?" he asked, stepping out and around to her side of the car.

"I'm ready."

The radio in his vehicle startled them with a burst of static, and then a voice came clear.

"Hellfire, it's the dispatcher from Gold Hill. I use the car phone in Plenitude, everyone knows the number."

He went back to answer it while she sat on the top porch step, inhaling the fresh pine smell of the forest around the house. As much as she admired trees, if it had been her house, she would have had the brush and trees cleared away farther back than they were. She rejected the thought of the dark figure lurking at the edge of the yard, staring up at that gabled window, waiting.

Betsy never saw that, did she? Kate looked up at the window of Betsy's room. The killer had stood close, too, looking up.

Dillon came back with a look of regret in his expression. "Reckon we'll have to make this another day. A prairie fire is out of control near Gold Hill and my men and I are all volunteers. They're asking for our help."

"Goodness, is there anything you don't do for the town? I hope they appreciate you."

"It's just something you do."

Kate touched his arm. "I want to stay here. It's early and it shouldn't take you long. You can come back for me." She prayed it would not be after dark. She doubted she could make herself stay here when the sun went down.

"It's not a good idea, Kate."

"Dillon, I appreciate your concern, but this is a house. Just an empty house. It's easy to understand why you would feel evil here, but the house is not the problem. The evil came here—and it's gone." She sensed agitation under his calm facade. Of course, he would hate to be here. It was better that he leave her alone. His strong negative feelings could block out any perceptions that might come to her.

"I know you're right, but—"

"Nothing is here to hurt me, unless you've got some bears roaming around the countryside." She tried for lightness and it worked a little. His rueful grin returned.

The evil came here, but it's gone. A premonition warned her that might not be the truth. She shook her head to dispel the thought. There was only one way to catch this killer and that was to out-think him. In order to do that, she had to immerse herself in the last place he occupied here in Plenitude.

"Well…" He was obviously torn between his duty and his fear for her safety. "You stay here. I'll check out the house first."

"Okay." She sat on the porch swing, forgetting to dust off the cobwebs and dust in her distraction.

It wasn't long before he pushed open the screen door, letting it slam behind him.

"No boogie man inside?" she asked more flippantly than she felt. Her heart went out to him. He never wanted to see this house again, that came clear and strong to her.

He didn't smile. "Nope. All clear. You sure you want to stay?"

She gave him a little push toward the car.

"Go. When you're finished, come back for me. I'll be fine."

"I'll leave the thermos of coffee. There'll be plenty at the burn site."

After he drove away, spinning wheels and radio crackling in his wake, the silence closed in around her. She sat on the porch a while, studying the landscape. It was not far, only a couple of miles back into town, only a few miles down that narrow, tree-lined gravel road, but she felt totally isolated.

Why would a young woman prefer to stay out here in this spooky old house? Maybe because she grew up in it and took comfort from that, with both parents incapacitated. Dillon had said Betsy should have stayed single, that it was in her blood to be a loner.

Kate walked out past the porch so she could look up at the window of Betsy's room. In her imagination, a slight movement passed in front of the window. Was it imagination? She shivered, looking out toward the road.

She wanted to run after Dillon and shout for him to come back. She made a step toward the driveway, but knew he would never hear her or see her past the bends in the road. It should be at least a couple of hours before he returned. She hoped it would be before dark.

This was absurd. The house was empty. Dillon checked it out. Alone, with no other impressions to interfere, the pervasive pain and anguish of Betsy's last few moments of life slowly began to invade her thoughts. She was responding to the premonition of intrusion that centered inside the house and struggled to push the negative atmosphere away. It was like swimming in thick sludge. The aura of death would be here a long time, maybe until the house fell down.

Walking back to the porch, Kate determinedly thrust the brief glimpse of the shadow in the bedroom from her thoughts. It could have been a residual manifestation of Betsy's spirit or Kate's own active imagination.

Neither one could harm her if she didn't dwell on the idea. She sat again on the swing and pushed her feet to get it going, bringing out an image of a prim little girl sitting on the swing drinking iced tea with her mother. The thoughts of Betsy as a child warmed her. For a moment, Kate set aside her feelings of Betsy and thought of her own situation. What would it be like to live in this community the rest of her life? She enjoyed Dillon's company very much and knew he was attracted to her.

It would take a special kind of man to accept her with her gift and not feel threatened. She would never be able to ignore it when someone called out to her for help.

She brought her mind back to the matter at hand, Betsy Albarade. Her spirit came through very strong on the swing, but as Betsy the child.

Kate moved to the middle of the long wooden porch. Across the open sides and front, the trees stood like sentinels. Some of the trees had lost their leaves for the coming winter. The pines stood thick and green beyond the edge of the lawn. She had the strange perception of them moving closer, like giant beings, picking up their skirts and scurrying forward an inch or two each night and then sitting back down again to await the next night's encroachment.

She rubbed her arms, which were suddenly cold. How silly of her, to be afraid of trees.

Betsy was afraid of what had been out there.

Betsy had sat looking out, feeling an obscure threat, a sense of being watched.

"Why didn't you tell someone, Betsy?" Kate spoke out loud, needing to hear the sound of a voice in the stillness. She missed talking to her cat.

The answer was clear. Betsy had grown into an adult who chose to live outside of town alone. Maybe she hadn't even admitted the uneasiness into her conscious thoughts.

"How long did you watch her?" Kate said the words, and then wished she hadn't. She wasn't ready to invoke the killer's presence. She was here to find out things from Betsy. It was unusual to get spiritual input without the benefit of her computer, but it was happening more often as she became receptive.

The machine rested next to her on the swing, but she didn't touch it. It was time to wing it, without looking at the monitor.

Kate opened the screen door slowly, her footsteps walked on Betsy's. Betsy's presence came in vividly intense. They shared the same feeling—as if eyes stared into their backs. Rushing inside, Kate slammed the door behind her, feeling safe in her own house. Her own house? Her thoughts were mingling with Betsy's.

Oh, God, was she going to relive Betsy's last moments? No! No! She couldn't bear to do that, not even to catch the killer. Kate closed her eyes and with a strong effort, struggled to break out of the heavy, ominous atmosphere surrounding her.

She felt it receding. Bathed in sweat, she pulled out one of the old ladder back chairs from the kitchen table, but restlessly moved away from sitting. It might be necessary to go into Betsy's last day sometime, but not now. If her death scene had to come through, if it was information she needed, let it come with the computer. It was safer, more controllable that way.

To enter into the domain of the killer was not what she wanted to do. She knew Betsy had never really seen her killer until that last moment when he turned her around and looked into her face while he finished his work.

She rummaged through drawers in the roll top desk, touching Betsy's possessions. Dillon had never returned to the house to sort out her stuff. Kate found a book. Maybe it was a diary or journal. That would bring her closer to Betsy than anything. She held the book and received a warm feeling, a comforting sensation. It was a copy of the book in Dillon's shop.

When Kate spread her palms, the book opened to Dylan Thomas's poem, *Death Shall Have No Dominion*. The words leaped out at her from the worn page. Was it a sign from Betsy? Maybe a sign that she had been thinking good thoughts of Dillon toward the last?

Didn't death have dominion over us—over those we love? Kate thought of her husband, her daughter, all those she loved. They were still with her, in a way, weren't they? They would always be. The poet said that though lovers be lost, love could never be lost. Was this somehow tied up with the killer and his thoughts? It seemed a very strong possibility that although the killer may never have heard of Dylan Thomas or his poem, it could be the essence of what was driving him.

Kate decided it was time to use the computer. She brought it inside and put it on the table, and sat in the chair she had pulled out before. When she flipped open the lid and her bookkeeping program came on first, she stayed away from the keys, waiting for the screen saver.

Watching the pulsing, throbbing colors always reminded her of a kaleidoscope her father had sent her when she was a child. Her father and mother divorced when she was six and she only remembered him by his presents. He never came to visit and she never knew what happened to him.

Abruptly the screen took on a softly-muted rose color and Betsy appeared in a field of flowers, wearing faded jeans and a T-shirt with a big sunflower on the front. While she painted on a large canvas, her long dark hair blew softly about her shoulders in a gentle wind. Kate felt the serenity and pleasure in the scene.

The picture shifted—zooming into a circus big tent, a flash of a trapeze swinging in the center—a man falling to his death on the hard-packed ground. The screen went to blood-red splashes and Kate put her hands over her face as if she could feel the warm blood pelting her. He said he had killed his father.

When she dared look up again, the scene had shifted to greens. She was looking at a small khaki-colored tent set in the middle of a wooded glen with a river in front. It had to be the Dells and the tent of the woman in the river.

She studied the area, but saw nothing unusual. There was the outline of the woman brushing her hair in the lamplight. Kate closed her eyes a moment, praying she wouldn't have to go through this death again.

Again, the scene shifted back to the circus tent. Kate steadied herself, waiting for the man to fall again, and the splash of blood, but this time a woman stood on the platform high up, shrouded in shadow. She was middle-aged, not agile, should not have been up there alone. Kate felt the woman's fear and despair.

'*I killed the bastard for what he did to Christine. When my mother found out, she leaped off the platform and died.*'

The words splashed across the scene, and the woman and the circus tent disappeared.

Then: '*Leave me alone, bitch!*'

The same words repeatedly filled up the screen, pulsing, striking her eyes with jagged slashes of brilliant lights. She tried to type, to ask a question, but nothing else came onto the screen, just those four words exploding in blood-red colors.

'*Leave me alone, bitch!*'

Kate knew it was the killer. He wasn't trying to contact her, toy with her as he had before. This was different. She was experiencing his intense rage, like blood pounding in his veins. She had intruded on his thoughts and secret memories and he knew it.

She was getting close. But how? Nothing made sense. She was sure neither Betsy nor Lenore knew the killer or had any idea where he came from so she was not getting any information from them. What did she see that disturbed the killer? The man falling off the platform hadn't seemed to trigger anything. The woman standing on the platform, trembling and afraid had provoked his anger.

The older woman was not similar in any way to the two dead women. Why had he chosen them for death?

Kate closed her eyes, looking inside herself for answers. When she opened them, the computer showed a scene that shocked and dismayed her.

It was night. The cat-like figure of a man crept toward a partially opened window of a house she had never seen. It was not a house such as would be in Colorado. She saw a low-framed, flat-roofed, colorfully-painted outside, not the usual white paint or redwood shingles she was used to seeing here in the town of Plenitude. The night felt warm and muggy, as though it was about to rain. The man was dressed in black clothing, wearing a black stocking-cap, dark, dark, everything about him looked dark.

He had no problem navigating the house once he was in-side. He knew where he was going. He had been there before. Back, down the long hallway, Kate followed in his footsteps.

He moved toward the bedroom. She wanted to stop. She tried to move her fingers toward the computer switch, but nothing worked. It was as if her motor control had become inoperative. She couldn't turn away from watching.

Wake up! Wake up! She tried to call out, to wake the sleeping house, but no words came. She was under his control, following in the predatory footsteps of a hunter.

He came to a door and paused, listening. She sensed his anticipation, the flash of white teeth, his eyes gleam-ing—tiger's eyes—in the puny glimmer of a nightlight in the hallway, near the floor.

The door was ajar and he pushed it open. Kate followed him into the room. The woman lay sprawled, pathetically vulnerable on the bed, one arm curved upward, one arm flung outward, with long dark hair spread over the pillow.

Oh God! *Wake up*! *Wake up*! Kate tried again to shout until her throat swelled with the effort. Was this happening now, or in the future, or in the past?

The hunter crept closer, bent, and picked up a length of hair, holding it between his fingers, rubbing it softly, like a lover might do. He leaned closer and touched his hand gently to the inside of her left arm, as if he saw something there that moved him.

Kate sensed his sudden change of emotion. He became angry, filled with hatred.

Christine couldn't hide from him. He always found her.

The woman stirred restlessly.

Wake up! *Wake up*! *Give yourself a fighting chance, at least.* Kate tried to croak out a warning. The woman continued to sleep.

When he tired of his little game, he eased down onto the bed and in one swift motion, flipped the sleeping woman over onto her stomach.

'*With the greatest of ease.*' He had said those words before and they rushed into Kate's thoughts now.

Kate tasted the sourness of vomit as it rushed upward from her roiling stomach. Yet, she could not tear herself away. Some force held her to the scene, compelling her to become a witness.

He had the wire out. Holding onto the little wooden ends, he draped it around her neck as she tried to scream. Her body thrashed. She kicked her legs, but his knee bent into the center of her back as he pulled tighter and tighter. At the last moment, he turned the top of her body around so they could see each other, as if he needed to feed upon her terror, see himself mirrored in her dying stare.

Kate mentally broke away from his hold on her, spun out of the woman's bedroom, hearing his mocking laughter follow her. She glanced at a digital clock on a dresser just before leaving. It said 1 a.m., and the date showed four nights ago.

Waking to sudden reality, seated at Betsy's kitchen table, she slammed down the lid of her computer, as if he could follow her from out of its bowels, and tore outside onto the porch. She leaned her head back, gulping deep of the fresh air for a long time.

With rising excitement, an idea formed in her thoughts until it was clear. She had the key all along and didn't recognize it.

He flew through the air with the greatest of ease.

That was how he was able to move about the country, strike like a phantom, and then disappear. He traveled with a circus and now moved toward Georgia and Florida. She had read of a winter home in Sarasota for circuses. Wasn't the circus dead? Occasionally the bigger ones appeared at Madison Square Garden, so there had to be some vestiges of it left in rural America.

When she saw Dillon, she would ask if he remembered a circus visiting Plenitude last summer.

With the killer's supreme arrogance, he had to show her how he did it. To show her how he was going to do it again and again until he found the person he was looking for.

Christine was the young girl who had made love to her brother. The killer had to be Nikki, Christine's brother, and he was searching for her.

CHAPTER 18

By the time Dillon returned, it was dusk, and Kate was more than ready to leave Betsy's house. She had considered starting down the road, but the trees came together overhead and the path lay in somber murkiness, so she stayed put—away from the house, sitting on a bench in Betsy's garden.

She and Dillon went back to the house and sat on the porch steps before he asked about her hours spent alone.

"He showed me another one, Dillon. It was horrible. I followed the Catman inside while he did it."

"He did it here again?"

"Not here, somewhere else. I stepped into his world, followed him with the computer."

Dillon pulled her close, nestling her into the crook of his shoulder. She felt his kiss on the top of her head.

"Ah, Kate, this can't be good for you. When this is over, you have to give up this thing that drives you. Throw away the damn computer."

She considered how it would feel to have someone strong and decent like him protecting and cherishing her. The thought gave her the warm cozies, until reality intruded. Everything came with a price. Giving up her independence, ignoring calls for help—if she received others—would take some serious pondering. She didn't think she would be able to ignore her gift until it left of its own accord. She had a gut feeling that would happen someday.

"The killing was four nights ago." She moved away from him so she could concentrate on what to tell him. "The night was warm and muggy with the feeling of rain in the air." She described the house and the portion of landscape she managed to see in the dark.

"The clock showed 1 a.m. If you could find out if a woman fitting the description was murdered approximately that time four days ago..."

"That's a tall order. Sounds like it could be somewhere down south, like Florida or Louisiana, or Texas. Lots of places are warm this time of year."

"Warm and muggy?"

"That narrows it down a little, but not a helluva lot. The whole Eastern coastline is likely to be warm and humid. Texas probably gets that way."

"No, it's on the East coast, I'd swear to that. You said Florida or Georgia. That sounds right. Can you try there? Send faxes to police stations? Try one state at a time. I know it's farfetched, but if we could find out what direction he's going, or how he's moving around, that would be a start." She was about to tell him what she had seen of the circus, but stopped, knowing she had to have more to go on first. Like who was Christine. If she waited one more day, the computer might bring her enough answers to tell him all about the circus.

"He doesn't hide the bodies, that's a help," Dillon said.

"Except for Lenore. He hid her in the river. He picks out single women, isolated women. It could be days before a body emerges, before someone is investigated as missing."

"It's a long shot, but we don't have much else to go on," Dillon admitted.

"He killed the last woman in her house. Someone's got to miss her." Kate stopped in time before she asked how long it had taken to find Betsy.

"I'll do my best," Dillon promised. "Does he know you followed him?"

Kate heard the underlying tension behind Dillon's words. "Yes, he knows. He did this on purpose, sort of thumbing his nose at me. I doubt he has found a way to reach me physically. He's psychic, but he has to have some kind of source to grab onto my thoughts. I use the computer. He's using my willing-ness to let him in."

He had gotten to her once before. The missing afternoon returned in bits and pieces. The thought of his erotic knowledge of her body made her blush. She couldn't let him possess her like that again.

"You need to check on and around the date you went out to investigate the tent in the Dells. I think someone might have seen the murder. Someone hunting for game in the night."

"I'm doing that. I have to wait until this bunch gets back from their family reunion trip, then I'll question Hank. He's head of the little group of poachers and there is no use asking anyone else. They're probably more afraid of him than they are the law."

"Do you think the town will accept Betsy's place for the historical society after what happened out here?" she asked, changing the subject, needing to get away from that scene with the latest victim.

"I don't know. It will take a while. People here are superstitious. I had no idea she willed the house to me. I sure as hell don't want it. I don't want to have to keep up the property until they decide to accept it, either. That could take years. I've shut off the electricity and phone, but later, before it freezes, I will have to come out and turn off the water, drain the pipes and put up storm windows. It's not worth it."

"Someone has to take care of the place," Kate said.

"I expect the town will accept it eventually." His voice sounded resigned, as if he didn't believe his own words.

"It's really a nice old house, valuable antiques."

"The house never set right with me. Now it feels diseased."

"The house isn't sick. It's the residue of what took place here."

"I know the truth of that, it's just hard accepting it. It's been a big help, being able to talk to you about it." He touched her shoulder and dropped his hand to his side.

"I almost forgot. I found this in a drawer. Hope you don't mind my rummaging around." Kate handed him the little book.

"I've been meaning to get back here, pack stuff away, but can't get into the idea."

Memories, so many memories for Dillon.

Kate avoided telling him that spirits generally left a place when they were at peace with their death—and Betsy was still here. Kate felt that quite clearly.

Dillon took the book and opened it to the poem. "Funny, I didn't see this when I investigated."

"Maybe there were too many distractions."

"By the way, there's something I've wanted to ask you."

"What's that?"

"Sometime before your vacation's over..." They both smiled at that one. "I'd like you to come out and look at my grandfather's place with me. I thought if I had someone come with me the first time, I could get it behind me."

The odd touch of vulnerability in his voice charmed her. "It's not your grandfather's place. Its Dillon Albarade's place," she reminded him gently. "Of course, I will. Thank you for asking."

"It's a few miles out of town, just over that rise of hills to the east. We could take a picnic lunch."

He sounded eager. It wasn't hard to imagine him as a young boy, alone on the big ranch, torn between his mother and grandfather, no kids to play with. So sad.

The shadows were lengthening by the time they got up from the swing to leave. "Ah, Dillon, could you please go inside and get my computer? I left it on the table."

"Sure thing. Have to lock the door. Although I don't know why, no one comes out here." He walked up the steps two at a time, making her heart ache at knowing how familiar he once was with Betsy's place.

He came back holding the computer.

"Let's go, now. Put the computer on the floor by my feet, please?" She didn't want to touch it, afraid of triggering another vision. She had only had one sighting in front of Dillon, but all along, she felt an awareness, as if someone was watching them.

She opened the car door and sat down, relieved to be away from the persona of the old house. Dillon stepped up into the driver's side and spun out of the narrow circle and onto the road. Dust flew up behind them, blocking out the sight of the house and trees when she turned back to look.

Kate had gradually felt a presence while Dillon sat at her side on the swing. Whether it was Betsy's dissatisfied essence or the killer's spirit, it was an oppressive entity. She couldn't have stood it another moment.

After some time, he said, "I'll tear the old house down, that's what I'll do," as if he guessed her thoughts.

"That would be a shame." Kate looked at his stern profile, wishing she could ease his pain. "The bad atmosphere will dissipate in time. Betsy's not there anymore, her spirit's at rest." That was a lie and she hated to say the words, but he needed reassurance more than truth.

"How could her spirit rest?" He hit his open palm against the steering wheel. "We haven't caught the bastard."

"Doesn't matter to a spirit sometimes. I don't think the soul, or whatever you want to call it, harbors emotions like revenge or cares about justice. That's just my spin on the subject."

"I don't like this, God knows I don't. All this talk of spirit worlds and craziness like that. But if there is such a thing, I would be glad to know Betsy's at peace. 'Cause I sure as hell am not."

"Don't you see? Betsy never called out to me, the woman in the river did. Lenore wanted someone to find and bury her. Now she's content, or will be when we bury her." She hoped Betsy would be appeased then, too.

"If everyone is so goddamned content, how are we going to catch him?"

Kate understood his anger and frustration.

"Through his arrogance, if we're lucky. He's the one I am in touch with now. He has been moving through the country with complete immunity, doing his evil. It's beginning not to be enough for him. As he sees it, there is no recognition for his superior intelligence, his ability to outsmart everyone. He needs more. He wants someone to know."

"That's where you come in?"

"Right. He has an audience. He can preen and show off and he thinks I can't get to him. He'll get careless in time."

Did she have that much time?

'I will come to you when the first snow falls.'

It was a cryptic reminder coming from inside her head. Could the killer communicate with her without going through the computer? The computer was only a machine she could cover with a pillow, hide under the bed, and throw away. If the murderer learned who she was, where she was, he might insinuate himself into her thoughts and gain control as he almost did before.

Kate turned to look back at the narrow road leading to the old house. She never wanted to come here again, but knew she would have to. The killer had left something of value behind in his haste to leave, and he had to return to the house.

On the paved road, Dillon, too, sounded relieved to be away from Betsy's house.

"I'll contact Hawkins in Denver. They can fax the counties along the East Coast from Georgia to Florida. By the time that gets in the system, there may be a missing person or a corpse at the morgue."

"That's good. We've got to stop him before he kills again."

Or before he comes for me.

e⁄ɔe⁄ɔ

Kate waved to Ralph when she hurried up the stairs to the sanctuary of her room. She should have waited for his latest weather bulletin. Ralph was sure to offer one if she hadn't rushed away, worried that he would ask questions.

Inside the room, Kate paused, chin in the air. Had someone entered her room? She sighed in relief, not sensing another's presence. Feeling tired, but not tired enough to sleep, she wanted to work out the puzzle. There was no way she was going to wait around for this madman to come for her. She had to try to find him first. Maybe she should have told Dillon about the circus, but she felt very strongly that she needed to put the pieces together before she sent everyone off on scattered searches that might dead-end. Then she would lose her credibility for sure.

Going over the list of what she knew about the stalker, some of the fragments that had come to her over the computer made no sense. The circus scenes with the man who fell to his death and the older woman—God only knew what happened to her—what did it mean? And then there was Christine.

Kate thought about Dillon's offer to take her to the ranch, a positive sign that he was growing more accepting of his heritage. Was that important to her? She considered the idea, wanting to take her mind away from Betsy and the house.

Surely there were local women who wanted to spend time with Dillon. He still had a life, if he would only reach out for it. She couldn't see how she might ever be a part of that life, a part of Plenitude.

Wasn't love supposed to reach out and grab you? Shouldn't it be thrilling, exciting, and heady—or was that just for teenagers and first loves? So far, she hadn't felt that sort of turmoil toward Dillon. She had it pretty darn good with Mac. Then no one until Slater. His was not a blinding, crashing love either. He helped her get over a rough time. Could be a lot of her feeling toward him had been gratitude.

Dillon only needed a little encouragement. He would be quite a catch, with his handsome looks, his big, sexy body and his quiet, steady ways. He was a rock, always there for the one he loved. She recalled their lovemaking and a warm glow permeated her body.

She got up and made a peanut butter sandwich, smeared some jelly on top of the peanut butter, and poured a glass of orange juice. It was dark but stars shone in the Colorado sky and the clouds had blown away. That gave her a little more maneuvering time before it snowed.

There was another key to this puzzle. The sum total of the parts didn't add up to the big *why*. Why did he do it? "If you find out the why, sometimes it leads you to the who with psychos," Slater had often said.

Dillon was a good honest cop, but out of his league. Being a sheriff was more of a hobby than a real job in Plenitude. She would have to find the answers on her own.

As soon as Kate finished the snack, she took out the computer and put it on the bed. Taking a deep breath, she opened it and pressed keys to bypass the spreadsheets to get to the word processor.

I have long, dark hair. I work in a circus. Kate typed the words, thinking as she went along. The woman was young, pretty, if the victims were any indication. Both Betsy and Lenore had the same type figures, athletic, full, and womanly. Was it a sweetheart who left him? A wife who ran off with someone else? Was it his sister?

Her hands paused at the keys and she concentrated on the image of the woman. Her fingertips grew warm, a name splashed across the screen.

Christine.

There was a lover involved. A woman who left him for some reason and he couldn't get past it. He had to be torn between love and hate to go so completely off the deep-end into this spree of violence.

Kate typed the name Christine, repeating it over and over, filling the screen, and waited.

After the two-minute time lapse, the screen saver came on, sucking up the words on the monitor. Her mouth was dry. She was not ready to talk to the Catman yet. She hoped she wouldn't have to.

It wasn't the killer. The next scene flashing on the monitor ran like a video with the sound off. A young woman walked forward, looking remarkably like the dead women, only this one had a lot of make up on, like stage makeup. She had a hard look about her eyes, a knowing, too-old look that didn't match her youthful body.

Kate knew this was Christine.

A thought struck her as the woman continued to walk forward.

"Let me see the inside of your left arm." Kate repeated the sentence, sometimes out loud, sometimes concentrating on the thought.

With a little smile, Christine stretched out her arm. Kate strained to see. A small tattoo with the name "Nikki" showed on the arm. Was that the name of the killer? Was he trying to erase his name from the arm of each dead woman?

Kate didn't say the name aloud, fearful of invoking the killer. She needed to find out more about Christine. This was the weapon she needed. This was the key.

Where are you, Christine? She typed the words on her keyboard and watched them flash onto the screen.

There was no answer. The woman turned and began to walk slowly away.

No! Don't go! Please. I need to talk to you. Kate typed furiously, concentrating her thoughts.

Slowly, Christine turned back. Her eyes filled with sorrow, her mouth tight with despair. *'He'll never find me...never find me.'*

The words seemed to come from everywhere and nowhere, from Kate's fingers on the keyboard. She didn't know how they came, but it would be impossible to forget the grief in the woman's eyes. Kate stared into the screen as Christine disappeared into infinity, a dot on the horizon of the screen.

She would not be back. Christine did not want to be found.

Tomorrow would come soon enough and, with it, perhaps the first snowfall. She wasn't ready for the killer, but she felt he was ready for her.

Touching her fingers to her neck, she could almost feel the cold wire there. Kate leaned back in the chair. She didn't remember turning off the computer, nor how long she sat in silence. Finally, she crossed the room to put the computer on the table and crawled on the bed, falling immediately into a deep sleep.

CHAPTER 19

Kate barely contained her excitement the next morning. She had to see Dillon first thing, tell him what she had learned last night. The question was how much to tell him. Dillon would be duty bound to pass on information to the police in Denver. If they acted prematurely, they could frighten the killer away.

As soon as she was dressed, she headed for the diner. The air felt soft and mushy, not as cold as it had been, with dark, low clouds bubbling in from the north. She pulled her jacket closer around her neck and ears. When she entered, the little diner was crowded as usual with men. Didn't women prepare breakfasts for their husbands anymore, or did the men get up too early?

Kate remembered when it had been her habit to sleep until almost noon to avoid sleeping at night. What a dreadful waste of time that had been.

Most of the patrons nodded politely to her, some smiled. She acknowledged them and thought how great that was, not to panic when strangers looked at her.

Since she had been meeting Dillon nearly every morning, no one ever sat in the seat next to him. That gave her a comfortable feeling.

"I've got a lot to tell you, but I guess it will have to wait," she began, sliding onto the little round seat.

"Well, hi to you, too, Ms. Macklin." Dillon rose off the stool, saluting her with two fingers to his forehead.

"Oh, I'm sorry. I get caught up in my thoughts. Please, sit. Good morning, Dillon."

"When you get caught up with your coffee, we'll go to the shop. I don't open to customers for another hour."

They sat in companionable silence, drinking and listening to the idle chatter around them. Buzz, buzz, clank of dishes, with country western music playing low in the background. Nice sounds early in the morning. She would never be able to hear music like that again without thinking of Dillon.

"It's pleasant to sit with you and not have to dredge up clever conversation," Dillon said.

"I noticed that. I like it, too. I'm not good with small talk, I bog right down."

"Me, too."

They finished their coffee and, after Dillon paid their bill, he helped her on with her jacket. She pulled her stocking-cap down over her ears.

"Hey, you look like a little girl with your hair sticking out, and the rest of it hidden under that cap."

She laughed up at him and for a brief second her heart drummed an extra beat or two. The blast of chilled air struck hard when they opened the door. She hid herself behind Dillon's broad frame a moment, out of the wind.

He looked at the sky. "Shouldn't be long now. Everyone waits in longing and dread for the first snowfall."

Dread. He didn't know the half of it. But she couldn't tell him. If nothing else, he would want to keep her in jail to protect her. She had to be free to work on a plan.

When they reached Dillon's shop, he laid a fire in the fireplace and soon had it roaring. She watched him move and wondered how she had ever connected him to the killing of these women. It might have been a normal assumption with both he and the killer being dark and graceful, but the Catman was an acrobat, with muscles swelling across his shoulders and upper arms that a normal man would not have. She had caught impressions of his strength and prowess when he climbed agilely up the tree in front of Betsy's room. He was an amazing specimen.

By the time they sat down at the scarred table, Kate was ready to tell him some of what she had seen on the computer.

"You say a circus may be involved?" Dillon wrinkled his forehead in thought. "A circus came through Plenitude and stayed for almost a week in July. The chamber of commerce or the newspaper would have the exact date."

"That's coming through to me. Do circuses usually stay so long in one place?" she wondered out loud.

"Don't know. As I recall, the weekend was coming up and they camped on Joe Flynn's ranch, out near the highway. Reckon he made them comfortable. What with his six kids, he was probably tickled to let them camp there."

Kate felt a weight shift from her shoulders.

He killed with the greatest of ease.

"'He flies through the air with the greatest of ease.' Remember that old tune, Dillon?"

"'The daring young man on the flying trapeze'?" he finished.

"That's how he does it!" Kate strode to the fireplace and stared down into the embers as if it could tell her something, but she already knew. "I think he's a trapeze artist."

"You're on the right track, by God. He'd have to be familiar with heights to make that leap from the tree onto Betsy's roof and down into her room."

"In each little town or village he checks to see if *she's* there. Let's say he thinks he sees the woman he is looking for. He could sneak away from the circus and track her down. That should be easy in a small town, to hide in bushes and spy on her. In his blind obsession, he thinks he's found her."

Dillon's eyes flashed with excitement. He was catching on fast. "He leaves when the circus moves on, but they don't travel far between these little towns. He sneaks back a couple of nights later and makes his kill."

"And by the time the body's discovered, there's nothing to tie the death with the circus which has moved on."

"I'll be gone to hell!" Dillon exploded, leaping to his feet, pacing back and forth. "It's a perfect setup. The excitement of finding the body, the small town police without a clue. God! I've been so stupid!"

"Don't beat yourself up, Dillon. He must be doing it all over the country. No one has ever connected the deaths with the circus as far as I can tell."

"But why? Who does he think he's killing? Why is he doing it?" The cry was wrung out of him. Kate knew he was thinking of Betsy.

She told him about the computer scene where the boy and his sister made love. "She has a small tattoo with the name Nikki on her inner arm. I think that may be her brother's name and he's the killer." She wanted to remember a last name, too, but that escaped her memory so far.

"That's so twisted," Dillon said.

"I know, but we have no idea of the circumstances involved. I have a gut feeling he killed this older man, maybe his father. What if the father had been molesting the sister and Nikki found out? Do you suppose his name is Nicholas? That should narrow things down a bit."

"This is mostly supposition, isn't it?"

"Well, some of it," she admitted. "I saw some scenes on the computer. I know the sister's name is Christine. In mulling it over in my mind, it could be that he is punishing Christine for something she did that hurt him badly. Maybe she ran away and left him behind. I think she's dead."

"If he's psychic like you say, wouldn't he know that?" Dillon asked.

"For one thing, he's not thinking rationally, and for another, he may not be that good of a psychic. If the circus trained him to read crystal balls for example, he might be limited in what he can see. And I know for certain, she doesn't *want* him to find her."

"So you think he's searching for his sister who abandoned him or left him? And you think he killed his father? That should make things easy to track."

Kate shook her head and took off her jacket. It was warming up with Dillon's roaring fire. "I don't think it will be that easy. I think he is very clever and covered his tracks well. There was something else, a brief glimpse of an older woman, about the same age as the man who fell to his death, and I think she is dead, too. It may have been his mother. It's all connected, but I don't know how. I just feel that this Nicholas person has to punish Christine for leaving him. The wire garrote might be part of his working apparatus and he thinks that's a suitable way for her to die."

She sat next to Dillon, and he pulled her close, squeezing her shoulder gently "Kate, I have to tell you, the way it looks, finding this S.O.B will be a miracle, but making any of this stick against him will be even harder. He probably has all kinds of alibis. I can check out the name of the circus that came here. If they have a Nicolas working there, it should come up." He released her and leaned back in the wooden chair. "If he does it the same way every time, he's never left a clue behind, I'll lay odds to that."

"I'll keep trying, that's all I can do," she said.

"That's another thing. I hate the thought of you involved in this weird game-playing, mind-thing that's going on be-tween you and the killer. You don't know for sure how strong his psychic connection is."

No, she didn't, and the thought of the killer continuing his murdering spree in such a terrible way was too much to dwell on for long.

∽∾∽∾

Later that afternoon, Kate walked past the sheriff's office and noticed a light in the window. The sun had receded behind the forest on the west side of town.

"Kate. Good to see you." Dillon greeted her entry with a grin, and kicked back his chair to stand, a warming old-fashioned gesture. She sat in the chair nearest his desk.

"Anything new?" she asked.

"Looks like you were right about a lot of things. A woman matching the description of the other victims was found in her home in a little town in Georgia. Same M. O.

"Do circuses still winter in Florida?"

"I'm sure they do. If what you say is right about his circus connections, he probably won't do his dirty work in Florida. Too close to the source, like fouling his own nest."

Did that mean he has turned around, to come back toward Colorado? "Remember I talked about his comfort zone? If the circus winters in Florida, then maybe he only kills women in the summer, when he's on the move. This woman in Georgia might have been his last until next season."

"That makes as much sense as any of this," Dillon said. "I'm working with the Federal Bureau to pin that down. Maybe they can track his moves. Now that it's become an interstate crime of violence, we can ask for more help."

"The feds are notorious for not wanting to share information. You can turn all this in to them, and you may never know what happened with it."

"I know," Dillon said. "I haven't had a lot of dealings with the FBI. It's hard enough working with the Denver police. Still, you are right. They play their cards close to the vest."

Kate liked the way Dillon looked so at home behind his sheriff's desk. She didn't know why that would cause a sudden sting of sadness, but his next words gave her no time to analyze the feeling.

"I have to know something," he said. "You told the Denver bunch the killer would be back for you. Did you mean that literally? Or through your computer?"

Kate began to hedge, knowing Dillon did not want to hear that she needed to go back to Betsy's house. She had to contact the killer, interrupt his movements, break into his habit pattern before he left the South and turned back toward Colorado. If she could find out where he was, Dillon could tell the authorities.

"It just came off the top of my head." she said. "I couldn't tell you why I said that." It wouldn't do for Dillon to have even a remote idea of her intention. He would never let her go on with it.

"He's certifiable," Dillon said. "How do you fight some-one who doesn't think like a normal person?"

Suddenly the room seemed small. Dillon's pacing back and forth caused her to draw her legs up tight against the chair. "You fight by getting the killer on your turf and by forcing him out of his rigid behavior pattern to do something extraordinary. This kind of killer is not so clever when he does something that breaks his own formula." She had learned that early on in the last case.

"You sound as if you have a plan. I hope—"

Kate interrupted before Dillon could lay down guidelines she was not prepared to follow. "I don't have a plan yet. I'll let you know when I do." He must not be so protective of her that he could stop her once she set an objective in motion.

So far, her interference had been part of a game to the Catman. Kate felt she would have to fight the battle in Pleni-tude. She and Dillon could go to Florida, she supposed, but she wasn't ready to fly yet. She hadn't conquered all her phobias, just put most of them in limbo until she worked on them one by one.

That would be just what the killer wanted, sucking them down into the vortex of his own world. Let the federal people go to Florida and work on it from that end, with the circus.

"In the meantime, what about going out to the ranch with me today or tomorrow?" He touched her shoulder. "I want to show it to you and I'd like to be with you again."

She looked into his eyes and knew he wanted to make love to her again. She wondered how to stall him. She needed more time. Dillon's interest wasn't casual, nor was he the kind of man who did or said things without thinking them through. He had kept his distance since finding the body in the river and since he knew she witnessed Betsy's death. It probably wasn't comfortable to be that close to her for a while. Now that he had re-considered and wanted to be close again, Kate wasn't so sure.

"Maybe later, Dillon, let's focus on this first, okay?"

She reached to touch his cheek and the sadness intruded again. Part of her longed to have him make love to her again, part of her needed separation until this was over. She knew it was not a good time. She should stay close to town, gathering all her energy to focus on the killer, without distractions.

The killer would hunt by his own timetable. He wouldn't wait for her to be ready.

CHAPTER 20

For two days, Kate stayed in her hotel room, except for meeting Dillon each morning for breakfast. She felt the pressure of time, of a clock ticking away. Every moment the killer didn't think of coming to her, he could be stalking another victim. She had to draw him in. It was only a matter of time before he returned to Plenitude. What had he left behind?

She worked on one of her bookkeeping accounts until late at night, trying to put her mind in a state of tiredness so that the stalker might appear. Even though some of the profit and loss statements were not due until about the time she had planned to go home, she enjoyed working on private bookkeeping jobs for small businesses in the suburbs. It used up time and provided her with extra money beyond that of Mac's life insurance. She might even work up the nerve and buy a car one day—learn to drive again.

She had never wanted to drive since Mac's death. Their car was old and she sold it first thing to clear out the garage.

Over the years, her fear of getting behind a wheel built up along with the fear of leaving her house.

For the first time, she was impatient with the work before her. She wanted to flow into that sleepy state before bedtime when she was ready to turn the computer off for the night. That's when she used to have her best visions on the computer screen.

After two days of spreadsheets, profit and losses, and pay-roll tables, and allowing her screen saver to work continuously when she was not at the keyboard, she knew the killer was not playing the game anymore.

Why? Did he sense she wanted to trap him? Was he so cunning that he shut her down so he could get close to her first? It would be easy. She didn't know what he looked like beyond the idea that he was dark, with a wiry build. It wasn't as if she'd recognize him if he sat next to her on one of the benches on the street, especially if he hid his physique, his overdeveloped shoulders, and arm muscles.

But if she ever looked into his eyes, she would recognize him in a heartbeat. She would know those darkly-gleaming tiger-eyes.

Dillon said the FBI was checking the circuses in Florida, but in the end, that wouldn't solve a whole lot. The killer could hardly be the only dark haired, swarthy, muscular aerialist in the circus. There were probably hundreds of men fitting that description. Even if the FBI connected him to someone named Christine and the man who died on the high wire and the older woman who Kate figured had leaped off the platform, there was still no proof implicating him as the strangler. He was clever enough to know he had to have an alibi each time he killed. He would never overlook something so obvious—in spite of his ego that had given her the first hint.

She knew these truths with a sinking heart, with a feeling of anguish for future victims. Never in this lifetime, would he ever find Christine. She was lost to him forever and maybe that was what drove him irrevocably forward to kill.

The third morning, lowering clouds slid onto the horizon at daybreak. Last night's paper predicted snow soon. Maybe that was why she couldn't contact the killer.

Nicholas was on his way to Plenitude.

On the street, going to meet Dillon at the diner, she smelled the air, which had warmed, and a light mist like silk feathers touched her face. Mist she could not see but knew could turn into snow.

'*I will come for you when the first snow falls.*' Again, she heard those bone-chilling words. They had connected without the benefit of her computer, and that scared the hell out of her.

In the diner, she considered how to tell Dillon of her idea to return to Betsy's house and try to reach the Catman with the computer, find out where he was. Would Dillon go along with her idea? Everything depended upon it.

"Dillon, I need to go out to Betsy's place one more time." They had begun sitting in a booth now, for privacy.

He looked at her, his steady gaze speculative, searching. "After what happened to you out there? Hell, woman, you don't have to be a psychic to feel the poison in that house, like a cancer eating up everything good that Betsy ever accomplished in her life. It's a sickening thing."

He had a right to feel this way about Betsy's place, but the intensity of his emotion, his expressing it to her so openly, made her worry about him. His perception amazed her. A down-to-earth straightforward man, Dillon was not a person to harbor such anxiety toward an inanimate object like this house. No doubt, he had hated his grandfather, but those emotions centered in his childhood, not in the present against some illusive evil that only she could see. It was plain he was uncomfortable with the whole business and she didn't blame him.

She touched his arm, seeking to calm him, as they left the diner. Outside the air was close and still.

"You're right," she admitted. "There is that feeling in the house. I was hoping never to go back, but I've tried to reach the killer for two days and nothing's happening."

"Why would you want to reach him? It's dangerous."

"I'll never make contact with Lenore again, she's at peace. I've felt Betsy's presence, but our minds or souls never came together. That leaves Nicholas. You don't want him sneaking in here unannounced, do you? That could happen." She might as well get it out in the open.

"Does that mean you're trying to bring the killer here? In person?"

She cared for Dillon very much, but his questioning made it difficult to deal with the situation as she felt she had to. "No, not him personally. I only want to contact him, find out where he is. I may be able to goad him into telling me. All you have to do then is make some calls and let the FBI catch him."

"Still, it sounds dangerous. We don't know what he looks like except you said he was dark and muscled. If he hid his body beneath a heavy jacket, there's a whole street full of people around here fitting that description. You almost believed it fit me. It fits Hank's description. He's the poacher, I told you about. They're not back yet, so I haven't talked to him."

"Forget about Hank. He's not involved, although he may be a witness to testify when we catch the killer. If he's like you say he is, he probably won't endanger his livelihood by telling what he was doing out at the Dells."

"He'd be afraid the Denver crowd will turn on him and blame him for the killings. These people who've lived here for generations don't trust outsiders much."

"Right. Tell me about it."

"What?"

"Oh, I was just mumbling. So you'll take me out there?"

"I could. But I won't leave you alone."

"Then it won't work! He will know. I need to lure him—his spirit—whatever you would call it. Maybe his mind. I need to bring his thoughts here to me. I'm only doing it through the computer, he can't reach me." She was not so sure after that hazy afternoon she tried so hard to forget. This time she was prepared. Knowing what he was capable of, she would stay wide-awake and as ready as she might ever be. The first snowfall meant something to him. He probably wouldn't come back until then.

They passed by Dillon's shop with the big *Closed-gone fishing* sign on the glass door.

"You put the same sign up even when you close for the day or the weekend?"

He grinned. "It's an inside joke. It's what you do here when you get a minute or two to spare, and Hilda found the sign in Denver one day when she was there."

"Hilda? She's the waitress at the diner, isn't she?"

"Damn fine woman. She's raising two kids after her old man took off for greener pastures. She was mad as hell at him for a while, but she never let it get her down."

"I liked her the first time I saw her," Kate said. Even when she entertained an odd thought or two of how it would be to become involved with Dillon, she had felt Hilda's strength and goodness. She wondered why there was no irritation at the waitress's obvious attraction to Dillon.

Shouldn't that have been a warning that she and Dillon had to remain friends, not lovers? If you love someone, you wouldn't want any woman to touch him like that with her eyes.

"I still think it's a crazy idea, going out there, but you're the most get-it-together person I know."

She took a deep breath, amazed at his words of praise. Get-it-together person? Kate Macklin? Since when? She thought of what he said and, in all truth, it was happening for her. She had worked through a lifetime of phobias and handicaps, and felt good about herself.

"Thanks, Dillon."

"I'll take you out there, but I want you to have contact with me at all times with a cell phone. You can call when you're ready to leave and I'll hear the message in the car or the office, wherever I am."

"Only if you promise not to call me. I could be right in the middle of something important. I must not be interrupted."

He growled a response that she took as an acceptance.

They crossed the street to the jail, which also housed his office.

"What happens if—when we catch him? Will he go to prison for a long time so he can't kill again?"

"Who knows? If the attorney general's office in Denver can accumulate enough evidence on him, he could get life for what he did here in Colorado. The FBI will compare dates of the circus along with homicides during that time. They can do that on their computers and take it across country."

"If they narrowed it down to one man they could search his premises. I'd bet he's saving trophies somewhere." Kate had read a lot about this kind of killer. The sick ones always kept a hidden cache of their macabre souvenirs. It was the last thing they ever destroyed and sometimes they held onto it until it became evidence.

"You're good at this, Kate. How long are you going to keep it up, chasing after your visions?"

"As long as I have to," she answered simply.

The expression on his face told her he was not happy with the answer. It was true. She'd had a lost, frightened feeling at the beginning, when the computer first called on her, immersing her in evil, drawing her into a nether-world she had no business being in. The up-side was the strength and courage she had gained from the experience. She had become a functioning human being, with only a few garden-variety phobias to call her own. It was a good feeling.

He pulled open a drawer and retrieved the spare phone. "My car phone number's been programmed in. All you have to do is hit this button. You won't need to dial. Here, we'll take this leather thong off my nightstick. Wrap it around the phone, just so, and keep it on your person at all times."

"But—"

"No buts. If you lay it somewhere and wander up stairs, you couldn't get to it in time if you needed to. That's another thing. Do you have to go upstairs?"

She wouldn't know until she went inside. "Does the house have a cellar or an attic?" The question popped into her head.

"Both. The cellar is dark and musty. Betsy kept some of her paints down there, also garden tools, rakes and stuff like that. When she was a kid, her mother used it as a vegetable cellar. The old woman canned a lot of fruit and vegetables. Betsy was always going on about how good things tasted. But there is no way into it except for the front door. No way out either."

"And the attic?"

He flinched and then grinned as if to dismiss his apprehension. "God, I hated that attic. She used to drag me up there to show me what she called the treasures. Old stuff brought out here by her parents from back east. It amounted to a couple of trunks filled with dried up, rotting clothes."

Kate's mind had shut off his words, concentrating on the flash of recognition that had just leaped out at her.

Treasures. Instead of conveying a positive image, the word made the skin crinkle at the back of her neck. Had the killer left behind some of his trophies in Betsy's attic? Could he have hidden away locks of hair and pieces of skin from the woman in the water, too? Had his lapse of orderly conduct disorganized him so much? His breach of rules might have thrown him off so that he hadn't completed his ritual of taking away his precious treasures.

She might be going off the deep end here. Sometimes it was hard to tell when her imagination left off and the visions began.

"Didn't you hear a word I said?" Dillon shook her gently by the shoulder.

"I'm sorry, I was thinking of something. What did you say?"

He moved away and sat down behind the desk. He looked at home there, a solid man, doing solid work. There may not be much law enforcing necessary in a town like Plenitude, but he did it to the best of his ability. He would probably become one of the town's leading citizens one day when he was older and rid of some of his lingering nightmares.

"I said I'll come get you in an hour."

"That won't be enough time. It's only a mile or two into town, takes you, what, three minutes to drive it?"

"I'm a fast driver but not that fast." He smiled and lost some of his worry lines. "Whatever you think it takes to get your vision or whatever you call it. I'll wait until you call."

"Yes, please, do that. It may take a lot of concentration to contact the killer. He doesn't want to talk to me anymore. I think I am getting too close and he knows it. He's afraid of being stopped before he finds her."

Dillon stood and moved to her side, cupping his hand behind her neck, rubbing her cheek gently with his thumb, as if he needed to have her complete attention. "We are talking about visions here, aren't we?" He had asked a question before.

She nodded, unable to look into his eyes and tell a lie. She didn't know for sure. A lot depended upon the arrival of the first snow.

When he took his hand away, she put space between them. It was easier to skirt around the truth that way. "If I can zero in on the killer's location, you can tell the police where to find him." She had to draw him here before anyone else died.

Funny how she had never seen the killer's face except through a hazy veil, but she knew his thoughts as if he deliberately shared them with her. He didn't share everything. He was a closed book to everyone but his sister. Christine was probably the only person he had ever let get close. That's why she had to be punished for deserting him.

On the way out to the house, Kate and Dillon were quiet until Dillon commented on the weather. "The road's slippery as hell, that light rain last night put black ice down. I hope it snows."

"Snow?" That was the last thing she wanted. "Why snow? Won't that make it worse?"

"Nope. When it snows, the temperature rises and melts the ice."

She wasn't as worried about the road conditions as she was hoping the snow stayed away—until she contacted Nicholas on the computer, until she satisfied her curiosity about the attic. She wanted to be wrong about that. The last thing she wanted to do was to open a trunk and find his grisly collection of treasures.

The computer lay on her lap and the phone strapped to her wrist. The phone was heavy and uncomfortable, but she would put up with it to please Dillon.

When he pulled into the driveway, she opened the door to step out, turning back to say goodbye.

"Not so fast." He was at her side before she could move. "I'm going in with you to check things out. Here is an extra flashlight. It's heavy enough to use as a club if you need to. But you said you were talking to his mind. Didn't you?"

Kate moved away before she had to answer. Dillon made her feel small, delicate, and protected. She wished with all her heart that might be enough. Why wasn't life more certain and choices easier?

He turned the key in the lock. She knew that gesture meant something positive to Dillon. The Catman didn't need a key.

They started inside but she froze on the threshold. The killer's presence screamed at her. Had he been in the house since she and Dillon left?

Kate stayed close to Dillon as he walked her through the entire house including upstairs, checking each bedroom and the bathrooms. At the narrow, twisting stairs to the attic, Dillon paused.

"We'll go up and have a look around if you want to."

She knew Dillon did not want to go up there. She closed her eyes to concentrate. The cold feel of the Catman's presence had disappeared. It had probably just come for an instant with her memories.

"No, it's okay. I'll sit in the kitchen, mostly. I hope I won't have to come up here to the bedroom. I'm the same way about that room as you are about the attic."

Downstairs in the kitchen, Dillon knelt and took a lamp from a cupboard. "Here's a lantern and matches if something happens to the flashlight. I'll be here well before dark, whether you call me or not, but it doesn't hurt to be prepared." He pulled a revolver from his jacket pocket and put it on the kitchen table near the flashlight.

"I don't want a gun, Dillon, I've never touched one in my life."

He shrugged her protest away. "Doesn't matter. I'm leaving my Colt 38. It only has a 2-inch barrel. You can put it in your pocket. It has a five shot cylinder and it's ready to go. Here, let me show you."

She felt warmed by the look of concern on his face. "I can't think of any reason I'd need that."

"Me either, or I wouldn't leave you alone. It's just a precaution." After showing her how to hold the weapon with both hands and telling her to just squeeze the trigger, he held her close and kissed her. A nice kiss, not blinding but sweet and gentle. She stood on the porch, waving to him as he turned in the drive and headed back to town. She watched the car's tail lights recede into the distance. The sky seemed close enough to touch, and her heart skipped a beat for every two it took, but there was another feeling that edged forward in her thoughts. A feeling of power and strength came over her. She would face this ordeal and not panic—see it out to the end.

CHAPTER 21

Kate went inside and opened the computer to wait, but in spite of the whirling, pulsing colors of the screen saver, nothing happened. The killer was blocking her, wouldn't let her in. She pushed the chair away from the kitchen table, thinking of how to goad him into talking to her. His obsession was with Christine. She could play on that idea.

And there was the treasure. He was coming back to this house because he had left his treasure behind. The thought became a surety instead of an ethereal idea. It was as clear as if he'd spoken the words out loud.

She wanted to postpone checking the attic. If a man like Dillon did not want to go up there, she wasn't all that brave either. She grabbed the flashlight and headed for the cellar door, what she hoped to be the lesser of two evils. She felt brave but not foolish. No way would she have even let Dillon go if she would felt any more of the Catman inside the house. But that part seemed okay.

Still, her hands trembled on the rail and her legs wobbled when she slowly descended the shaky steps. The cool, earthy smell rose up to strike her in the face, as damp as a grave.

Why did she have to think of that? She glanced up at the dim rectangle of light above her. She had left a chair propped against the door to make sure it stayed open. Dillon did say there was no way into the cellar except for the front door, but that meant no way out either.

She paused a moment on a step, trying to marshal all her senses, but it was difficult. The odors were so strong, the dank mustiness so prevailing.

At the bottom, she aimed the flashlight into the corners. The light flared out on empty shelves lining the walls. The floor was hard packed dirt.

Her heart thudded in her chest. Did she hear a noise from over in the corner? She aimed her light in that direction, but nothing moved. Mice and rats lived in cellars. Fear of rodents paled beside her apprehension of meeting Nicholas down there.

She skirted the perimeter of the room, kicking her feet into any dirt that looked soft and diggable. Even though the police must have gone over the house extensively, they weren't thinking along the lines of the killer digging a hole to hide his treasures until he could return for them.

A scraping sound came from above her head. Was it the wind on the windows? Her legs trembled and she forced herself to take two more steps and then two more. Enough! She couldn't do it. It was like a tomb down here. She turned to rush back toward the light, afraid of the cellar door closing on her. She slipped on the worn bottom step and holding the flashlight tight with one hand, swung around and crashed into an old desk at the edge of the stairs. Her elbow felt bruised, and she rubbed it to take the numbness away. It hurt like hell, but the injury wasn't serious. She touched the phone hanging from her wrist. Bless Dillon. The thought gave her the courage she needed to climb the stairs again.

She took a deep breath when she stood on Betsy's cheerful tile in the kitchen. She slammed the cellar door shut and shoved a chair up against the knob. Just in case. It was a dumb idea. If anyone had been hiding down there, she couldn't have missed him. It felt good, just the same, to put the chair in place.

The screen saver still flitted across the computer monitor when she glanced in that direction, but nothing else showed.

The house was cold. Dillon had offered to lay out a fire in the pot-bellied stove, but she hadn't wanted to take the time. There was no way she would stay here after dark.

Outside, the temperature was icy cold. Good. It wouldn't snow until the air warmed.

The key to the puzzle had to be why Nicholas wanted to come back here, and Kate didn't think it was only to settle the challenge she threw at him. He was smarter than that. Christine was part of the key, but not all.

She tucked the flashlight under her arm and started up the stairs. The telephone banged painfully against her bruised elbow, causing her hand to lose a grip on the banister. Without pausing to worry about the pros and cons, Kate ran back down, slipped off the leather thong and laid the phone on the table next to the computer.

At the top of the stairs, she crossed the creaking wooden floor to the landing, listened and turned to go up the narrow attic steps. The stairs were dark and twisted off to the right near the top. She didn't want to waste the flashlight batteries, and forced herself to move ahead in the semi-darkness. The thought that the killer could be waiting anywhere in the house made her stop, her foot almost missing the next step. He was a hunter, and he enjoyed the chase.

In spite of her misgivings, Kate continued up. When she faced the attic door, she paused, reluctant to go in. '*No time, no time*,' a voice whispered in her mind. She put a hand on the knob and with a wild squeak, the door opened. If the cellar had been damp and clammy, the attic was the opposite. The air in the closed room was dry, and multi-hued dust motes sifted past the narrow windows when she flashed the flickering light around the room.

She picked her way across the floor beams and let her senses tell her what she needed to know. The presence of the killer was very strong, but somehow it didn't feel threatening. As if he had been here. His aura had touched the entire house, but in the attic, it was as if he had left a part of himself behind. She pictured him sitting, hiding up here, and listening to Betsy moving around in her bedroom on the floor below. She shook off the chills. It was not a thought she wanted to harbor.

In the corner, under a dusty heap of clothing, she found a round-topped old steamer trunk. She played the flashlight beam across the cover, and saw that there was less dust than covered the rest of the room.

She turned, wanting so badly to leave, that it had become a physical hurt to stay. Her limbs trembled, the arm she hurt throbbed, and every sense told her not to open the trunk. Yet, she had to.

Fingers shaking, she lifted the lid and shone the light across the bottom of an empty trunk. Disappointment warred with relief when she sat on the dusty floor and leaned against the trunk. She jerked away, sensing his touch on the trunk. Nicholas had opened it, looked in. Why? Sweat soaked her clothing, in spite of the cold. When had she started to think of him as Nicholas? She had seen the name Nikki on the tattoo. Was the full name just a natural development of her thoughts? His last name had never come back to her memory, try as she might.

She made her way down the stairs. The computer was the only thing left for her, the only way to find the key to what made Nicholas tick and where he was hiding. In the kitchen, she sat at the table, looking at the screen saver, concentrating. Nothing came. She moved away from the table with restless energy.

"I want some fresh air." She said the words aloud, needing the comfort of a voice to break the heavy silence.

Outside on the swing, she zipped up her jacket. It was just past noon. The attic had been cold, but outside was colder, especially when the light wind insinuated its way against her skin and damp clothing. While she sat wondering what to do next, an overwhelming smell of roses encircled her; the cloying sweet scent of blood-red roses. She caught a brief glimpse of them in her mind's eye.

She peered over the edge of the porch at Betsy's garden. Sere browns, dark earth, all dry and waiting for winter with no flowers of any kind in sight. Still, the odor was overwhelming and she hurried to the garden.

One rose bush at the corner of the garden looked alive, just barely. Kate snapped off the end of a twig and saw green beneath the brown of the limb. The smell was still with her, but gradually fading.

Grabbing up a flat, sharp stone, she knelt and began scraping and gouging at the foot of the rose bush. She struck something solid. Frantically, she grasped the top corners of a little box and, sitting down on the hard, frigid ground, she opened it gingerly, trying not to touch it too many places.

Lying side by side were two dark locks of hair, two separate arrangements, each tied neatly with a narrow blue ribbon in the center of the long hair. Next to them lay a folded plastic bag. The ordinariness of the zip-locked bag warred with the contents, which looked like dried strips of jerky, but instead had to be pieces of skin from the inside of a woman's arm.

Kate closed the box and sat for a long moment holding her middle as if she would break in two. She clutched the box in spite of icy fingers, although she would have liked to throw it as far away in the woods as she possibly could. She knew Dillon would have to examine the contents. That was his job. There could be fingerprints even after such a long time and being buried with soft dirt all around it.

This is what Nicholas had left behind in his haste to leave Plenitude and why he had to come back. She closed the lid and stood, her knees aching from the exposure to the cold ground. She had to reach him on the computer, make out his location and stall him before he came here to find his gruesome treasure.

He promised he would come by the first snowfall and she had a feeling he was one who always kept his word. Not like his sister who had betrayed him. Kate was hanging her life on her trust in his fixation on the truth. There was never a certain time when this strong personality trait of his came to her thoughts, but it was there now.

The clouds above the treetops were so low, that she saw only darkness and the cold increasing every moment. Running up the steps, she carried the box in the front of her shirt so as not to touch it again and set it in front of the computer. She pulled up a chair, opened the computer lid, and began typing as fast as she could. She typed the same sentence over and over on the keyboard.

I am here, Nicholas. Christine is waiting for you.

She was sure about the name Nicholas. The thought came to her, like the scent of the roses. Betsy and Christine were helping her.

Nikki. Nikki, you have been a bad boy. Look what I have here. Your treasures. Why did you leave them behind? Did you want Christine to find them?

Kate waited, hardly daring to breathe for fear of disturbing her concentration.

'*Christine! I've searched for you. I miss you so. Have you come back to me?*'

Kate's typed words exploded off the screen and the new words swept trembling across in irregular, wispy edges. Her fingers paused at the keyboard. It was so crucial to get it right. She would never get another chance.

I want to be with you, Nikki. Let me come to you. I want you to brush out my hair for me and rub my shoulders like you used to. I'm so tired.

Before he could answer, Kate saw Christine, lying in a casket. She closed her eyes, trying to block off the sight from Nicholas but Kate didn't know how good she was at blocking. The young woman wore long sleeves, yet the slashed wrists showed through in Kate's vision. What a terrible irony, that Nicholas had searched for his sister, killed those women, and she had died by her own hands. Would he tune into what she just saw? That would be the end of it all, he would never come to her.

A long pause. Was he going to answer?

'*I love you, Christine. Why did you leave me? I've searched so long for you. You put all those imitations in my way, to fool me, to test my loyalty to you.*'

Kate's fingers moved over the keyboard without needing her thoughts. *Shame on you, Nikki. You are a naughty boy to leave your treasure behind.*

'*I couldn't help it, Chrissie. I was so sure I found you twice there, but that was a mistake. I had to catch the train. I didn't want anyone to see my treasures.*'

Tell me where you are. Tell me.

A long pause. '*I have to come for you.*'

No! Tell me where you are. I'll come to you.

The screen faded, her last typed words shaking as if the monitor blurred. He was leaving! She couldn't let him go. Not without knowing where he was.

Nikki. Don't leave me. Tell me you've missed me, please, I need to hear it.

Kate thought he was gone. Nothing came onto the screen for a long while, not even the screen saver returned, only the crackling static of a blank square stared back at her.

'*I didn't leave. You left me.*'

She wanted to stall him, get him off the subject of coming to her. She had to get him going again, so he might drop his defenses and tell her his location.

Slowly the screen filled with color. Kate could almost hear the loud circus music and smell the sawdust. A slim figure of a man and a voluptuous young woman soared through the air with the orange tent ceiling above them. They leaped, somersaulted, and grabbed the swaying trapeze bars with effortless grace. Then the screen went dark. He had left behind his last thoughts.

He was on his way to Plenitude.

CHAPTER 22

Elbows on the table, chin resting in her palms, Kate stared at the screen moments after it turned black. As if waking from a dream, she shook her head to clear it and glanced down at her watch. Such a long time had passed! He tricked her.

Kate scraped back the chair, and leaped to her feet. She had schemed to trap him, find out his location and he out-maneuvered her. He was coming here, on his way now—or—the thought chilled her to the bone, he could be here now. He would come for Christine, and for his treasures. She could feel him rushing toward her. In a quick swipe of vision, she saw him carefully lifting up a window. Which window?

A scraping sound came from somewhere in the house. The wind, the tree limb brushing against the roof, she had heard the noise when she was in the cellar. Was it the exact same sound? Fear made the veins in her temples pulse and she thought of the front and back doors. She hadn't thought about locking them.

Reaching for the phone lying at her fingertips, she punched the code for Dillon. A crackle on her computer screen made her turn to look. She saw Dillon's vehicle tilted on the side of the road, up on a jack, and he was changing a tire. Snow came down all around him. Dillon wouldn't be coming soon. His phone was inside the insulated cab of the car and he couldn't hear her.

She left the key on the phone punched down. When he went back into the car, she prayed he would hear the buzzing and know she wanted him—if the batteries on her phone held out.

Kate dashed around the house, locking windows and doors and remembered the one in the cellar. Dillon told her there was no other way into the cellar but she remembered seeing a narrow window near the top of the room. He never thought of it as an entrance but she knew how slender and wiry the Catman was. She opened the cellar door. Could she do it? She had to. The lamp Dillon had lit for her was brighter than the flashlight. She picked it up with shaking fingers, and edged down the flimsy stairway. The dank, musty smell was stronger than she recalled. No time to be afraid. He could be blocking her, but she didn't feel his presence here.

Not yet.

The chair fell twice when she climbed up on it. Her fingers trembled when she pulled the lock together on the little window at ground level. Not pausing to look around at the dark corners, she ran up the stairs, slammed the door shut, and shoved a chair under the doorknob.

She needed to go up to the second floor now. She ran up, to check the locks on the windows in Betsy's room. In the room, she saw the window had no lock. She looked around for something to wedge it shut. She was wasting valuable time. She couldn't do anything about the other windows on this floor. That realization came through loud and clear. That meant none of the other windows upstairs or in the attic had locks. Her one consoling thought was that if Nicholas ran true to form, he would probably come up through the tree, as he had done to get to Betsy.

She hurried down stairs and paused at the front door. No! Stay inside something warned her. But she had an idea, and had to brave going outside. He could be out there, waiting, lurking at the edge of the trees.

Dashing off the porch, she ran to corner of the house to the water spigot she had noticed when Dillon brought her here the first time. If she splashed down the attic roof, it would buy her time. Had Dillon shut off the water already?

Kate turned the handle. At first, it wouldn't budge, rusty and cold as it was. Finally, with strength born of panic, she turned it and the water trickled first and then gushed out of the hose end. Most of the hose appeared buried in the ground, to keep it from freezing she supposed. It hadn't frozen yet, but she felt the cold increasing every second.

As soon as she pulled the remainder of the long hose out of its coiled position, a sharp crack echoed across the tree-encircled lawn. Water poured out of the broken green line. The hose had snapped. Her throat felt tight, her stomach churned.

The attic. She would carry buckets of water from the bathroom to the attic, reach out as far as she could and throw water upwards. It was far from a perfect plan, but she had to slow him down until help came. The perfect scenario would be for him to slip off the roof, hit the ground, break a leg and lie trapped until Dillon brought the troops.

She shut off the water and ran up the steps into the house, slamming and locking the front door. Rummaging through the lower cabinets, she found a tin bucket and a pan with a handle. That would have to do. She raced up the stairs, hesitating only a moment at the landing leading to Betsy's bedroom. He couldn't be here yet. They were attuned to each other now, and she would know when he came.

In the upstairs bathroom, she found an old fashioned bathtub with legs. Rust stains etched the front of the tub beneath the spigot and around the drain hole. Water dripped. Thank God, the water coming into the house hadn't frozen. She turned on the tap and rusty, smelly water poured out into the bucket. Grabbing up the bucket and slopping water all the way down the hall in her haste, she hurried up the narrowed stairs to the attic and opened the door. It was dark inside the room. No sun slanted through the windows. She checked the window ledges to make sure, but there were no locks.

An icy blast of air hit her when she opened the window. The sky was still leaden, overcast, but the air was colder. A good sign, no snow yet. She leaned way out of the window and awkwardly tossed up the water.

She pulled her head back quickly in case it all came down like rain. With extreme satisfaction, she saw that only a small amount of water slid down over the eaves. It was so cold the patina of ice stayed in place, freezing immediately. It took four buckets before she was satisfied. There was a little left in the last bucket. She looked downward, over Betsy's tiny balcony and tried to aim the water toward the ledge. She used the flashlight to knock off the tell-tale icicles that had formed on the edge of the roof above her and left the attic.

Was he psychic enough to know about the ice on the roof? She had to hope not and if her mental block had worked before on him with Christine, it should work again.

CHAPTER 23

Kate sat gingerly on the edge of the bed in Betsy's room, with a good view to the tree outside the window. The sky had turned cloudy but it wasn't near dusk. Waiting was hard. If her judgment was off, he could be downstairs creeping upward for her. The thought made her blood run cold. She swallowed the sour bile that lay on the back of her tongue.

Chances were what life was about. If you didn't take chances, if you stayed safe, you were dead anyway. Her gaze never wavered as she stared out the window. She had done everything she could do to prepare herself for his coming. The window was wedged shut with a screwdriver she found downstairs in one of the drawers.

The flashlight lay across her lap, and her trembling hands held the revolver Dillon had left her. He'd said it was loaded. She could use it if she had to. She could, she could.

"I can do it," she whispered, needing the reassurance of her own voice to fill the dreadful silence.

Her heart leaped into her throat when she saw snow flurries start to fall, flakes big and soft, like white corn flakes. Snow brought warmer temperatures. The ice would melt and there wouldn't be a chance in hell he would slide off the roof and fall to the ground.

The revolver dipped in her grasp and she felt so tired. She might as well lie back on Betsy's bed and surrender to her fate.

A dark flash in the tree passed her vision. She almost missed it.

He was here!

A figure moved up the crotch of the tree. A psychic would know someone was here, waiting. By now, she was certain his deranged grasp on reality let him imagine Christine waited for him.

His sister, Christine. What a pathetic, twisted life for both of them. Kate's vision of Christine showed the sister had committed suicide by slashing her wrists, probably not long after she left her brother.

Slowly crawling upward in the tree, he moved so sure, so stealthy. If Kate hadn't known what to look for, she would never have seen him. At the last limb above the window, he poised for the impossible leap, a giant panther from the jungle, all muscles and bone and sinew, a predator after his prey.

Kate tried to swallow past her dry throat. She knew what it meant to be frightened out of her wits, mesmerized, unable to move a muscle if he flew on top of her.

He seemed to poise, concentrating on his jump, sizing up where he must land on the roof to balance his slide onto the tiny balcony. When he launched himself upward, she almost missed the dark blur through the sky.

She waited, holding her breath, not daring to let it out for fear he would hear her, sense her presence. It took only seconds, but it seemed like long minutes until she heard the impact of his body on the roof and then a slithering noise. The hairs on the back of her neck ruffled, and she shivered when her acute hearing brought the sound of his nails frantically scratching for a hold on the sharply slanted roof.

He was sliding down, helpless. He hadn't seen the black ice, which had formed beneath the light covering of snow.

She held the gun pointed at the glass, with both hands as Dillon had showed her. At the last possible moment, he slid off the roof, poised with his feet delicately balanced on the thin banister of the balcony. His body vibrated for a second and then—he leaned forward in a graceful arc, his feet still on the banister, and peered into the window, staring directly at her.

Backed into the shadows, Kate was not sure if he saw her until he smiled. The most evil spreading of lips, she could never have imagined anything so malevolent as that smile and narrowed, gleaming cat's eyes staring directly into her own. They were soul to soul, with nothing separating them but the flimsy window.

The gun wavered in her hand. '*You can do it, you can do it,*' the whispered litany sounded in her brain, but her fingers refused to tighten on the trigger. Her thoughts slipped backward for a split second to the pools of blood left on the ground after her daughter had died.

Blood. She let her hands fall limply into her lap. No blood. She couldn't do it. Frozen, she waited her doom, knowing she was minutes from death. The bitter taste of defeat began rising deep within her throat, choking her.

His hands slipped down the window, leaving behind narrow, red trails. His nails were broken off to the quick, bloody nubs where he had tried to keep his hold on the roof. He pulled on the widow frame, the screwdriver fell out onto the floor, the window was loose and he had his fingers underneath the narrow opening, his muscles bulged, ready to lift upward.

When she saw his bloody fingers curl beneath the window frame her terrorized shock ebbed away, replaced with a lust, a terrible hunger to live. She rushed forward, and raising the flashlight, she smashed his fingers with all her strength.

The look of surprise on his face disappeared from her view and he lunged backward in shock, teetered for a long moment with both feet on the ledge and then with what must have been for him a curiously awkward movement, disappeared from her view.

Running to the window, she looked out in time to see the dark graceful form somersault backward off the edge of the roof, plummeting toward the ground. Like a giant cat, would he land on his feet?

She rushed downstairs to the kitchen window with a full view of the garden. Expecting to see him rise to his feet and come for her, instead, she saw his wracked body sprawled on his back, arched in the center. He had fallen directly on the largest rock in Betsy's garden.

Minutes passed. He didn't move. What should she do? He was so like a cat, maybe he had nine lives.

It wasn't hard to imagine his dark, shadowy form crawling toward her, broken and injured but invincible with his hatred. Her fingers trembled but she punched the button again for Dillon's car phone. He must have been waiting, he answered right away.

"Ah, God, Kate, I've been out of my mind. I caught your signal, and I'm heading your way now, almost there. I had a flat."

"I know. Dillon, come quick, please."

"I will. I didn't know what your signal meant so I called in all my deputies, the fire truck and the ambulance. They will all be pulling in any minute. You okay?"

"Yes, yes I am now," she whispered.

She set the phone down and waited at the window. Outside the snow had begun to fall again, thicker this time.

Kate turned to look at the computer on the table. She had forgotten it was still on. The gyrating, pulsing colors and shapes from the screen saver had disappeared. In its place, words moved across the screen, arranging themselves into patterns, waiting for her to look at them. A delicate, soft smell of roses came with gentle warmth and settled around her shoulders, comforting, calming her.

She sat down at the table. As soon as she did that, the words moved into order.

Death shall have no dominion. We have the dominion.

A feeling of contentment poured over Kate. The uneasy feelings of restless disquiet, the tension she felt in the old house since the first moment she stepped inside were gone. Betsy was free.

The shrill sound of sirens invaded the quiet. She wondered if Nicholas was dead, but she didn't want to look again. Her plan had been so thin, but in a twisted way, it had worked. She made him come to her, but not in the way she expected. In her heart, she knew no one would have caught him otherwise. Not until he'd amassed more victims.

For a moment, it had seemed as if his somersault might have enabled him to survive unharmed. He would have come inside for her then. She had taken chances. It had been the only way to catch him. Thank God, she was learning to take chances.

"It's me, Kate. Open the door." Dillon startled her by pounding and yelling. She hurried forward before he broke it open.

"Are you all right?" He stopped to hug her against his chest and then held her away. "What happened? You look like you've been drawn through a knot-hole."

"He's out there." She pointed. "He's in Betsy's rock garden, hurt or dead."

Dillon pivoted around and signaled to his men. They drew their weapons and rushed toward the garden. She followed slowly, staying on the porch, not wanting to get close, as if he might still reach her.

She watched Dillon gesture toward the ambulance attendants. The firefighters ran up to look, the lights flashing on the big yellow truck.

Dillon walked back up to the porch and stood next to her, watching.

"There's a box on the table. I wish…I wish you didn't have to open it."

He went inside. She brought him the lit lamp. He had to do it, she knew that. He lifted the lid with a pencil tip and stared down at the contents.

Dillon raised his head to look at her. She had never seen such torture in anyone's eyes in all her life. Damn Nicholas to death. He was a monster.

"Kate." His voice was low, hoarse. He wrapped the box carefully in a towel. "Take this and go to my car. Wait for me."

What was he going to do?

She was distracted momentarily when her attention turned to the white-coated ambulance attendants carrying a stretcher toward the vehicle.

When she looked back, Dillon had walked halfway up the stairs with the lantern in his hand.

"No! Dillon, don't! The house is empty. There is nothing bad here. Betsy's at peace." She watched in stunned fascination as he raised his arm holding the lamp.

She turned to the deputies. "Can't you stop him?"

They shrugged. One spoke. "It's his house, ma'am. Likely he can do as he pleases with it. The fire truck's here. They won't let it get out of control."

'*Go, Kate. Leave now. This is something I have to do. For Betsy.*' She hadn't heard his words out loud, but they came to her mind in a muted whisper, ruffling the hair against her ears.

They heard a soft explosion and saw the flare of light through the door and windows. Dillon ran out, leaving the door open to create a strong draft. He carried her computer tucked under his arm.

Maybe he should have left it behind.

They all moved back to the ambulance parked in the driveway. The house was old and dry. The flames licked and caressed it, devouring the wood in liquid swallows so quickly, she could hardly believe what she was seeing.

The ambulance attendants had brought the stretcher to the vehicle door, ready to load the man inside.

"Is he dead?" Kate forced herself to look at Nicholas and saw the yellow flicker in his eyes. The emergency team had strapped his body down, all the way up to his shoulders. She knew that wasn't necessary. A slight movement of his hand, caught her eye. Neither his head nor his body moved with his spastic hand motion.

"Can you prop him up? He wants to see the house one last time." Their souls were still connected. She knew he needed to look. She couldn't ignore his silent plea.

Kate turned toward the house to see why he was staring.

Framed in the window, floated an ethereal form, silhouetted by the flames in the background. It was a young woman with long dark hair. Christine. Kate glanced at the deputies, the ambulance drivers, at Dillon, and knew they had not seen the vision, only she and Nicholas had seen it.

Kate heard a low gurgle of anguish come from behind her, as Nicholas tried to call out Christine's name. In a second, the window had exploded with the intense heat and they all moved back instinctively. Kate felt the connection between her and Nicholas break apart like a snapped wire.

She hadn't noticed when the soft, wet sleet began to fall. With the combination of the firefighters and the sleet, the surrounding forest would be safe.

Dillon motioned to the ambulance attendants. "Get him to the hospital. Don't remove the straps until he's safe inside and don't take your eyes off him," he ordered the two deputies riding in back.

"If he survives, I want one of you in his room and one just outside at all times. I can deputize some help if we need it. I won't have him escaping."

Kate shook her head. "He can't escape, because he is trapped inside his body with a twisted spine and useless legs. He's doomed to lie like a vegetable as long as he lives, with only his brain alive." No more Catman. Kate shivered, thinking what a horrible living death that would be for him. Was this a part of death having no dominion?

The fire truck stayed behind when the ambulance pulled away, the lights not flashing. The air had warmed and the heavy sleet turned to snow, this time in earnest with big, thick heavy wet clumps. She knew this was truly the first snowfall. The other had been false, a trick of nature. The Catman should have waited. He could have made the leap and come inside Betsy's room safely.

She and Dillon waited, until he saw the firefighters had the blaze controlled. She moved away to let him say his good-byes to Betsy.

"It's ironic, isn't it?" She finally spoke, hating to break the hush of the forest. "He made a mistake again today, his second breach of rules. This is the first snowfall. The other snow earlier was a false snow that didn't last a half hour. If he had waited, he could have made it inside the window. His first mistake in killing the woman in the river started the beginning of the end for him."

She wasn't sure if Dillon understood all the implications, or even if he was listening.

The snow began to cover the outbuildings when he took her arm to guide her toward his car.

CHAPTER 24

In the vehicle, Dillon turned to Kate and put his hand under her hair, around the back of her neck, rubbing his thumb gently beneath her jaw line.

"I don't know what to say, Kate. I've never known anyone like you. You are one of a kind. If it hadn't been for you, Betsy's killer would still be out there, looking for new victims." His voice hardened, his cop's voice. "But goddamn it, you took chances. If I'd known…"

She reached her hand up to touch his, leaning her cheek into his palm. He bent and kissed her, a strong, searching kiss, a good kiss.

She didn't love him, not with that earth-moving excitement she had known with Mac and thought she'd begun to feel with Slater. She was comfortable with Dillon. It wouldn't be difficult to live the rest of her life with him. Was comfort and security enough? She searched for that all her life and finally realized she had to find it within herself.

Plenitude was a nice town. The people would accept her eventually. Could she think of spending the rest of her days here?

And there was Rasputin. Her cat would love it out here—for about fifteen minutes. Then he would want back in a room with walls. They were two of a kind, not used to all this open space.

She kissed Dillon a little longer, as if to force a stronger feeling, but none came.

He must have sensed it too. He pulled back a little to look at her. "You aren't staying, are you?"

She shook her head, unable to put it into words.

"You sure about this?"

"Yes. I think you are too."

"Maybe," he admitted reluctantly. "Still, I'd like to give us a try."

Even now, he couldn't say he loved her. Neither could she have said the words.

"I know. But we aren't made that way. It's either all or nothing, isn't it?" At his hesitant nod, she put her hand over his.

"You're going to leave yourself open to more things that come to you. I should have left that damned machine in the house."

She smiled and leaned against his broad chest. "No good, it always finds me."

"I'd never let you do this, I guess you know that. Endanger yourself like you did. It's crazy."

"I can't refuse to help when someone calls," Kate said simply, knowing the truth of it.

"I'll come to New York," he promised. "I don't give up that easy."

"Thank you, Dillon. I'll take that as a promise. I hope you can settle your mind about your grandfather's place. That would be such a waste if you don't accept it."

Sometime in the future her priorities could change or his might. It was possible she just had some more living to do before settling down to serenity and peace. When the visions stopped, her life would change, too. He might be here waiting.

"Denver is returning her body tomorrow. You'll stay to see that through?"

She knew he spoke of the woman in the river—Lenore. "Of course. I won't be satisfied and neither will she, until she's settled properly."

"We could have a memorial service for her. Wouldn't many come, but my deputies and the volunteers who helped bring her up, they'd be there."

"Good. She would like that. I'll look up Sarah, she'd come."

"Ralph will be there," he added. "He doesn't miss many funeral services, says he's keeping in practice for the big one, meaning his own, I suppose."

She smiled at the thought of how the hotel manager would probably hear about the service without anyone telling him. "We can include Betsy in the memorial, too, if you'd like. I know you've already strewn her ashes, but…"

"That's a good idea. I wasn't there the first time. Physically I was, but mentally I was too hurting, too mad. Betsy deserved a life!"

"I know. They both did. All his victims deserved to live and so did Nicholas and Christine. But it's gone for all of them now. We have to accept that."

He started the car.

"So, after the services, you'll be going."

She looked at his profile, so lean and hard, so strong. Her eyes misted and for a second she could barely see him through the haze of near-tears. "Yes. I've got to go home."

"You and your computer and your cat," he said.

The computer, my cat, and me. That didn't sound half bad, in fact it sounded darn good. She smiled when he put the car in gear and headed back to Plenitude.

THE END

About the Author

Born in Phoenix, Arizona, Pinkie Paranya traveled all over the U.S., Alaska, and most of Mexico with her late husband. Ever since she can remember, writing has been her passion. After completing her fifteenth novel, trying to discover the genre she loved most, she still hasn't decided.

Paranya enjoys romances with their intrigue and uplifting happy endings, but she has also published two paranormal psychological suspenses, a cozy mystery, and an Early American Alaskan trilogy.

Visit her website, www.pinkieparanya.com.